SIGNATURE

For more books by
Jeff Carson
go to…

www.jeffcarson.co

SIGNATURE

Jeff Carson

Cross Atlantic Publishing

Published by
Cross Atlantic Publishing

Signature
© 2016 by Jeff Carson

Chapter 1

The creature must have heard them coming because a shrill cry filled the night.

"Oh ... did you hear that?" A pair of tiny arms latched onto Wolf's leg as the plastic bin lurched again.

He bent over and shone the Maglite through the cage of the hockey helmet, illuminating the six-year-old girl's eyes locked on the trashcan.

She gripped his leg harder and took a step back, trying to pull him with her. For all the fuss Ella Coulter had made wanting to be his wingman, she was starting to crumble.

"David!" Her mother's voice came from the house and echoed into the forest beyond the barn.

"It's okay!" he said.

"Do you know how painful rabies shots are?" Lauren Coulter asked, her shapely silhouette shifting in the kitchen doorway.

He had never had the privilege.

An outbreak of barking came from deep within the house behind Lauren. Jet, Wolf's adopted German shepherd, had informed them of the current problem and then lost his usefulness. At twelve years old, the dog was normally slow, living out his twilight years comfortably seated or lying down, but when it came to raccoons he became a rabid beast. He was probably clawing a groove into Wolf's bedroom door right now.

"Mom! I'm okay!" Ella said, releasing her death grip on Wolf's thigh. She adjusted the mittens, straightened the puffy winter coat and pointed. "Let's go. He's probably so scared. You have to get him out."

Wolf shone the flashlight beyond the downed trashcan. A single raccoon was edging closer along the barn's red exterior wall—clearly the mother who was refusing to leave the area with her baby in such a predicament.

In an effort to keep wildlife out of this particular trash can—the one without a heavy duty bear-proof fastening system like he had on the others—he'd strapped a simple thirty-inch bungee cord from handle to handle across the lid. He had been lulled into complacency about this particular bin. Though he'd found it on its side more than once over the years, it had never been opened. Apparently it was time to invest the $22.50 at Rascal's for a secure model.

There was another shrill cry, this time longer and more desperate, and it drew the mother raccoon closer.

"Stay here."

Wolf's tone froze Ella in her tracks, and she stood obediently under her pile of protective clothing.

It was enough screwing around. It was three in the morning and he needed sleep if he wanted to function at all tomorrow, so he made straight for the can.

The mother raccoon went mean, trotting alongside the wall at full steam now, both of them making for the target without slowing.

I am a man.

With a deft movement he straddled the can, at the same time swiveling it so the lid pointed at the mother, keeping his flashlight pinned on her shining eyes. The cold wetness of the plastic soaked through the fabric of his pajama pants.

Shit.

The mother raccoon bared her teeth now, raising her front claws with each running step.

He felt the animal knocking against the bin under him, heard the rustling of plastic bags inside. There was another cry, this time sounding as if Wolf had put it in a headlock.

The mother started screaming—short shrieks that said there was about to be blood.

"Let him out!" Ella shouted.

"David!"

Dropping the flashlight on the dirt, Wolf gripped his left hand on the bungee cord that ran over the length of the lid, trying to pry his fingers underneath. It was trivial, mundane movements like these that made him miss his pinkie finger, which had been blown off by a handgun last year. The dexterity of his hand was reduced by a digit, and thus his timing was slowed that extra millisecond to allow the mother raccoon to get too close.

"Stop!" He pointed at the animal.

The mother skidded to a stop, peeling back her lips as she shuffled side to side.

Pulling the bungee cord, he released his makeshift lock and popped open the lid with his other hand.

A ball of fur darted out, knocking the flashlight along the ground. The beam of light twisted and landed on the receding mother and child, who joined a lingering pack at the corner of the barn. The family of raccoons then turned and disappeared into the woods.

"Yay! Ha ha!" Ella jumped up and down. "Ha ha! Did you see that, mommy?"

Wolf plucked the flashlight from ground and illuminated Lauren's face, who was now standing a foot behind her six-year-old daughter, her arms retracting back to her own sides.

"Yeah. I saw that." Lauren's chest was heaving.

"Oh, hey." Ella turned around. "Can I take this off?"

Lauren took the helmet off her daughter and watched Wolf straighten the garbage can against the barn.

Free of her helmet, Ella pulled off Jack's old mittens and swiveled a glance between the two adults. "That was so cool. David saved him."

Walking back to the house, Wolf rolled his shoulders and puffed his pectoral muscles, making a show of stretching one side of his neck.

Ella stared in smiling awe while Lauren rolled her eyes.

"See you inside," Wolf said.

***

Three hours later, a thin hand grasped his shoulder, gently pulling Wolf from his sleep. Warm lips tickled his earlobe.

"My hero," Lauren whispered, running a hand down his side, causing him an involuntary muscle spasm.

Wolf turned, catching her facetious smile. If Wolf had learned one thing about Lauren Coulter in their last year of dating, it was that she relished every moment she could make Wolf lose even the slightest bit of control, which meant all she had to do to get her fix was to touch him.

Her jade eyes narrowed as she looked at his lips. Without hesitation she reached around the front of him and went straight for the groin, massaging him through his boxer shorts.

"Good morning," she said.

Her lips pulled into a perfect-toothed smile, and then relaxed as they gravitated towards his mouth. The smooth skin of her thigh brushed across his legs as she straddled him, and then she was over him, kissing him on the neck as her fingernails tickled at the waistline of his underwear.

He gave another involuntary shudder as she reached inside with an eager, firm grip. With her other hand she hiked up her tee shirt and sighed. Coupled with her firm, warm body pressing against him, the sounds she made drove him wild.

Wolf pulled up her shirt, revealing her small, golden-skinned breasts and palmed them both. When he tried to pull off her shirt, she refused to unhand her trophy and they became a tangle of fabric and limbs.

They both laughed. Her smile was perfect. Even after a night of closed-mouth sleep, her breath was intoxicating.

The doorknob rattled and the door swung open, banging against the wall. An eighty-pound German shepherd strode in with a six-year-old girl in tow.

Lauren collapsed onto Wolf's chest. "Hey, baby."

"Hi," Ella said in that conspiratorial tone she used first thing in the morning. She was there to speak to her mother, not to Wolf.

Sticking true to her routine, Ella rounded the bed, her feet pattering on the carpet to the far side where Lauren had been sleeping three or more nights per week, for months now.

Lauren slid her hand out of Wolf's underwear in the most erotic way possible and bent towards her daughter.

Wolf heard soft whispering and a tiny giggle. He knew the gist of the conversation well, though he never heard it outright:

"Can I have some milk?"

"Yes, you can get it yourself."

"Can I take Jet outside?"

"Yes. Be careful."

Ella left in a run, and Jet left on her heels, a wagging tail thumping the doorjamb on the way out.

"Race?" Lauren asked, straddling him again.

When the kitchen door thumped closed Wolf and Lauren made love furiously. It was a game they had played in this exact scenario before. Lauren had once called it a race to the finish. Either Ella wins or we win. Who will it be?

Three minutes later, they were both already spent and panting heavily by the time the hinges of the kitchen door squeaked back open. They always won.

After a quick shower, Wolf changed into work clothes, which consisted of his second-favorite pair of worn Levis, a lightweight flannel shirt, and lace-up leather Gore-Tex work boots that had seen more miles than the tires on his SUV.

He went to the kitchen and poured a cup of coffee from the steaming carafe. There was a half-eaten bowl of chocolate Cheerios on the table, and a cooling piece of toast on the counter. Lauren and Ella stood on the front deck marveling at something in the meadow.

Wolf sipped his coffee and walked out the front door to the deck.

The valley wall to the west was ablaze with sunshine, the highest peaks veined with thin tendrils of dirty snow that clung to the shady crevices.

At 7:20 a.m., the sun's rays had yet to hit the valley floor on Wolf's acreage, so the air had more than a nip to it. Mid-August at nine thousand feet could host all sorts of temperatures and weather extremes during the day, but it was always cold in the morning.

With the overnight rains, the air was heavy and the meadow grasses matted down with water, the trees high up near the tree line dusted with snow. Two elk grazed in a thin veil of fog that hung motionless to the south.

Ella was on the railing, staring in awe at the two beasts. "They're huge."

Lauren smiled at the view, sipping her own coffee, then slapped Ella on the back. "Okay, back inside. It's cold."

"Do you ever see bears here?" Ella looked at him, her imagination already running wild behind her eyes before he could answer.

"Yes."

She shot her mom with an I-told-you-so look and stayed put on the railing.

"Let's go," Lauren said. "You have to finish your breakfast, and I have to butter my toast."

"Didn't I butter your toast earlier this morning?" Wolf asked.

Lauren blinked. "Butter my toast?"

"You did?" Ella asked.

Lauren walked inside, pulling a strand of her strawberry blonde hair behind her ear. "You're a dumbass," she said just for him on the way by. He watched her hips sway under her flannel pants as she walked inside.

With great reluctance, Ella followed her mother. "I love your house. It's so much better than our new place in town."

"Ella," Lauren said.

"What?"

Wolf shut the door.

"Come inside and eat your Cheerios. They're getting soggy."

"That's how I like them."

Wolf was frozen for a few seconds, watching the beautiful woman with the tattoo behind her ear and her beautiful daughter do their morning routine in his kitchen.

Finishing a glaze of butter on her toast, Lauren turned to Wolf, catching him staring. She did the hair thing again, averted her eyes and went red in the face. "Do you want some toast?"

"Sure."

"Eggs?"

"Sounds great."

Ella stared up at him, at her mother. "Do you know what?"

"What?" Wolf sat down.

"I want to be a bear when I die."

Wolf raised his eyebrows and sipped his coffee, unsure where to begin with a response.

"When you die?" Lauren turned from cracking an egg. "Where did you hear that?"

"Nowhere. I just told you. I want to be a bear. Do you know why?" She waited for Wolf to answer.

"Why?"

"Because they're huge and fierce. And they can scare mean raccoons away, and they don't have to answer to anyone."

Lauren scrambled the eggs in a bowl. "Who told you that you could come back as a bear when you die?"

"What?" Ella chomped a spoonful of Cheerios, dropping half of them on her lap. She looked up at her mother, then at Wolf. She was trying to figure out what she'd said wrong.

"Nothing," Lauren said.

Wolf winked at Ella. "You like bears, huh?"

"Yeah. We saw one on the road last month."

"I know. You told me about that. That's so cool."

"Yep." She dove back into her Cheerios.

Lauren slid a plate of steaming eggs and toast in front of Wolf, and then kissed him on the temple. "I have to go pee," she declared and left the kitchen.

Ella dropped her spoon and squinted one eye. "Do bears have mommies and daddies?"

"Yeah."

"They do?"

"Well, yeah."

"Then why is there only one big bear with the little bears when they're walking around?"

"That's the momma bear. She takes care of the cubs."

While Ella thought on this, Wolf heard a sound just outside of the kitchen, and then Lauren's receding footfalls.

"So … what do the daddies do?"

Wolf shoved a forkful of eggs into his mouth, brainstorming for an answer.

"Can daddies change?"

"What?"

"Can like, you have one dad, and then another dad comes and becomes your dad?"

Wolf gave a noncommittal shrug and took a bite of toast. "Yeah. They can."

"I wish you were my dad."

"Ella." Lauren was standing at the entryway, her mouth hanging open. "Jesus," she muttered under her breath as she walked behind Wolf. There was a loud clank as she fumbled something in the sink.

Once again looking like she was wondering what she'd done wrong, Ella stared at her mother's back and chewed a mouthful of food.

Wolf stood and put a hand on Lauren's shoulder.

"Sorry," she said.

"For what?"

His phone started vibrating in his pocket, which sounded as intrusive as a buzz saw in the awkward silence.

She looked at his pocket and flipped on the faucet. "Better get that."

The phone said it was MacLean calling, which meant something was going on. The sheriff rarely called Wolf's phone. He preferred talking through the channels of one of his underlings rather than to Wolf himself.

"Hello?" He answered and walked into the living room.

"We have a DB."

He walked out the front door to the porch, letting the information bounce around in his brain.

"You there?"

He shut the door. "Yeah."

"I said we have a dead body."

"Where?"

"Start driving down the river. When you cross the bridge, she'll be on your right. Next to a shitload of cops."

Chapter 2

Wolf shut off his engine and got out of his SUV. A southerly breeze came off of Williams Pass, smelling like river water and soaked mountain foliage. Low clouds polka-dotted the sky, blocking the morning sun for moments at a time.

He zipped up his jacket and shut the door, then walked to the fluttering crime scene tape strewn from guardrail to guardrail, blocking his access across the Chautauqua River to the highway. Deputy Yates stood with a clipboard, looking like he had plenty to say about the situation and couldn't wait to start talking.

"Yates," Wolf said.

"Sir." Yates turned and gestured with the clipboard. "Got a DB."

"So I heard." He nodded past the deputy at the cluster of people in the center of the bridge wearing navy blue windbreakers with F-B-I in traffic light yellow scrawled across their backs. "Why are they here?"

"They were here first."

He raised an eyebrow and Yates nodded.

MacLean failed to mentioned the FBI on the phone. More of them mingled on the other side of river, along with a dozen SBSCD deputies.

Three black Chevy Tahoes were parked nose to tail, blocking access onto the bridge on the other side. Down river, along the highway shoulder above the water, was a line of SBCSD vehicles, all with turret lights flashing.

He recognized three of the FBI agents at the center of the bridge as men that were stationed at the Denver Field Office.

"When was this called in?" he asked.

Yates shrugged. "An hour ago. The race supervisor called it in. He's across the bridge giving a statement, I think."

The math didn't add up. "And they beat us here?"

"Yeah. Me and Wilson got here first, and they had three of them big black Tahoes parked like that. Then they started ordering us around, telling us to make a perimeter and push the crowd back down the road. Assholes."

A feminine figure emerged from the cluster of agents and waved in his direction. Special Agent Kristen Luke had a cell phone pressed to her ear, her mouth moving, her eyes fixed on him.

He raised his chin.

She gave a single impatient wave and turned around, resuming a heated conversation into her cell phone.

Yates saw the interaction and pulled up the crime tape. "Go ahead."

Boots crunching on the wet gravel, he made his way across the bridge, the white rapids of the Chautauqua billowing underneath with a low roar.

Down river, a banner strewn high above the river said *5th Annual Adrenaline Games—Rocky Points*. The now too familiar logo of a mountain biker flying sideways through the air was splashed next to it.

Rocky Points had been blessed with this year's tour stop, which had been in Breckenridge the year before, Keystone the year before that, Steamboat Springs the year before that, and Vail the inaugural year. If history was to repeat itself, the fanfare promised to bring a lot of money to local businesses, excitement to throngs of people, and a lot of headache for the department.

Crowd control and risk mitigation had been the topics of the last month at each and every situation room meeting. Planning for the event took precedence over everything else. Man-hours were adding up and there were a lot of overworked deputies getting overtime pay.

A corpse and a dozen FBI agents were a hell of a way to kick start the opening weekend.

He walked up onto a circle of agents, who looked at him like an underclassman walking into a secret meeting about stealing the rival school's mascot.

One agent broke away and eyed his SUV in the distance. Wolf's SUV was dark gray, unmarked, but clearly a department vehicle to the trained eye.

"Can I help you?" The agent asked.

"I don't know," Wolf said. His badge was on his belt underneath his jacket, but he made no move to show it.

The agent had the delta shaped torso of a special forces soldier. He creased his forehead and eyed Wolf up and down. Raising a finger, he pointed at Wolf. "You check in with the deputy down there?"

Wolf turned to the railing and took the first opportunity to study the scene below.

Now it was clear why they were all standing here, because this was the only place from this vantage point they could see the dead body. Like parted curtains, there was a gap in the tall reeds and bushes, and on the ground was the corpse of a woman. She was lying on the right side of the river—the far side for the patrons that would be gathered up along the highway to see the race.

Forensic suits circled and bent over her, their progress with the scene blocked by a pop tent they had erected with zip-sides that flapped in the wind.

The corpse, lying on dark, lush green grass, almost matched the snow-white fabric of the forensic suits.

"Stand down, Special Agent Hannigan," Luke said. "This is Chief Detective Wolf."

Turning to the man, he held out a hand, a little surprised to see the big agent had stepped so close, like he had been entertaining the idea of tossing Wolf in the water below.

"Special Agent," Wolf said with a nod.

Special Agent Hannigan's face showed anger, resentment, and thoughtful contemplation as he wondered if the detective in front of him could somehow get him in trouble, and then he settled on a smile that fooled nobody. "Nice to meet you."

He shook the man's thick hand and turned back to the railing. "My deputy said you guys beat us here."

Luke tilted her head side to side. "We were in the area."

Wolf's lips were moving, and the sound coming out of his mouth was just stalling. Meaningless details. The real question filled his body with dread. "Who is it?"

"We don't know yet."

One of the men down at the body towered over the others. Six inches of black socks demarcated the end of his forensic suit pants and the beginning of his booties.

"That's Dr. Lorber," Wolf said.

"Yes."

He looked at her and frowned. "You're using our forensic team?"

"Yes. We have an assist team on the way up from Denver."

"There were going to be a lot of people standing on this bridge." He pointed to the highway. "A lot of people lined up on the side of the road to watch this race."

"Yeah, there were. And they were arriving in droves when we got here. Lorber and his team were quick with setting up that tent, but I'm sure the Twitter-verse is going ape shit with pictures of the body."

"Let me see her."

At the sound of crackling tires, Luke looked past him and narrowed her eyes.

"Shit." Wolf stiffened. A silver Audi SUV sat idling next to Wolf's SUV. Deputy Yates was talking to someone through the open driver's side window. "It's Lauren and her daughter."

"Tell them to go a different way back into town."

"There is no different way."

"There has to be."

For them to turn around and take the county road to the east, the only access back to the north toward Rocky Points was following Pine Trail, which was a two-track road that cut through the forest with plenty of elevation change. Seven years ago this bridge had flooded out, and Wolf had taken the route to work for three weeks while they re-built it. It was suitable for a dirt bike or an adventurous 4 x 4 enthusiast, impossible for a nurse with her six-year-old daughter in her booster seat in the back. Especially after a night of heavy rain.

"There's no other way. I'll drive them through."

Special Agent Hannigan had both his hands out. "Whoa, whoa. Wait a minute."

"What?"

"What's going on?"

"You're going to have to allow traffic across the bridge. There's no other way into town from this road."

Hannigan made like he was thinking about something, then nodded. "Okay."

Wolf walked to the crime scene tape, ducked under and went to Lauren's window.

"What's going on?" Lauren's eyes were wide with concern, her voice low.

"Why are there so many coppers?" Ella was in her booster seat directly behind her mother.

Wolf put on an easy smile. "We're helping with the river race."

"Oh, cool! Can we watch the race, mommy?"

"It's cancelled for the day. That's why we're here. Sorry."

"Why?"

He flicked his head to the side. "Can I talk to you a second?"

"I'll be right back." Lauren left the engine running and stepped out.

They stepped a few feet from the car. "We have a dead body down in the river. Just off the right side."

She put her hand to her mouth. "Someone drowned? Was it in the race?"

"No."

"Then when?"

"It was … something else, we think."

"What do you mean?" Her eyes bore holes into his. "Jesus … she was murdered?"

He nodded. "Listen, it's visible when you cross the bridge, off the right hand side. I need to drive you across. You can sit in the back seat with Ella and block the view. It should be out of sight when you get across the river."

"Should be?"

"Just put a hand over her eyes if you have to. Once we cross, they have a tent set up to block the view from the public. I'll drive you until the whole thing is out of sight."

They did the dance. Wolf drove with Lauren in the back seat. She sat close to Ella, square-shouldered to her daughter, pointing out the left side of the vehicle at random things. Ella was having none of it. There were cop cars and people with FBI jackets and commotion on the other side and the questions gushed out of her.

Wolf deflected, and a quarter mile later he pulled to the side of the road and let himself out. Any suspicion of any deception by Wolf and Lauren was gone from Ella's consciousness, because she was now firmly concentrated on the skateboard competition in town.

"…and they have a ramp that's like, two hundred feet high. That's what Melody said. Her brother is a skateboarder …"

Wolf shut the door and went to Ella's open window. "That's going to be awesome. I can't wait to see it."

Ella smiled brightly. She had her mother's sea green eyes and squint when she smiled. Ella Coulter was going to have a lot of boys chasing her in life. "Yep," she said.

Wolf ruffled her hair and met Lauren coming around the back of the car with a hug. Her arms were limp at first, and then she gave him a quick one-two count embrace.

She tried to duck past him but he caught her, putting a finger under her chin and tilting it up.

Her eyes were wet, her lips quivering.

"See you later, okay?"

She nodded, sniffing and wiping her nose. "Yeah."

He let her go and she opened the door. "Talk to you later."

The door thumped and they were gone, the expensive imported engine purring into the distance.

"What happened to that girl up there?" A shirtless man with swim trunks, long hair and tanned skin edged towards Wolf.

Wolf saw no breaks in the clouds covering the sun. The man had to be pre-hypothermic. He scrolled through his mental Rolodex of generic quips. "Thanks for your patience. We're working on it." With that he marched back up the road toward the bridge.

"Yeah, good answer," the guy said under his breath.

A black BMW SUV blew past toward the bridge at unsafe speed for the amount of people milling around. Wolf recognized the car, and if there was any doubt, the driving style told him it was District Attorney Sawyer White.

He jogged the quarter mile back to the bridge. Out of breath and now sweaty, he stepped up to one of the Chevy Tahoes and watched as Special Agent Luke, Hannigan, DA White, and Sheriff MacLean walked away from the rest of the group toward his parked SUV on the other side.

They ducked under the tape and cut left behind some bushes.

"Hey, what's happening?" Detective Tom Rachette appeared next to him.

Wolf gave him a double take. The detective was a squat and muscular man and was normally quick to break into a sweat during rigorous activity, but he looked like he'd been swimming in the river his shirt was so soaked. "What happened to you?"

Rachette shook his head. His breathing was heavy. "Frickin' FBI and MacLean. They've got us on crowd control. I've been running up and down the road, telling people to back off, making them get in their cars. It's a nightmare. More people just keep showing up."

"Where are they going?"

Rachette looked over his shoulder. "I don't know. To the DB, I guess. And I tell you what, that DA White is one real prick. Almost ran over me on the way in. Then he got out of his car and told me to move out of the way. Almost drop-kicked him right there."

Wolf nodded absently. "Okay, you're off crowd control. Instead, figure out who in that crowd was camping around here and interview them. Did they see anything? Hear anything? Figure out what they know."

Rachette nodded.

"I'll see you in bit."

He ducked under the crime scene tape and jogged across the bridge. The group of FBI agents watched him pass.

"Sir." Yates straightened. "Uh ... I'm not supposed to let anyone else down there."

"Then don't." Wolf walked past him and cut into the brush.

He caught up with DA White, MacLean, and special agents Luke and Hannigan on the eastern bluff above the river.

DA White was taking the rear, his suit jacket flapping in the wind, and he turned with a start as Wolf's footsteps crunched up behind him. "Where have you been?"

"Wolf," Sheriff MacLean said with a nod.

"I was detained for a moment."

"You been briefed?" White asked.

"That's what we're doing now, right?"

White's eyes narrowed before he turned and continued onward. It mattered little what people said or how they said it, the man seated in the most influential office of the county always had a problem with the way people spoke to him.

Luke eyed the exchange and followed behind Agent Hannigan, who had kept walking and was now making his way down the bluff in the distance.

When they were even with the body below they shuffled down the same path. Luke took the lead, sticking to a game trail that switched back and forth.

Wearing black dress shoes that shone with reflections of the clouds, White fell twice, but Wolf and MacLean gave him the courtesy of ignoring him. At the bottom of the incline they reached a copse of coyote willow, and then it was straight bush whacking toward the sound of moving water.

Breaking free of the brush, the scene was just a few yards ahead of them.

White sniffed. "Ah."

The wind had died down, and the air was saturated with the stench of dead human.

Dr. Lorber, the Sluice-Byron County medical examiner stood up from a crouched position, rising above the rest of his team by at least six inches. "Hold it there."

The M.E. walked to them, stepping carefully around plastic evidence tents, his thin, long legs like a crane. When he reached them he looked at his rubber-gloved hands and shrugged. "I'd shake, but …"

"Just … show us what you have," DA White said, his unblinking eyes staring at the body.

Lorber raised his eyebrows and flicked a glance at Wolf. "Right. We have a female. Between eighteen and thirty years old, but I'm guessing on the younger side of the scale." Lorber put two long fingered hands on his hips and stared over his shoulder. "Kind of hard to tell."

"Jesus." DA White cupped his hand over his nose, then quickly dropped it and looked up toward the bluff on the opposite side of the river.

Wolf knew the man was looking for cameras that had possibly caught his moment of weakness.

Agents Luke and Hannigan stepped forward, and Wolf stepped around MacLean and White to get a closer look.

"If you don't mind," Lorber said, "let's keep it at that distance."

Even from ten yards away, they could see enough detail to haunt their dreams for the next decade or two. The woman was naked, lying on her back with her legs open and her arms extended from her sides. Palms up. The symmetry of the pose was striking, like that Vitruvian man drawing by Leonardo da Vinci.

Lorber pushed his glasses up on his nose. "We found a few footprints, totally unusable after the rain of course, coming down from the road to the river. They're large prints, so I'd say we're looking at a man as the culprit. He must have walked along the banks to this point.

Looks like he carried her by the lack of scrape marks. Then he put her down, strangled her, left her here in this position. Move this tent here and you can see she's pointed straight at the registration area on the other side of the river. The guy was clearly putting her on display."

"You have a time of death?" Wolf asked.

"Rigor mortis hasn't set in. By the cleanliness of her body, we're saying she's been out here since before three a.m."

"By the cleanliness of her body?" White asked.

Lorber nodded. "Gene!"

A member of Lorber's team stood up from next to the body, picked up an aluminum case and jogged over. "Yes sir," he said in a breathless whisper.

"You've met Gene, right?" Lorber said to Wolf. "My new assistant?"

Wolf had met Gene at various points over the last year. He was Dr. Blank's replacement, and the new ME's assistant had seemed like a stand-up guy, but he was something more altogether to Lorber—like the close little brother he'd never had.

"Hi, yeah, we've met," Wolf said.

"Hello." Gene's mouth stretched wide, revealing a smile that would have been contagious in any other setting. Behind John Lennon style eyeglasses, his brown eyes were dark like strong coffee, his eyebrows matching his hair—black flecked with gray like static on a television.

Just like Lorber, the man was ten years Wolf's senior, and just like Lorber, he was a man stuck in the wrong era.

"What do we have?" White said with a *get on with it* wave of his hand.

"Gene, we were talking about the cleanliness of her body, and I was just going to explain our theory. Would you like to give it a go?"

White shook his head. "Why don't you explain it to me, Doctor. I'm not in the mood for Magic School Bus right now."

Lorber straightened and nodded. "Right. Let's move closer, until I say stop."

The M.E. led them toward the body. Agents Luke and Hannigan followed first, followed by Wolf, then MacLean and White.

As they approached, the smell of putrefaction grew stronger. Lorber held up his hands and they stopped only a few feet away.

Bending down next to her head, Lorber pointed his finger like a yardstick. "The lividity suggests she died where she is. The bruising on her back conforms exactly to the contours underneath her. Clear signs of throttling and I'd say by the strong hands of a male. You can see the marks on her wrists and ankles."

"Tied up," Agent Hannigan said.

Lorber nodded. "Probably strangled while she was tied up so he wouldn't get any defensive wounds on him during the kill."

"Christ," White said as he stepped nearer. "Where's her ear?"

They all crowded next to White to get the same angle view he had and saw a red hole where her ear used to be.

Agent Luke and Hannigan gave each other an unreadable look.

"Jesus Christ," White backed into Wolf. "You never said anything about her ear being cut off."

Lorber pulled his eyebrows together. "We're just now processing the scene, sir. I'm not sure—"

"He's here?" MacLean turned to Agent Luke. "In Rocky Points? That's who you were chasing? That sicko from down south?"

Luke blinked. "That's what we're here to find out, Sheriff."

Lorber shrugged. "Van Gogh killed by strangulation and left women with severed ears. Put them on display." He looked at Luke, and then Wolf. "Looks like his work to me."

His work.

Gene turned to them and swallowed, adding his own nod.

"Shit," White said, looking left and right along the river.

The Adrenaline Games banner flapped on a breeze, and the side tarp on the tent snapped and lifted up, giving any people across the river who happened to be looking at the time a perfect glimpse of the corpse.

Wolf watched a woman put a hand over her mouth and turn into the man next to her.

Shit indeed.

Chapter 3

"Hey, it's me," Wolf said into his cell phone. "I guess you're working. Listen, I'm not going to be able to go to the fair tonight with you and Ella."

He walked to the window of his office and gazed down at the scene below. Main Street had been converted into a skateboard and BMX bike park a block or so down to the south. Directly underneath the window there were dozens of tents set up. A tinny voice over a loudspeaker barely penetrated the triple pane glass and the soft howl of the air conditioner vent that shot cold air up the leg of his jeans.

"It's … about this morning," Wolf continued. "I have to work on this. Anyway, give me a call, okay?"

He pushed the call end button on his cell and shoved it in his pocket, and within seconds it started vibrating. Pulling it out, he hesitated, vaguely recognizing the phone number on the screen.

"Hello?"

"Hi, Detective Wolf? This is Lucretia Smith." She stopped talking and let the silence take over for a few seconds. "Are you there?"

"Yeah."

"You remember me, right?"

"Vaguely," Wolf lied.

She blew into the phone. "I was calling to see if we could meet."

"About what?"

"About the dead girl that's everywhere on the internet. You don't want a bunch of idiots on Twitter writing your story for you, do you? I figure you want to get on the record, let everyone know that Rocky Points is safe for the Adrenaline games this weekend."

Wolf formulated a response, and then exhaled instead. He sure as hell wasn't going to mention the ear thing. He'd done a search on the internet and found any pictures of the victim's body to be fuzzy and pixelated when zoomed in on. It was impossible to see if her ear was there or not, though the killer seemed to have turned her body to make it clear. There had been no mention of it, so for now the secret was safe.

"I have a source telling me that she had a severed left ear."

Was safe.

"Where did you hear that?"

She laughed and it sounded like a hyena. "I don't give up my sources."

Wolf said nothing.

"I know you want the story to be accurate so your department isn't shown in poor light. And … I know you're a smart man, Detective Wolf, but I'm just going to come out and say it. You owe me."

Wolf paused. "For what?"

She scoffed into the phone. "If it wasn't for me you'd all would be sweating for November right now. Wondering if you even had a job."

"Last time I checked they had a law on the books preventing anyone getting fired if a new Sheriff came into office."

"Are you being serious right now? Because of my piece that law was put on the books."

Wolf was not being serious. He knew what Lucretia Smith's "piece" had done for the department. Earlier that year she had cracked a case involving Sergeant Deputy Greg Barker, candidate for the sheriff's office Adam Jackson from Aspen, Colorado, and councilwoman Judy Fleming. They'd been caught conspiring against the department, trying to make it look bad in order to make themselves look better for this year's elections on November 17th.

However, they had made one mistake in targeting Wolf to be the pawn in their game. A game that ultimately cost lives and the career of Detective Hernandez, who could never fully use his shooting arm again, and who had to be let go from the department because of it.

Wolf and MacLean had found out the truth about the collusion, and the tables had turned, but since that day Deputy Barker had still been in the department. Sheriff MacLean was a crafty politician, and keeping Barker on as a deputy meant Barker's father would be happy and would be forced to support MacLean in his next bid for another four years in office. The wealthy rancher and his influential tongue would have no choice but to support MacLean on any and all of his viewpoints and decisions.

Adam Jackson's power play and infiltration of the department through Barker had been a double-edged sword. On the one side Wolf had been introduced to Lauren Coulter. On the other side, Lauren Coulter and her daughter had been put in mortal danger.

MacLean had played his hand, keeping Councilwoman Judy Fleming, the "Aspen Wonder" and Deputy Barker in play for future use. But every day Wolf saw these corrupt faces walking around town was one day too many.

So that's when Lucretia Smith of the Denver independent Press association received an anonymous packet of detailed information about the massive corruption from an anonymous source named *Black Diamond*.

Black Diamond had been a persona invented by Wolf, Patterson, and Rachette.

As for Lucretia Smith's part in it all, it had been a lazy, lottery-winner-esque bit of investigative journalism that had boosted her career as a freelance writer, landing her on CNN and Fox News for months to come where she pushed her new book.

Wolf owed her nothing.

"I have nothing for you," he said. *And who the hell told her about the ear?*

"Nothing?"

There was a knock on his door and Special Agent Luke poked her head inside.

Wolf held up a finger. "Bye, Miss Smith." Wolf hung up and pocketed his phone.

Luke walked in and collapsed on the chair, bringing in the flowery scent of her shampoo. "I'm exhausted."

"How did you guys beat us to the body? Why were you here without me knowing?"

"Without me knowing?" She raised an eyebrow. "Last time I heard you threw the race for sheriff and now you're a lowly detective."

"MacLean knew?"

"Of course he knew."

He eyed the door, considering storming down to MacLean's office.

"Listen, let me follow my orders and I swear to you you'll know everything I do within twenty-four hours."

"Not good enough. Time is of the essence here. You know that."

When she said nothing, he paced in front of the window. "You knew Van Gogh was in Rocky Points, so you guys rolled into town … tried to find him. But you failed and now we have a dead body. Maybe a local girl, whose parents are …" Wolf realized why she was there. "You have an ID."

She nodded. "Sally Claypool. You know her?"

"No." The roiling in his stomach was no less. This girl was a part of his small community. There would be many affected people.

"Twenty-six years of age. Lived with her parents here in Rocky Points."

My God. Her parents. What they must be feeling right now.

"We have a favor to ask."

He stopped and looked at her.

Luke closed her eyes and exhaled. "We need somebody to tell the parents."

"Shit." He left for the door.

"Patterson has the address," Luke called after him. "And bring them to county. We need them to ID."

"Of course you do." He muttered under his breath.

Chapter 4

"You all right?"

"Yeah. Yeah," Rachette said, but he was feeling anything but all right.

Failure was no stranger to Tom Rachette, but this was getting ridiculous. These days, failure was a constant underlying feeling, a background noise that drowned out half of everything else. He was slow to react to quips in the squad room, even slower to dole out a good beauty. Not like him. And now this?

He looked at Wolf. The man was clearly not buying it.

"You don't look all right," Wolf said.

"Well, I just screwed up the whole thing with the parents. So …"

"Ah." Wolf twisted the windshield wipers and the blades slowed.

Another curtain of rain was coming up fast. A bolt of lightning struck on the flat expanse between the two sides of the valley.

"You were okay."

Rachette rolled his head back. "Okay? I said, 'I'm sorry, but we found your son.' Your *son*."

The rain hit the windshield like a shotgun blast.

"And you corrected yourself. I think they got the gist of it. I don't think they're worried about your delivery of the news right now."

Rachette's face went hot. "I know. Sorry. I'm just … I guess looking at what happened today, things could be much worse." He rolled his shoulders back and took a sharp breath.

"You did well," Wolf said.

Rachette believed him, and warmth swirled in his chest. At least Wolf cared about him. Three words, and the guy could make you feel like an invincible god sometimes.

Nothing like his father. The guy stayed in Nebraska for a fish fry instead of coming to see his son get married for God's sake. A fish fry.

The pattering of rain peppered with the occasional piece of hail hammering into the roof kept them company for a while.

No words.

It was the words Wolf held back that were as important as the ones he said, Rachette decided. The guy got it. He didn't want to talk about it. Patterson would have been chattering right now. Would have been talking about it *again*.

Eyeing the rearview mirror, Wolf let up on the gas.

Rachette leaned forward and checked the side mirror. The guy's headlights were two orbs flickering behind the mist kicked up by Wolf's SUV. Bright blue sky was behind them, making the vehicle a shifting silhouette. It was like a metaphor, them driving into the darkness to identify their dead daughter.

"Damn," he said. "I'm just glad their neighbor volunteered to drive them. Can you imagine being in that car right now?"

Wolf said nothing.

Rachette leaned back and inhaled the rain-soaked air coming through the vents.

They passed a sign that read *Sluice-Byron County Hospital – 4 miles.*

His phone vibrated in his pocket and he checked the screen. It was Julie again. What the hell did she want from him? Get your own life. Stay out of mine.

"Who's that?"

"What?"

"The phone call."

"My sister." Rachette hit the call end button and put the phone in his pocket. He gave it two to three minutes, at least, before the phone vibrated indicating she was done with her third ranting text in the last three days.

"Huh. All okay out in Nebraska?"

"Define okay. Like, are my parents finally putting their foot down with my sister and she's finally, after four years, moving out of my parents' house okay? Or, she's calling me to come stay with me for God knows how long okay?"

A hint of a smile cracked through Wolf's stony face.

"What?"

The Chief shrugged. "Might be nice for you to have Julie in town for a while."

"Why?" He felt a stab of betrayal.

Wolf said nothing.

"She's a mooch. She'll be sleeping on my couch for four years, eating my food, watching TV, probably …" he let the sentence die.

Truth be told he was embarrassed by his little sister. She was loud. Obnoxious. And if he was considered outgoing, then his little sister was an infomercial saleswoman, up in your face and talking non-stop.

Patterson liked her, which completely confused him. But when Julie had visited two summers ago, he felt right back in ninth grade, when he was a freshman in high school and she was still in elementary school and still tagging along, tripping him up literally and figuratively every single day.

Come stay with him? Live with him? Hell no. His life was too complicated right now as it was.

They had passed through the heaviest of the rain when the glass façade of County hospital rose from the side of the valley.

He felt his blood pressure start to go up. His breathing escalated. He'd shot and killed a man, had been shot in the shoulder, had witnessed violent death first hand. But something about standing next to the corpses. It made his gag reflex come alive. Last time he'd been in the morgue with Lorber poking at those Cold Lake victims he'd felt vertigo sweep over him and barely escaped without puking.

Wolf slowed and pulled into the parking lot.

Underneath the covered drive in front of the glass entrance doors stood Special Agent Kristen Luke with some overblown meathead in a suit. *Hannigan*, he remembered.

The two agents stopped talking with one another and watched them approach.

Damn, Kristen Luke looked good. Her hair was lighter now, bleached by the sun or chemicals, Rachette didn't know, but it was hot.

It was cut shorter, split in the middle of her tanned forehead and tucked behind the ears. And that body. He would spend an entire night in Lorber's morgue for one hour in the sack with that woman. Wolf was the luckiest man alive, ever.

A vision of Charlotte bending over him in bed, her wide mouth smiling, flashed in his mind.

They parked and got out. It was quiet, the air smelling of pine and sage oils released by the rain.

Sally Claypool's neighbor squeaked to a stop right next to Rachette. Through the water beaded windows he saw three faces drained of life.

Sometimes this job was the worst.

Sally Claypool's stepfather was the first out of the car and stretching his arms over his head, like he was silently complaining for the distance they had to drive to identify his dead stepdaughter.

Rachette opened the back door for Sally Claypool's mother.

She had her purse on her lap, a wad of used tissues in a fist. Her eyes were bloodshot, red rimmed.

"Help you up, ma'am?" He held out a hand.

She ignored him and got out on her own, walking away toward the back of the car, as if she was beginning a long journey across the sage field ahead, then up into the forest to go disappear.

Wolf came to her and took her arm. Firm, turning her the right direction and uttering something to her. So gentle.

With more than a little relief that Wolf had taken over, he took up the rear and thought about corpses. His mouth began watering instantly.

"Place is a lot bigger than I remember it."

Nobody reacted to the stepfather's pointless statement.

Special Agent Luke broke away from her big partner and walked toward them with confident strides.

Sally's stepfather hitched up his pants and nodded to her, and Luke walked right by him to Sally's mother.

"Hello, Mrs. Trawler." Sally's mother had taken the last name of step-dad. "I'm Special Agent Kristen Luke with the FBI. I'm so sorry for your loss."

Sally's mother looked down and nodded, began a new wave of sobbing.

It was too much. Rachette closed his eyes and sucked in a breath. It was sweet, tangy with pine, but only made him feel worse.

When he opened his eyes he flinched, because Kristen Luke was a foot from him, leaning in to speak.

"Hey, we need to talk," she said.

She clutched his tricep and led him away. She smelled like flowers and lotions, and it was all he could do to resist flexing his arm underneath her warm grip. That would have been weird.

"How are you doing?" she asked.

"Uh, good."

"Good. Listen, we need you to stay out of the identification process. Okay?"

Like Superman must have felt when somebody finally removed the kryptonite handcuffs, relief washed over him like a bucket of warm water. It was almost orgasmic.

He nodded, trying to keep his expression neutral. "Okay. No problem."

She slapped his arm. "Thanks."

Rachette watched her walk away, pulling up her jacket to tuck her blouse into her belt line. He swallowed at the sight of her panty-lines.

Two   nights   in   the   morgue.   Two.

Chapter 5

"That's her."

Doctor Lorber lowered the sheet back over Sally Claypool's face, flicking a glance at Wolf.

Wolf didn't react. There was no need to. It was clear neither her mother nor stepfather had seen the severed ear. They had set up Sally's body with her missing ear on the far side, brought the parents in from the correct angle and Lorber had lifted the sheet just so.

It was a deception Luke and Hannigan insisted on. Wolf was still on the fence about it. If Lucretia Smith ran with her source's information, then everyone was going to know soon enough it was the Van Gogh killer—one of the most infamous monsters that ever lived in Colorado. Just not right now.

Sally's mother backed away and looked desperately behind her, ready to get out of the room.

"Please, come this way Mrs. Trawler." Luke led her by the arm out the swinging doors and into the hallway. Another doorway later and they were out of the formalin stench and into the disinfectant odor of the hospital's east wing.

The first floor waiting room was deserted, so they went to the far corner near the windows and took a seat.

Sally Claypool's mother was the first to sit, and her husband sat next to her. His eyes climbed all over Luke and then settled out the window. He planted a cold, dispassionate hand on his wife's shoulder.

Luke sat down in the row in front of them and Wolf sat next to her. His seat rose a little when Hannigan landed in the chair next to him.

"Ma'am," Luke said. "When was the last time you saw your daughter?"

She dabbed her nose and gazed out the window. "Yesterday. In the morning."

"Was that … before she went to work?"

"She was in between things. Didn't work."

Luke nodded. "And when she didn't come home last night, did you think anything was amiss?"

Mrs. Trawler shook her head.

"We thought she was out with Jeremy." Sally's stepfather pointed vaguely at Wolf. "She's always out with that dude. Don't see her half the nights of the week because she stays over there."

Luke turned her head towards Wolf but kept her eyes on Sally's mother. "Mrs. Trawler. Who's Jeremy?"

"Attack? What's his—"

"I'm asking Mrs. Trawler," Luke said, locking eyes with the stepfather.

Mrs. Trawler swallowed, wiped her nose again. "Jeremy Attakai. He's a deputy with the Sheriff's Department."

Wolf kept his expression neutral. "She was dating Jeremy Attakai?"

"Yes. Had been for a few months."

Hannigan slid forward on his chair and the plastic seat groaned under his weight. He eyed Luke, who pointedly did not return his gaze. She kept her eyes on Sally's mother.

"For a few months," Luke repeated, and then she slid forward on her seat, too. For a moment her eyes glazed over, and then she stood up.

Hannigan stood up in unison with her.

Mr. and Mrs. Trawler looked surprised, and Wolf just managed to hide his confusion.

"What's wrong?" Sally's mother asked.

"Ma'am." Luke used her gentle voice, but Wolf could see she was straining. She was itching to move, and nothing was going to stop her and Hannigan from leaving right now. "We thank you very much for coming in today to help us. Again, we're so sorry for your loss. Detective Wolf, will you please join us outside," she produced a card and held it out. "Mrs. Trawler, please call me if you think of anything else that might be of importance."

"Who did this?" Sally's mother asked. "You're leaving? You're all leaving? Tell me who did this."

"Ma'am. We intend to figure that out. We just need to speak outside, and these detectives will be back inside shortly to answer more of your questions."

Wolf stood and narrowed his eyes at Luke. She ignored him.

"Jeremy?" Sally's mother put some pieces together in her head. "You think he did it?"

Luke patted Wolf on the shoulder and walked away briskly with Hannigan on her heels.

"One second please." Wolf followed behind them into the lobby and out the automatic doors.

They walked in silence, past Rachette, who was waiting outside, past some people walking in from the parking lot, and then stopped next to Luke's black Tahoe.

Wolf stared at her expectantly.

"We need to go," she said.

"What's happening?" Rachette walked up.

Wolf studied the agents' faces. "You think it was Deputy Attakai?"

"Attakai?" Rachette turned to Wolf. "It was Attakai what? Who killed Sally Claypool?"

Luke's face twisted in annoyance and she glanced back toward the automatic doors. "Keep it down. And keep in mind they're still on the other side of those windows watching us."

"So talk without moving your lips," Wolf said, "I don't care. Just tell us what's going on. She said Sally was dating Deputy Attakai and you guys flipped out. Why?"

"We can't say. And now we have to go."

Wolf and Rachette watched the two agents slip into Luke's black Tahoe, Luke already talking on the phone as she climbed behind the wheel. With chirping tires, she backed out and drove away.

"What the hell was that?" Rachette stood next to him.

"That was us getting pushed out of an investigation."

"Why? They can't just do that. Local law enforcement needs to formally request their help. Not the other way around. That's bullshit."

"You know Jeremy Attakai?"

"The guy from Durango?" Rachette shrugged. "Talks about hunting and fishing, and that's it. Why?"

"He was dating Sally Claypool."

"Really? I don't really hang out with the guy. He used to hang out with Barker. So ... screw that."

"Wait here."

He walked back into the hospital and found Sally's mother talking to her neighbor in whispers in the waiting room. Her stepfather was purchasing a bag of chips from the vending machine in the hallway.

For the next few minutes Wolf gave his condolences, his assurances, and his card, and then he left out the front door of the building, and into the blazing sun.

"What are we gonna do?" Rachette gazed down the highway to the north, as if he could see Luke's car, which was miles down the road by now.

Wolf pulled out his phone and dialed Patterson.

Chapter 6

"Hooooooo! Drink it! Drink it!" Saliva shot from the man's mouth as he egged on his companion.

Finished gulping his beer, the man slammed it onto the bar counter and raised his hands in triumph.

There was a three-deep row of partiers facing the bar with cash in one hand and a dwindling glass in the other. Music pumped out of the speakers so loud it was impossible to hear a scream in your own head, yet everyone did just that—they were leaning into one another, telling stories that took so much effort veins popped from their necks. And they drank. Just breathing the air inside Beer Goggles Bar and Grill gave Wolf a buzz.

He pushed his way forward, keeping a firm hand on the butt of his Glock.

"I need to talk to you," Wolf said, pushing between two college-aged women wearing tight tee shirts with no bras.

"To me?" The woman on his left looked up, then saw his badge on his belt and looked like she'd been caught cheating on her final exams. "Why? What did I do?"

Wolf ignored her and nodded at the bar owner, then thumbed toward the front door.

Jerry Blackman pushed a sloshing beer across the polished stone bar top, wiped his hands on a rag and nodded back to Wolf.

"Back outside." Wolf turned, but Rachette was gone.

"… and it's really just about helping people," his detective was yelling into a girl's ear. She wore a sports bra with a CU Boulder logo and leaned away at the same rate Rachette leaned in.

Wolf slapped his arm. "Hey! Let's go!"

Wolf and Rachette wormed their way through the crowd. As detectives, they weren't obligated to wear uniforms, so they didn't. But even with button up shirts and jeans, the badge and gun on their hips were enough to get the crowd parting like the red sea, giving them a clear pathway back to the door.

Patterson had arrived and was wandering around outside. "Geez, there you guys are. I was hoping I didn't have to go in there."

"It's rockin' in there." Rachette looked longingly back at the windows.

"Yeah, so I noticed."

"What are the feds doing?" Wolf asked.

"I don't know. But I give it a few minutes before they figure out she was here through her phone data."

For the moment Wolf and his detectives were running down a lead the feds didn't have. It was little consolation considering they were no closer to finding Sally's killer, but it was something to be ahead of the information for once.

"And what exactly did her phone data say?" Wolf asked.

"Called Hal at Summit Wireless, had him access the GPS. The last time it was switched on was last night at 11:42 p.m." She pointed at the ground. "Here."

"Probably in her car," Rachette said.

"Have you guys checked yet?" she asked.

"Nope. Been inside getting Smokey the Bear." Rachette squinted and toked an imaginary joint. "Speaking of …"

The noise from inside swelled and Jerry Blackman stepped out. "Hey, guys."

"Hey, Jerry." Wolf shook his hand.

Jerry Blackman was the owner and manager of Beer Goggles, which was arguably the most famous business in town. Travel magazines included the log-built tavern in top lists—Top Ten Places to do Après Ski. Top Seven Colorado Mountain Bars.

How Jerry had made such a thriving business was a mystery to many. But Wolf spent his fair share of time here and knew Jerry was the genuine article when it came to making food, and the atmosphere was second to none, situated right next to the rushing Chautauqua River among the pine trees. The place was clean, and the beer selection was borderline too many choices, and all of that sat well with the locals as well as the visitors from Denver.

Jerry flinched at a low passing bird and failed to notice Patterson's and Rachette's extended hands. "What can I do you guys for?"

"We need to ask you a few questions," Wolf said.

"Yeah. Sure." Jerry sighed and wiped his forehead. Sweat slid down his face. His ponytail was drenched. "I could use a break. But I don't have the manpower in there to hold this crowd for long."

"Good business, this Adrenaline Games, huh?" Rachette asked.

"Yeah." Jerry's smile disappeared. "Adrenaline games?"

Two men came out as loud as a cannon blast, with unlit cigarettes in their mouths. "Hells yes! I don't give a shit what she says, I'm gonna—"

"Hey, bro!" Rachette said. "No smoking within fifty feet of the entrance to a public restaurant. So beat it."

The two men squared up for a confrontation, then eyed the guns and badges and left into the parking lot.

"That's the name of the extreme sports competition we have going on in town this week." Patterson narrowed her eyes.

"Yeah, I know," Jerry said.

She blinked.

"Jerry." Wolf pointed to the parking lot. "Why don't you come with us for a second."

They stepped into the densely packed parking lot, keeping their feet on the rocks and gravel to avoid the puddles, and stopped at a beat up blue Ford Fiesta.

"You called this in earlier this morning?" Wolf asked.

There were two bright orange stickers: one on the driver side window and another on the passenger side. The stickers said, *Warning, please move this vehicle immediately to avoid towing.* They were official SBCSD stickers and had been affixed by a deputy. And in this case, said deputy logged the warning into the department computer system to be checked on twenty-four hours later. If the car was still there, it was to be towed.

Patterson's thorough check had uncovered that red flag, which had matched Sally Claypool's license plate number from the DMV records, giving them the location of her car to add to the last known location of her phone. Both her phone and the car location had been the same place—here.

Jerry thought about it for a second. "Yeah, I called it in. I don't like people leaving their cars overnight. I need the space as you can see."

"Do you know Sally Claypool?" Wolf pointed at the folder Patterson had brought with her.

She opened it up and produced a printed picture of Sally Claypool's driver's license photo.

Jerry's furrowed brow told it all. He was terrible with names. Copious amounts of THC ingested every day for decades did that to a person. He took the paper from Patterson and pulled his glasses down his nose.

He shook his head. "No. I don't think so."

"Did you see her last night?" Rachette asked, letting a little impatience creep into his voice. "She was here. This is her car."

"She was?" Jerry scratched his beard. "Shit, there were just as many people here last night, too. Well, not as many. But a lot. Tons. It's the best two days of business I've ever had."

A car rolled past them, sloshing through the deep potholes. It parked in front and let out a half dozen giggling women.

Jerry stood on his toes and watched them go inside. Another blast of thumping bass and screams echoed through the trees, snipped short by the shutting door.

"Who else worked last night?" Wolf asked.

Jerry went wide-eyed, and just when it looked like blood might start oozing from his ears he said, "Cherry. Veronica. They were here."

"And are they inside?"

"Yeah," Rachette answered for him. "They're in there."

Wolf took Sally's driver's license photo and gave it to Rachette. "Go in there and ask them."

Rachette smiled and snatched the piece of paper. Without another word he was jogging back to the front door.

"Thanks for the help, Jerry. Can you please check credit card receipts for Sally Claypool and give the information to Rachette? And otherwise, we'll leave you be. You can head back inside."

"This that girl who was killed last night?" Jerry asked. "That picture? This car?"

Wolf nodded.

"So … she was taken from here?"

"We're here to find out. We'd appreciate it if you kept this quiet." Wolf nodded. "Thanks again. Have a good rest of the day."

Jerry hesitated for a moment and left.

Looking in the windows of the Ford Fiesta, Wolf listened to the rhythmic crunching of Jerry's footsteps recede and disappear into the sea of humanity.

"This is where she was taken, isn't it?" Patterson stepped to the other side of the car, looking at the ground.

The ground on Wolf's side was a blank canvas, wiped clean by inches of violent downpours over the last twenty-four hours.

"I'm not seeing a phone in there," Patterson said. "Could be in the glove compartment. In the center console."

"Door's unlocked here." Wolf pulled some gloves from his pocket and put them on. "I see her keys on the floorboard by the gas pedal."

Patterson put on some gloves and tried her side. "Locked here."

As he lifted the driver's side handle, the door popped and sagged open on screeching hinges. It smelled like old fast food and stale cigarette smoke, with a hint of perfume.

The car bounced as Wolf sat on the driver's seat and reached over to pop the passenger side lock. He opened the center console and found a fistful of change, small junk—scraps of paper, gum wrappers, a lollipop stick—and a makeup kit.

Patterson opened her side door and checked the glove compartment. "No phone."

"None here either." He bent over and made to pick up the keys, then thought better of it. "Better get out of here. So far it's the only piece of evidence that hasn't been hit by rain."

Running footsteps came from the bar, and then a splash. "Shit!" Rachette came up shaking water off his boot. "Cherry says she saw her last night. Says she was drinking at the bar," he looked at his notes, "with a girl named Gabrielle Hammond. She says she doesn't remember her talking to any men. Veronica says the same thing. Saw her talking with the same girl, Gabrielle Hammond. Both say they don't remember Sally leaving. She was there, and then she was gone. Sally paid her tab at 11:40 according to her credit card receipt. I asked if they had her phone number. That was a negative."

"When did Gabrielle Hammond pay her credit card receipt?" Wolf asked.

Rachette's mouth dropped open. "If she had one."

"Go check it."

He ran back to the bar.

Wolf shut the car door and stepped toward the hood, gazing down at a clearing next to the river.

Patterson mirrored his movements. "What are you thinking?"

There was a short decline in front of them, then flatness covered in long, lush grass, underbrush and pine trees, all soaked and dripping from the afternoon rains. A few paces beyond, the river was a white ribbon of burbling water.

"If the killer took her phone," Wolf said, "we'd be able to track it, and track him. So he either shut off the phone and kept it, or left it here somewhere."

He sidestepped down the hill and Patterson followed.

They zigzagged back and forth, their pant legs soaked to the skin after only a few minutes, scanning each square inch of the ground slowly and methodically. Pushing aside long grass with their feet, checking near the stalks of bushes and grass, they also checked in and around the pine trees, getting soaked with a deluge of water on their necks with the slightest touch of the branches.

"Got it." Patterson stood looking down with her hand up.

Wolf walked to her.

It was an iPhone lodged in the branches of a rock jasmine bush.

"Bag it."

"Might want to make it a bag of rice," she said. "That thing's gonna be toast with all the rain."

"What are you guys doing?" Rachette was back and standing near the bumper of Sally's car.

"Get an evidence bag," Patterson said.

Rachette was breathing heavily. "Gabrielle Hammond paid at 12:45 a.m. Over an hour after Sally Claypool. But thanks for asking."

"Oh yeah," Patterson said in a mock interested tone. "Can you please get an evidence bag?"

Their vehicles were down and out of the lot, across the bridge and a good fifty yards further along the access road that led to the highway.

Rachette looked like he was going to protest, then turned around and jogged away. Only a few seconds later he came back. "Uh … we have company."

Chapter 7

Wolf hiked back up the incline to the parking lot. A line of black Tahoes were idling behind Sally Claypool's car, an agent Wolf had never met sliding out of the lead vehicle's passenger seat.

"Hello. You must be Detective Wolf."

"And you are?"

The man smiled and nodded, seeming to approve of Wolf's defiance. Like he was comparing his first impression to what he'd heard. "Special Agent Todd. I'm the new Assistant Special Agent in Charge of the Denver F.O."

He was a good-looking guy, probably Wolf's age, just about the same height, with short brown hair that was sculpted like a trimmed shrub at a French countryside estate. His voice was low and smooth, like a radio announcer's. His eyes were light blue, which gave them an electric quality.

"You must be new," Wolf said.

"There are a few of us new guys this year. I'm a transplant from Chicago, along with Special Agent Hannigan, whom I think you've met."

Wolf pulled off his latex glove and shook the man's hand. "Yeah, I've had the pleasure."

"I see you found her car." Agent Todd gestured behind him.

Luke climbed out of the second Tahoe with Hannigan and they stood a few feet behind Todd, pointedly keeping out of the conversation. Agent Hannigan looked like he was wishing he had a bag of popcorn to go with the show.

"Kristen's told me a lot about you," Todd said.

Kristen?

Wolf nodded toward Sally Claypool's vehicle. "The bar owner called it into the department this morning. It was parked here overnight and he wanted it towed, but our deputy opted for warning stickers and logged it into our system."

"And how did you three come upon her vehicle?"

"Detective Patterson was checking Sally Claypool's DMV records, saw the match. So here we are."

"And you didn't tell us?" Agent Todd asked.

"Correct."

The ASAC smiled wider and shook his head; like this was classic Wolf behavior he'd heard about. "Have you found her phone?"

"Yes."

"Good work."

"Anything I can do to help," Wolf said.

"Look, I know this is awkward, our … entrance into matters here."

"Very."

Agent Todd nodded. Made a face. Nodded some more. "But I assure you we're here with only cooperation in mind. There was an ongoing investigation that drew us here. We requested the sheriff to keep our presence secret, because to let others know could have endangered our operation."

"Your operation?" Wolf looked at Luke, who averted eye contact. "Whatever your operation was, it ended with you guys rushing to the dead body of one of our citizens. As far as I'm concerned a dead girl that could still be alive if only you guys would have made it clear that you were in town in the first place, and why, and how, and when. And for whom."

ASAC Todd narrowed his eyes, dimming the blue bulbs to a cold stare. "In due time, detective."

"That's what I keep hearing. I think due time is long past."

"Where's her phone?"

Wolf stepped aside. "Down in a bush by the river."

ASAC Todd pointed. "Would you please show it to us?"

Wolf hesitated. "Of course."

He led them down the incline to where Patterson was still standing.

***

For the next two hours Wolf, Rachette, and Patterson helped with the rest of the processing. Or at least, those parts they'd been allowed to participate in. Which put them in charge of less important tasks, like calming down Jerry Blackman as his parking lot became a crime scene on the best business day of his life. A small team of FBI scientists, along with the agents on hand, took care of processing the rest of the scene.

All the while the clouds were clearing, pushing out on a freshening breeze from the southwest. As the sun grew hotter the air turned muggy next to the river, and more and more patrons of Beer Goggles Bar and Grill streamed into the parking lot. They walked by with cell phones pointed, firing stupid questions that went unanswered by tight lipped FBI agents.

The entire time Wolf ignored Luke. He felt childish, especially when she was close enough to touch, but he also felt betrayed by her so far today, and that was something she needed to talk her way out of. Not him.

Now, as Vince "Viper" Hurwitz of Viper's towing was jamming into position to pull the Ford Fiesta out of the lot, Wolf called Patterson and Rachette over.

"We're done here." Wolf smacked a mosquito on his neck.

ASAC Todd came over and ran a hand through his hair. "Thanks for the help. We'll be giving a detailed report tomorrow morning at your station. As I'm sure you've heard from Sheriff MacLean."

Wolf hadn't heard a thing from MacLean in the hour and a half they'd been there. He looked at his watch. 3:46 p.m. Things were heating up even more inside Beer Goggles, and it would be hopping on Main Street with the Adrenaline Games opening weekend fair going in full swing.

"We have to go," Wolf said.

ASAC Todd nodded. "I understand. You guys were already going to be busy without all this happening."

He and Luke made eye contact for a moment.

"Bye."

"Damn, I could use a beer." Rachette patted his belly as they made their way down the parking lot. "And a few burgers."

"Watching a bunch of people drink will have to do for now," Patterson said looking at her watch. "Theoretically we have fifteen minutes until our security shift."

"Well, people are going to have to watch my fat ass eat while I protect them."

Patterson eyed Rachette's belly. "Yeah, you're really working on something there."

Light footsteps came chasing after them, and Luke came in step next to Wolf. "Hey."

"What?"

Luke looked at Patterson and Rachette. "Do you guys mind giving us a moment?"

"I'll see you guys later," Wolf said.

She waited for them to leave and then took a hard breath. Looked back up the parking lot at the whirring tow truck. "This is a delicate investigation. There's a lot at stake with some of the people here."

"You don't have to tell me what's at stake. A girl's dead. A killer's loose in our town. Not yours. So cut the BS."

She nodded and looked at her feet. "Fair enough. Listen. Here's the reality. We've had a serial killer task force in place on this for two years now. You know that adding more investigators usually muddies up the water, confuses logistics." She looked up the parking lot again.

Wolf frowned. "What?"

"My ASAC up there has your DA convinced everyone needs to step aside, especially now that it involves one of your own. You know the drill. Internal investigations are usually outsourced. It's about due process and objectivity—"

"Bullshit. Because our guy was dating Sally Claypool, he's the guy? And what if it's not him? Then it's just us stepping aside while you people walk in here and investigate a murder in our town."

"Yeah, well … you don't know the half of it." She put her hands on her hips and stretched her back.

Wolf leaned toward her. "I don't? Then tell me."

"Just … have a little faith in me, all right? I'm working on it."

"Yeah, yeah." He waved a hand and left.

Chapter 8

Wolf knocked once and opened the door, not bothering to wait for permission to enter.

"Yeah?" MacLean waved a hand. "Oh, hey. Come in. Shut the door."

He stepped in and paused at the sight of D.A. White sitting across from the desk. He was heavy looking in the chair, his tie loosened, a button undone, and his sleeves rolled up.

"What's happening out there?" MacLean asked.

"That's what I was going to ask you."

MacLean looked at DA White. "Well, we have Deputy Attakai in interrogation room C talking to fed interviewers. Or should I say, not talking. He's not saying anything. Waiting on his lawyer, who should be here any minute. And you guys found Sally Claypool's car, which is getting towed into impound right now, and we'll be giving that over to the fed forensic team. You also found her phone, which we'll be—"

"Why are we rolling over and playing dead on this? Because it may or may not involve one of our own deputies?"

White frowned and stood up. "We're not rolling over on this. We're acting accordingly. This isn't a deputy having sex in the evidence room, a few bucks missing from a towed vehicle, a few punches thrown off-duty … this is a step beyond an IA matter. This is murder, and in case you had your eyes closed this morning, it's sick, twisted murder. And like you said, this might involve one of our own." White walked to the window behind MacLean's desk and looked down. "Look at it out there. We have every news outlet in the country already parked along Main Street. They came for a puff piece about the extreme sports, and now they're staying for the show."

"It makes no sense." Wolf's voice was louder than he wanted it to be. "What the—"

"Deputy Attakai's sister was one of the victims of the Van Gogh killer two years ago," MacLean said.

Wolf stood dumbly, trying to process the information. "What?"

"His sister escaped the killer's clutches. She was the only one ever to escape." MacLean upturned his palms. "Yeah. There's a lot more to this we don't know, okay? I'm in the dark just as much as you are, but I have learned that little tidbit. So it's more than he was dating Sally Claypool."

Wolf blinked. "So, you think since Attakai's sister escaped the killer … that Attakai is the killer … I'm not understanding."

"You're not supposed to understand," White said. "You don't know enough to be making judgments right now. So why don't you calm down."

Wolf faced the DA. "Calm down?"

MacLean stood and held up his hands. "Right now Lorber is doing the autopsy, preparing his prelim report, and he's going to present it to us tomorrow morning. At that time, our federal buddies have promised me a full and thorough briefing of what's going on. And then we'll all be happy. Okay?"

Wolf walked to the window and looked out. The rain was back. There was a curtain of green to the south and it flickered from within, but drops were already streaking the window. Through the triple panes he heard a constant rumbling outside. Vendors wrestled with flapping tarps and tents while patrons scuttled away like bomb sirens were going off.

"And if it's not Attakai?" Wolf turned around.

White shrugged. "Then somebody else will determine that."

"So we just have a sick, serial killer on the loose in our town, and you want to outsource the investigation?"

"It's a matter of due process and objectivity, Wolf."

"Cut the bullshit, Sawyer." Wolf said, raising his voice louder than he wanted.

The room flashed and there was an immediate boom of thunder outside.

"You know I can't cut the bullshit," The DA said. "It's all about the bullshit. The council is up my ass with making sure we come out of this doing the right thing. They've got pictures of that dead girl all over the internet for God's sake. I'm getting calls from reporters talking about the Van Gogh killer. And how the hell do they know about that little tidbit of information? You know what's coming up in November. Any screw-ups will mean reassessment of budgeting. And cuts in funding at any level would destroy way too much this county has invested in thus far."

Wolf eyed the condo building poking up through the trees to the north. Despite the electrical storm barreling into town, a group of men were still hammering on the roof, the threat of losing precious man-hours forcing them to play Russian roulette with God. More county investments.

MacLean cleared his throat. "Wolf. You did a good job today. There's nothing more we can do but wait for tomorrow morning."

"And then what?"

"And then what, what?"

"How are we assisting in the case?"

MacLean gestured to White. "At the request of the District Attorney's office, we are to turn over the investigation to the feds."

Wolf glared at White. "I'm not sure this is going to bring up your numbers, Sawyer."

White rolled his eyes. "You don't know what you're talking about."

"I don't? That's what's going on here, isn't it?"

Drops were pelting the window now, and another crack of thunder penetrated the silence.

White held his tongue, because anything that came out of his mouth would have been an obvious lie and they all knew it.

MacLean was sitting pretty for this year's election, running unopposed in November for his office of Sheriff thanks to the scandal that dropped the floor out from under Adam Jackson's campaign, but Sawyer White was anything but in the clear when it came to his job security. He had a woman named Blair Hanquist to contend with.

Blair Hanquist had started out as a laughable candidate for District Attorney, a mere pile of dried dog poop on the path to Sawyer White's third four-year term in office. Laughable, because Hanquist had entered the   race   talking   about   White's   heavy-handed   sentencing recommendations. He was too tough on crime, she said, and Sawyer White and his cronies laughed with utter confidence, dismissing Blair Hanquist's backward approach with a wave of their hands.

Sawyer White had been elected during a time when candidates were out-toughing each other, promising to put dangerous criminals away. And he proved to be very good at doing exactly what he promised, putting away a lot of young people for a very long time. Only his idea of what dangerous criminals were was not the same idea that the people of the tri-county district had.

Wolf had never told it straight to Sawyer White's face, but he was more inclined to think like Blair Hanquist when it came to sentencing a seventeen-year-old kid who'd been caught with a few pills. Rather than slap on intent to sell charges, ship him out, and lock him up and throw away the key down in Florence, he'd rather see that kid working up at the ski resort, down at the local grocery store, getting his life together with the help of a little professional guidance, good old fashioned talking, along with social pressure to keep him in line.

Or whatever they did to make the kid better. It was a case-by-case basis as far as Wolf was concerned. All he knew was that when his father was Sheriff, they had four beds in two cells in the old department building, and they were rarely occupied. Now they had forty-six beds in state-of-the-art cells, and they were crowded under the "recommendations" from Sawyer White. Rocky Points and the other small towns north and south weren't filled with criminals, and they needed to start acting accordingly.

"What's going on here, Chief Detective," White's voice was low, "is my official recommendation, which will be followed. If you don't like it, you can talk to Judge Richardson. I'm sure he'll be happy to spell it out for you."

"Gentlemen," MacLean said. "We're on the same side, here. Let's all just relax."

Wolf walked to the door.

"Seven a.m. meeting tomorrow," MacLean said before the door shut behind him.

Chapter 9

Hey Dad. How's it going? I hope all is well with you and everyone down in Points.

Things are going great up here. We had a visit from the Alaska State Patrol yesterday, some trooper looking for a guy skipping his parole or something, and I thought of you.

The ice fields are actually very warm, which was counter-intuitive for me. I sunburnt the roof of my mouth! Can you believe that? I was hiking with my mouth open and the sun reflected off the snow. Hurts like crap when I eat.

Anyway, the program is great and I'm glad I'm doing it. I've met a bunch of cool people and the professor is hilarious. And thanks again for helping me out with the cost. I owe you … but don't hold your breath while waiting for me to pay you back.

I'll email you again soon. We don't have readily accessible internet up here on the ice field, which is actually pretty nice for a change, so I'll probably talk to you again in a few days.

Love,

Jack.

Wolf closed the email and clicked back over the internet. Scrolling down the Durango Herald newspaper webpage, he commenced reading the next article in line.

The Van Gogh killer has struck again and the city of Durango is frozen in fear.

"We are following promising leads at this time," Sheriff Ron Mansor of the La Plata Sheriff's Department said early Thursday morning to reporters. What exactly those leads are, and how law enforcement and FBI agents are going to act on them is anyone's guess, because since Thursday morning nobody is talking.

Last Sunday morning Rose Chissie, 26, was found murdered and put on display in a park. A family who wishes to remain anonymous found her naked and mutilated body—"

The music outside started up again, ripping him from his reading.

He stood and stretched at the window.

Main Street below Wolf's office was hopping. The sun was back out, the black top street drying rapidly, and hundreds of patrons holding beverages had taken to the streets . The music pumped from a trio of speakers set up by an energy bar company. How they'd been put in charge of the music he had no idea, but it was less "extreme sport" and more "mountain rock" so he approved.

He used a scanning technique he'd learned in the army, eyeing a narrow band of vision from left to right, moving down a fraction of a degree, then back right to left, and repeating. It only took him a few passes to find Lauren with Ella.

His pulse jumped at the sight of her. Her hair looked redder than brown in the fading light of the day, and it was pulled back with silver hair clips, framing her tanned, beautiful face. Her smile warmed him through the fifty yards of air and three panes of glass. An older man was chatting her up and she had the guy in an uncontrollable laughing fit. When she walked away, the man gazed at her behind until his wife appeared and punched him in the shoulder.

It was a fact that every man Lauren Coulter came into contact with fell instantly in love with her, and they just had no control over it. He still remembered the first time he'd looked into her green, nebulous eyes, and the certainty that he'd found the one. The only one that could possibly hold a candle to his late Sarah.

It was dumb, but Wolf felt jealous for the first time in years. Jealous of the smile she'd given that harmless old man. Probably because she'd been ignoring his calls all day. He considered dialing her number right now to see what she would do with his own two eyes. Look at the phone and shove it back in her purse with a disgusted look on her face?

He blinked and shook his head, dismissing the thought. It was amazing the difference a few hours could make. They had made love in bed this morning with such insatiable desire for one another, and then she had gone cold. Flash frozen.

He knew it was Sally Claypool. It was having to face her own troubled past because of what was happening here and now.

Lauren had meandered through the crowd and was now talking to a good-looking man Wolf failed to recognize. He wore a short-sleeved shirt despite the post-rain nip to the air which had everyone else dressed in jackets, and his arms were well tanned and muscular. He was pointing at Ella while Ella smiled and hugged her mother's leg, and Lauren was bright-eyed and smiling, like she did when she and Wolf were having a particularly good time on a date.

"Hey," Rachette was standing with Patterson at his door.

"Feds've got deputy Attakai in interrogation," Patterson said. "Sally Claypool's car's getting worked by the feds forensic team."

"So I heard. How about the interviews with the campers?"

"There were three camps set up within a quarter mile of Sally Claypool's … resting place," Rachette said. "They all saw nothing. I sent you an email with the report."

"Okay," Wolf said.

Rachette walked to the window and looked down. "And with that, that means there ain't shit for us to do."

"Go home."

"Done," Rachette said, his eyes lighting up. "Well, I'm gonna head down and get a beer. You guys in?"

Patterson shook her head and looked at her watch. "I've got just enough time to go put Tommy to bed, kiss my husband and go to karate class."

Rachette scoffed. "Why not just stay home? Have a beer and relax after a day like this."

"With Scott's mother? No thanks. I'd rather go punch some stuff."

Rachette eyed Patterson.

"What?"

"Is she going to be there?" Rachette asked.

"My mother-in-law?"

"What? No." Rachette went red in the face. "Never mind."

"You mean Munford?" Patterson shrugged. "Normally is. She's a blue-belt now. Moving up fast."

Rachette stared out the window with unfocused eyes.

Wolf slapped him on the shoulder. "You go ahead. Drink yourself silly, but be ready bright and early. Seven a.m. sit room meeting. I'm going down to meet Lauren and her daughter."

"Right." Rachette blinked. "Right. See you guys tomorrow."

***

Steam rose from the black top of Main Street, thickening the normally thin mountain air. On it rode the smells of cooking meat and fried dough, and it made Wolf's mouth water. Breakfast had been cut short by the call, and the rest of the day had been without any food.

With a clear mission in mind—buy Lauren and Ella some dinner, stuffing his own face in the process—he made his way through the crowd toward the last place he'd seen her from his office window.

He smelled her before he saw her standing right next to him.

"David! Mommy, there's David!"

Wolf turned and saw Ella first. Her arms were out as if she wanted to charge him with a hug, but Lauren had a firm grip on her jacket. Ella stopped and looked up at her mother, and then settled back into leaning against her leg.

"Hi, David," Lauren said.

Wolf leaned in and kissed her cheek, and he thought he felt her pull away.

"How you doin', sport?" Wolf said, channeling his deceased grandfather, who used to say the same thing to him growing up.

"Good," Ella said. "Have you seen those skateboarders doing those tricks up the street?"

Wolf smiled. "No, I haven't. What kind of tricks are they doing?"

"Like, super huge ones. One guy was like, flipping and twisting in the air, and then he came down and just, shoom, went down the ramp, and then he went up the other side, and did more tricks …"

Wolf couldn't help but smile wider at her enthusiasm, but his smile dropped when he saw Lauren was staring at him with a blank face.

When Ella paused to take a breath, losing her train of thought, Wolf took advantage of the opening. "You guys want to get some food?"

"No thanks."

"Yeah!"

Lauren looked at Ella. "We have to go, honey. We're going to Aspen for a while."

Wolf blinked. "Okay. What's going on there?"

"What's going on there is what's not going on here." She raised her eyebrows. Got it?

Wolf got it. The relief that he knew what was troubling her instantly relaxed him. "I tried calling you today a few times. I wanted to let you in on what was going on."

"Hey!" Margaret Hitchens appeared out of the crowd, butting into their conversation. She was outgoing, probably the most outgoing of any person in the town of Rocky Points. It's what had made her tens of millions of dollars as a real estate magnate. She was also a good friend of Wolf's and had always been. And ever since he'd started dating Lauren, she'd taken to being their biggest fan of them as a couple. "Hey, Ella!"

"Hi, Margaret!"

"Hey, let's go get us a funnel cake. Let your mom talk to David here, okay?"

Ella's broke into a smile, and then dropped it so suddenly it was comical. "Mom? Can I go get a funnel cake?"

Lauren smiled despite herself. "Yes. Go ahead. Thanks, Margaret."

Margaret ignored her and disappeared with Ella into the crowd.

Lauren stood with crossed legs and looked at the ground.

Wolf reversed their day together in his mind. For the life of him he could not find what he'd done wrong, but he knew it was lurking there somewhere.

"Hey, David." A man came up and slapped Wolf on the shoulder. It was Mark Ponsford, a man who made his living as a ski patrolman in the winter and a ranch hand in the summer. "So what's going on with this thing from this morning? Is it true that it was Sally Claypool?"

Wolf was surprised at the amount of fear he saw. Mark Ponsford had an eleven-year-old daughter who roamed freely around town on her scooter. His concern was a punch to Wolf's belly.

Lauren had lifted her eyes and was watching Wolf's response.

"We're working on it, Mark. I promise we're working on it."

Mark stood nodding. Clearly unconvinced, but wanting to be. "Okay."

Swiveling his gaze to the crowd, Wolf realized there were ten people surrounding him looking at him the exact same way Lauren was.

If he were a man in a movie, he would have held out his hands, raised his voice over the music, and given a reassuring speech, but the truth was he felt ill-prepared to tell them anything of substance, and now he felt completely out of place at this fair when he should be out there finding a vicious killer. Wherever there was.

And what if the guy was here?

A few people looked like they were reading his thoughts, and they saw the uncertainty in his eyes, only magnifying the uncertainty in theirs.

"I'll talk to you later, okay, Mark?"

Mark nodded and left.

"Could we please walk so we could talk?" He grabbed Lauren's hand.

She pulled her hand away. "Look, we do need to talk. But not here. Not now."

He frowned. Her talk definitely had a different meaning than his talk. "You also want to talk."

"Yes."

"About what?"

"Us." Her eyes started to water.

"Okay." They stared at one another for a while. Could have been a few seconds, or an hour, he wasn't sure. "But you can save your breath. Cause I get it."

A tear slid down her cheek.

He eyed the crowd, and the sight of Lauren's discomfort seemed to move most of them along.

He leaned in close to her and lowered his voice. "I'll uh … I'll see you around. I think it's a good idea what you're doing. Get the hell out of town, because the truth is, we don't know who this guy is yet, and he's a sick individual. Definitely get out of here," he turned and left, making his way through the crowd.

Every time he looked up from the litter-strewn, wet street, there were people looking at him, so he kept his eyes down.

"Detective Wolf?" The voice was high pitched and familiar.

Looking up, he saw the petite, spandex-clad body before he saw the bubbly smile of Lucretia Smith. Her long blonde hair was pulled straight back, and it seemed to pull her lips off her teeth, her eyebrows back on her head, and her eyelids up along with it. It was like a shark wearing a thin mask.

Wolf continued snaking through the crowd.

"Detective Wolf, I just want to talk to you about Sally Claypool."

Wolf stopped and she ran into him.

"Oh, geez." She stumbled back and looked up. "Can I have a second?"

He lowered his voice and bent to her ear. "This is hardly the time or place to be discussing the corpse of a murdered woman. Do you see the children right over there? The parents?"

Her wide, enthusiastic eyes narrowed into knives. "Then let's go somewhere where we can talk. Like up in your office?"

He grabbed her bare elbow and led her off the street, past a tent, and behind a pine tree next to the sidewalk. "What do you want?"

"I told you, you owe me."

"I don't owe you anything."

Her smiled disappeared. "I want to know about the ear. I want to know why I saw a deputy being escorted into the back of the building by other deputies. What's his name? Attakai?"

Wolf felt his face flush.

Her smile returned. "Yes. I know about it all."

"Then why are you talking to me?" He left her next to the tree.

"I want to know about the truck they found in Durango."

He wanted to keep walking away, but the comment was so out of left field he had to pause. How the hell was she getting information he didn't have? He wanted to ask her that, but he didn't want to see the shit-eating grin.

"What's with the truck, Detective Wolf?" she asked to his back.

Wolf turned around and walked back to her. "This is what I'll tell you."

She pulled out her cell phone, pushed a button and put it in front of Wolf's face. "Go ahead."

"If you interfere with this investigation, print anything, or type it on a webserver or whatever the hell you do, and somebody gets hurt, then I'll …" Wolf looked at the cell phone inches from his mouth and stopped himself.

"I'm just looking for the truth."

"Me too. So back off, all right?" Wolf walked away.

"Wait, wait." She stepped up to him and pulled out the waistband of her spandex.

Wolf stared confusedly for a second, and then watched her reach in with purple fingernails, fish a business card out of her panties and hold it up. "Can you call me if—"

Wolf turned and left, back through the sea of scared faces, and into the automatic doors of the County Building.

"Hey, honey," Tammy said from behind the reception desk. "Looks fun out there."

Wolf nodded absently, pulled his phone from his pocket and dialed Agent Luke.

She answered after two rings. "Yeah?"

He walked to the waiting area near the windows. "Find a way to get me on that task force, or we're done."

Luke blew air into the phone. "You're threatening our friendship? A little full of ourselves, are we?"

"You heard me." He pushed the call end button.

Chapter 10

"Kiai!"

The right front knuckle punch came at Patterson. His weight shift had telegraphed the move, so she had no trouble dodging it with a quick step to the left.

Her opponent's glove whooshed past her ear with the uncontrolled force of a low-rank belt.

Zach Herring was a forty-nine year-old with plenty of facial hair and the body-type of a man who kept warm in the winter. He was an averaged height man, which was to say he was much taller than she was, which meant it was easiest to go for a hammer strike on his ribs.

So she did. Her padded glove tapped against his ribcage before he knew what hit him.

"Up!" Sensei Masterson stiffened and raised his hand nearest Patterson. "This fighter." He punched the air with a hammer strike. "Punch to the," patted his side, "ribs. Two points to zero."

Zach's face was a mask of anguish and disgust for losing two points in a row. She knew the real source of the scowl on his face was she was a girl half his size kicking his butt, even if it was a girl who'd been studying martial arts for over ten years of her life.

"You okay?" Patterson smiled.

Zach's eyes flashed behind the full-caged facemask and he forced a smile. "Yeah, yeah."

"Ready!"

She took a left half-moon stance and raised her guard.

He mirrored her position.

"Fight!"

Zach came in fast this time, as she knew he would. Shuffling forward, his eyes widened and his lips stretched with concentration.

Staying right where she was, she kept her gaze on his torso, letting him charge, entering her into the fight.

His right leg craned, and he thrust his foot forward. The front-ball kick came hard, again, too hard for sparring conditions.

Sidestepping, she simultaneously dodged the kick and was instantly in position to hit a number of open targets. In a real-life situation, with an opponent actually attacking her—without a spar helmet, a protective cup, gloves, and foot protectors—she would have gone with an elbow to the ribs, followed by a devastating knee to the groin, followed by an elbow to the nose, followed by a crippling, sadistic, thrust kick to the front of the knee, which would have probably put a real assailant in the hospital for a month and given him a lifetime limp. But instead, she threw a lightning fast back two-knuckle punch, tapping him on the chin.

"Up!"

The word failed to register in Zach's brain. She'd seen it before. The man had a combination already in mind, and his mind had already given the command to his body to carry it out. The second command—to make his body stop—was a full second behind and was going to show up to the party late.

Patterson's guard was up.

"Stop!" Sensei Masterson saw it coming.

So did Patterson. At least, half of it. He came in with a left, and she deflected it high with a forearm block, and then he came in with the second half—a right thrust punch which connected squarely somewhere between Patterson's nose and upper lip.

Instinctively, she closed her eyes and jerked her head back to lessen the impact, which sent her whole body arching backwards to the point she left the ground. Twisting, she landed on her hands and feet and bounced forward like a cat, coming up a few paces from Zach at the ready for more action.

Zach pushed his helmet up onto his forehead, revealing horrified, wide eyes. "Oh my God, I'm so sorry."

Patterson softened her face, flashing a mouth-protector smile. Sniffing, blood shot down the back of her throat and she gagged at the sudden flow.

Lifting her head back, she ripped off her gloves and wiped a finger under her nose, feeling the numbness of her slick upper lip. Her finger was bright red under the humming lights of the now silent dojo.

"Are you okay?" Gene Fitzgerald had been lined up against the wall. Now he stood next to her gripping her shoulder. "You all right?"

"Yeah, I'm fine."

"You're bleeding, bad." Munford came up next to Gene.

"What was that, Zach?" Gene said, squaring off with Zach. "Didn't you hear Sensei Masterson?"

"Don't worry about it," Patterson said. "He didn't mean to, did you Zach?"

Zach was blinking with an open mouth. "No. No, sorry. Geez, I'm sorry."

"Is it broken?" Munford was in her face now.

"Back, step back," Masterson said in a relaxed tone, like he was quelling excitable ten year-olds. He pointed a finger at Zach. "You need to learn to control your force." He snapped to a pencil position and raised an arm over Zach's head. "Fighter disqualified!"

It was a mock-tournament sparring match. Nothing to get too worked up about, but Patterson saw the utter disappointment in Zach's face. "I'm sorry." He mouthed the words, but no sound came out. The earlier fire in his eyes was replaced by shame.

The fresh coppery taste worked its way under her mouth guard. She took out the shaped piece of plastic. "It's okay. Really. Getting hit is part of the training."

Zach nodded and stepped in line at the side of the room, looking like he was trying to disappear into the wall.

"Gene and Charlotte, you're already out here. You're up next. Patterson, go get that washed up."

"Yes, sensei." Patterson bowed on her way out of the dojo and went into the tiny bathroom at the rear of the building.

With paper towels doused in mountain-cold tap water, she cleaned herself up, jammed a couple wads of toilet paper up each nostril and went back out just in time to catch the final point of Munford and Gene's fight.

The dojo was alive, the other nine members of the dojo laughing at some turn of events she had just missed.

Gene and Charlotte were circling one another in the middle of the room, both of them giggling, both trying to look serious.

"You're going down," Gene said with a laugh.

Munford stepped in and kicked him in the gut.

"Oh!" Gene did a nice job of deflecting the kick downward, but into his own groin.

The dojo erupted in raucous cheering.

"Up!" Sensei Masterson snapped to pencil position with a hand over Munford's head.

Munford had her hands over her mouth, her eyes wide. "I'm sorry, Gene."

"This fighter! Ball kick, to the—"

"Yeah! We saw the ball kick, all right!" Zach said.

"All right, all right." Sensei Masterson looked at his watch. "Line up."

They lined up and listened to Sensei Masterson give his parting words. Once class was dismissed, Patterson took her time getting her sparring equipment back in her bag, waiting for the dojo to clear out.

She was stalling, because outside Munford and Gene were talking and giggling some more in the parking lot. And also in the parking lot was her car, which would bring her home to her husband and son. And her mother-in-law, with her disappointed, judgmental glares.

"You okay?" Sensei Masterson was watching her with his hawk eyes.

"Yep. No problem."

"Have you been practicing for the test?"

She shrugged. "Not enough."

Sensei Masterson was seated at a chair in front of a computer screen. It was where he called out his goodbyes from, staring over crescent glasses as he pecked out emails one letter at a time with board-breaking strong fingers. Now he lowered his glasses on his nose, staring at her with icy intensity. "Not enough?"

The test was for sixth degree black belt, something she'd been working toward for the last eleven months since she'd committed to her karate practice again. It would prove to be a brutal test of mental and physical strength. If she failed, her black belt could be revoked.

Fishing her tennis shoes out of the cubbyhole, she sat on the bench and put them on. "Not nearly enough."

His eyes softened and he leaned back, crossing his legs. "Tommy?"

The sudden glossing of her vision startled her. "Jesus. I don't know why it's ..." she was going to say *bothering me so much* but nothing came out of her closed up throat.

Sensei Masterson stared at her, and then nodded like he understood. He did understand. The man understood everything. He always had.

For the last eleven months, Patterson had renewed her commitment to her martial arts practice. The reasons were many, but most of all it was an outlet for the stress that was damming up inside her. Apparently it was far from working.

Wiping a tear before it fell down her cheek, she nodded. "Yeah. Tommy."

She looked outside. Munford and Gene were watching her through the windows. They walked away further into the darkness of the parking lot, giving her and Sensei Masterson some privacy.

Or maybe they were going to go screw once and for all. What was she going to tell Rachette when she saw him back at the station? And he was going to ask. *Was Charlotte there? How about Gene?* The more she hung out with these two, the more she felt like a traitor.

"Parenthood will test you far more than anything martial arts can throw at you," Masterson said.

"I once heard somebody say that parenting is never done right or wrong. It's just done." She tied her shoes.

"And this is what you're thinking about while crying?"

Straightening on the bench, she shouldered her gear back and stood. "I should get going. I need to go home and sleep."

Sensei Masterson pushed his glasses up his nose and pecked the keyboard. "Later." The man wasn't exactly Confucius.

"See you Wednesday," she said.

"Practice."

"Yeah."

Nipping, but not biting, the air outside was heavy feeling with humidity from the river. She let her bag drop at her feet and pulled on her hooded sweatshirt, zipping it to her chin.

"Hey," Munford called from across the parking lot, her toothy smile glowing in the semi-darkness.

The crunch of Patterson's footsteps on pea gravel was faint against the low roar of the river.

The dojo was two streets off and across the Chautauqua from Main, in an old pizza joint that never survived the eighties. Past the rushing water, rear porch lights of houses built fifty years ago swarmed with bugs. Above them the sky glowed from light streaming off the Adrenaline Games festivities on Main. A guy was yelling something into a loud speaker over bumping bass.

"How's the nose?" Munford asked.

"Not bad." It sounded like *nod bad.*

Gene made a pained face.

She pulled out her cell phone and checked the time—8:06. "What a day, huh?"

Gene and Munford's chipper mood dissipated.

"Yeah. Talk about a rude awakening," Gene said. He looked at his watch. "Speaking of … shoot. I have to get back to the hospital to finish up the prelim with Dr. Lorber. We probably have an all-nighter ahead of us."

"Any earth-shattering news to tell us from the autopsy?" Patterson asked the assistant ME.

"Other than the severed ear, and working the first Van Gogh killer scene in two years?"

She chuckled humorlessly. "Yeah."

"We've been working all day on her," Gene said. "We just have a few more tests. Need to take some photos. You'll know what we know tomorrow. I'm a little nervous, standing up in the front of that huge room."

Munford put a hand on his chest. "Oh, you'll do fine. You have a lot of experience talking in front of classes, right?"

"I guess."

Patterson eyed Charlotte's hand on Gene's chest, and the way they stood so comfortably close to one another, and she suddenly felt like a third wheel. "Okay. I'll see you guys tomorrow."

Gene and Charlotte looked at her and nodded, as if she were already an afterthought.

She walked to her Jeep and got in, eyeing them laughing some more in the rearview mirror as she drove out of the parking lot. The news would not be good for Rachette. Things were definitely progressing, and she could hardly blame Munford.

Gene was the opposite of Rachette. If she wanted to date a grownup for once, more power to her. Even if the grownup were old enough to be her father. Albeit a handsome, young-looking father.

Her phone vibrated in her pocket and she pulled it out. It was Scott.

"Hey," she said.

"Are you coming home?" The earnestness in his question broke her heart. It sounded like he was holding back saying the words *ever again.*

"Yes. I'm on my way now."

Chapter 11

Wolf stopped at the bridge crossing from his side of the Chautauqua to the highway side and got out of his SUV.

The eastern peaks were silhouetted against the brightening sky. A symphony of bird noises filled the air. It seemed less like a crime scene today and more like a peaceful morning along the river, save the news van parked across the highway where a man scrambled to set up an umbrella light stand.

"Morning." Yates was sitting in a camp chair with a thermos of coffee perched on the ground next to him.

"You still here?" Wolf asked.

"Nah. I just showed up. Had Johnson here all night."

Wolf nodded. He thumbed to the north. "Mind if I take a walk?"

Yates cracked a smile. "Would it matter if I said yes?"

"No."

Wolf snaked through the dew-laden brush and made his way out to the bluff above the river. When he was about even with where Sally Claypool's body had been, he found the game trail and hiked down.

Through the reeds and bushes he went, and then he was back out on the beach where she was found.

Evidence of the crime scene processing was everywhere—holes and footprints, scrapes and indentations—but there was no evidence of the crime that had taken place.

With unblinking eyes, he stood in the cool air surveying the ground. He transported himself to two mornings ago, becoming an observer of the crime as it took place.

He saw a man parking, probably somewhere in front of where Wolf's SUV was now. He saw the man in a raincoat with the hood pulled up over his head, keeping himself dry against the curtains of freezing rain while he carried a naked, shivering, Sally Claypool over his shoulder.

He saw him struggle down the slope next to the bridge, down to the river, and then he saw the killer walk along the swelling banks to this point. Splashing. Stumbling.

He wondered if Sally would have been resigned to her fate, too far gone mentally and too taxed physically after her torture to care anymore about what happened to her. Or maybe she was kicking and screaming the whole way. She had been tied up. Sliced with a knife. He suspected she would have been no more than half-conscious for the moments before her demise.

He saw the man put her down. Saw him reach his hands around her neck.

Wolf shut his eyes but the vision remained. He shook his head to clear his thoughts and scanned the other side of the river. There were three news vans now with satellite dishes raised high on telescoping poles, and three reporters with their cameramen. One of the male reporters was live, gesturing over his shoulder toward Wolf.

Wolf turned around and made his way through the reeds and bushes again. Hiking back up the bluff, he took a breath at the top of the rise, taking a final look below.

Picturing her body on the grass and rocks, the angle at which she was set, he followed the line up to where the race registration tent had been.

The registration tent had long been removed. The race organizers were scrambling to set up another course north of town, over two miles away. Now, in its place, was parked a maroon sedan with a man standing at the back bumper.

The man had a black beard and shoulder-length hair, wore jeans and a black fleece jacket with a white North Face logo on the breast, or so Wolf thought. It was too far to tell.

A tingle swept through his body as he stared at the man.

The man looked to be preoccupied with the news teams and the crime scene below. He hadn't seen Wolf.

Wolf pulled out his cell phone and opened his camera function. When he swept it up the man was climbing back inside his car.

As the man's brake lights blossomed, Wolf started snapping pictures.

On his fifth photo, his phone seemed to shut down. "What the—"

It vibrated and Dr. Lorber's phone number was displayed on the screen.

He quickly pushed the call end button and the camera function reappeared. Raising it again, he pressed the button over and over, getting useless photographs of receding taillights that disappeared around a bend.

His phone vibrated again and Wolf answered. "Yeah."

"Hey, you coming in or what?" Dr. Lorber asked.

"Yeah, why?"

"It's almost seven and you're not here. I'm just making sure."

Wolf looked at his watch. He only had ten minutes. "Yeah, I'll be there."

Chapter 12

The department parking lot was packed with the full fleet of cruisers, black Chevys Tahoes, and then some. There was a gaggle of reporters being held back by two mute deputies at the rear of the building.

Ignoring the flurry of questions as he walked inside, Wolf made his way to the third floor. As he walked straight past his locked office, voices echoed down the hall, growing louder as he entered into the squad room. Deputies were bunched together speaking excitedly.

He spotted Patterson and Rachette, and they hurried over to meet him.

"Hey," Rachette said.

"We're not on the case?" Patterson stepped close to Wolf and put her hands on her hips. "We're cut out?"

Wolf straightened, and then craned his neck to see inside the open doors of the Sit Room.

The Situation Room, or Sit Room, was like a modest sized college classroom he'd seen at CU Boulder when he'd dropped Jack off last semester, with arced rows of seats that climbed up at an incline. A group of coffee-sipping suits and uniforms were conversing down at the front of the room, displayed behind them a huge picture of Sally Claypool on the projection screen.

"It's the first I'm hearing about it." Wolf's voice was louder than he wanted it to be, but the anger was boiling over. "Who told you?"

"Luke," Patterson said, backing away a step. "Wait. You didn't know about this?"

Wolf looked at her squarely. "About us getting cut out? No."

"No, Rachette and I are cut out. Not you. Shit. I thought it was your idea. Sorry. I …"

Patterson backed away, and only then did he realize she'd been squaring off with him.

Wolf took out his cell phone and gave it to Patterson. "Can you check out the last of these photos on my phone? See if you can get a plate."

Patterson took his phone. "Yeah. Sure."

Wolf noticed half the squad room was watching their exchange.

"Chief, you coming in?" Undersheriff Wilson was pulling the auditorium doors closed.

Slipping inside, Wolf skirted the rear of the room and walked down the side stairs near the windows. The men at the front of the room ignored his arrival, some of them conversing in hushed tones and more than a few of them preoccupied with Special Agent Luke's backside as she bent over a laptop computer, looking as if she was preparing to give a presentation.

He recognized ASAC Todd, Agent Hannigan, and a few of the others from yesterday. Then there was DA White speaking in hushed, serious tones to another elected official. Dr. Lorber sat in the front row with his new assistant next to him. Behind them sat four more elected officials Wolf recognized from the county council.

Sally Claypool smiled on the big screen above Luke. She looked vital and happy, holding an orange drink in her hand. It could have been her cell phone screen saver, her Facebook profile photo.

Luke looked up and saw Wolf, and then got back to tapping her computer. "Can you help me?" She pointed at Gene Fitzgerald.

The man pointed at his own chest.

"Yes, you. Are you good with computers?"

Dr. Lorber stood up. "If you need computer help, then I'm your man."

"Good, fine."

Wolf reached the front of the room and sat down, leaving four buffer seats between him and the nearest FBI agent.

Lorber was pressing keys and tapping the mouse, and then he tested a laser pointer-clicker. The screen switched to a power point presentation.

"Thank you." Luke put a hand on Dr. Lorber's arm, and Wolf felt the heat coming off the man's face from twenty feet away.

He couldn't blame him. Kristen Luke did look good, and it wasn't just his current rebound state of mind. Normally past her shoulders and pulled back with some sort of fastener, she'd cut her hair and given it some blonde highlights, and now it was just above her shoulders, pulled back behind her ears like parted drapes.

Her face was deep brown, like she'd been in the Bahamas tanning for a week before today, and her eyes sparkled. As ever, she was impeccably fit, filling out her pantsuit perfectly.

She was nervous and smiling a lot, and that was probably what did it for him. Wolf hadn't seen her smile since the last time he'd seen her, which had been over a year ago. She wasn't normally a smiler, but the prospect of standing up in front of a group of people did strange things to a person.

"Okay, okay," she said. "All right everyone. Let's get started." She stared down two men at the front of the room and they hurried to their seats.

"My name is Special Agent Luke. I'm the assistant lead investigator for the Van Gogh task force. Special Agent with the Denver field office. My colleagues are Special Agents Hannigan, Wells, and Shecter, and this is Assistant Special Agent in Charge, Brian Todd."

"Sally Claypool." She turned to the big screen and began pacing the front of the room. "I'm going to start off this meeting by giving up the floor to your County Medical Examiner, Doctor Lorber." Luke tossed a clicker to the front row and Dr. Lorber caught it with two hands, just avoiding being hit in the face.

She turned and walked straight toward Wolf and sat down next to him.

Her familiar aroma of shampoo and perfume swirled against him.

"Hello, friend." She spoke quietly without moving her lips, drawing out the word friend.

Doctor Lorber stood and flipped his ponytail back with one hand. He wore a white lab coat over black jeans and a blue-checkered button up shirt. The ensemble hugged his limbs, making his movements arachnid-looking.

With a wave Lorber summoned Gene to stand up with him.

Gene dressed much the same as his boss, with jeans and a button up shirt under his own lab coat.

The two men were opposite body types and it looked like a giraffe and a man were now standing at the front of the room.

The County Medical Examiner pressed the clicker and began comfortably pacing the room, while Gene looked lost for a moment and settled on facing sideways and standing motionless.

The picture changed to the naked, spread eagled version of Sally Claypool on the riverbank. It was white skin on green grass, brown river sand just below her feet. The picture had composition, almost like a work of art.

With another click, the picture changed to Sally Claypool lying on the cold steel table in Lorber's lab. The photo was focused on her neck, which was black and blue.

"Fractured larynx, damaged neck muscles, thyroid cartilage and hyoid bone were damaged. Cricoid cartilage is almost exclusively fractured in throttling, and all the other signs point to exactly that—death by strangulation."

Click. The victim's naked torso, dark nipples on white skin that was striped with angry red marks.

"Shallow slashing with a sharp blade."

Click. Her back, striped with angry red marks.

"Same thing on the back."

Click. A red mark on the back of her neck.

"I believe this is where Sally Claypool was injected with a knockout drug. Prelim toxicology suggests Fentanyl. Which is fifty times more potent than heroin. One hundred times more potent than morphine. Has a rapid onset, and a short duration. In other words, a perfect drug to incapacitate a victim upon first meeting. You found her keys on the floorboard of her car. Which suggests she was attacked, injected, right when she was climbing in."

Click. Her left wrist, which was deeply bruised and scabbed.

"She was tied up with hemp rope, which we found in her wrist tissue."

Click. Sally Claypool's left ankle, which was also deeply bruised and scabbed.

"Same thing with the ankles. By the abrasions, it looked like she was hogtied, with her hands lashed to her feet behind her back."

Click. A close up of her fingernails.

"Analysis of the dirt under her fingernails did not match the dirt composition of the area she was found in, which suggests she was brought somewhere else for a short while before she was taken to her final destination. Gene?" Lorber tossed his assistant the clicker.

Gene was gazing up at the screen and the clicker bounced off his chest and clattered to the floor. He bent over and picked it up, and when he rose his face was so filled with blood it looked like his head might pop.

"The dirt is, uh, a conglomeration of many geological strata found in the Quaternary Alluvial fan in the Chautauqua valley—the different types of rock dumped out of the steep canyons onto the valley floor."

Gene cleared his throat. "We did a close examination of the dirt at the scene and compared it to under her nails. The dirt at the crime scene, on that entire section of the river and to the south, has a high iron content. Hence the reddish color of the dirt south of town. The dirt under her nails does not have high iron content. We know through the composition that it is from the alluvial fan that came out of the Rainbow Creek valley and flowed north, in the same direction of the Chautauqua River."

"Which means?" MacLean pointed his pen in the air.

"So the killer took her somewhere north of where Rainbow Creek comes out of the mountains," Wolf said.

Gene nodded and pointed at Wolf. "Yes. The dirt indicates she was taken north. Held for a short period of time, and then taken to where she was killed."

The assistant ME tossed the laser clicker back to Lorber like it was a live grenade.

Lorber caught it without looking. "Rainbow Creek got its name for a reason—because it has so many minerals and other materials running down it from those mines up the valley. We found all those minerals under her nails."

"Okay, I got it," MacLean said.

Click. A side view of Sally Claypool lying on her back. The underside of her body was deep purple.

"As you can see, the blood pooled in her back, at the same angle of the slope of the riverbank she was found on, which suggests she was brought there alive and strangled where she lay. It's also suggesting the killer then put her in this pose."

Click. Back to her on the riverbank.

"And he left her for the river rats to find the next day. Clearly a display. Rape kit was clean, no sexual activity within the time of her incarceration."

Click. Indentations in the sand next to the river came up on screen.

"These are shoe prints of our killer, but unusable except to suggest it was a man with a sized nine to twelve shoe who brought her there.

You can see some washed out scrape marks, suggesting he placed her body on the ground and pulled her into place. Other than that, they tell us nothing. The rain erased anything useful such as shoe tread pattern and exact size."

"As far as the rest of the scene," Lorber shook his head, "Clean as a whistle. It rained at least one inch two nights ago, and it cleaned her and everything else in the vicinity. We found little save the hemp fibers embedded in her wrists, and the dirt under her fingernails. Otherwise, we're looking at too much environmental interference. Absolutely nothing at all from the perpetrator. Except for what he wanted us to find. Her."

Lorber gestured to Luke.

She stood and walked to the front of the room. "Thank you Dr. Lorber."

"And I take it there was no DNA under her nails?" Wolf asked.

Lorber shook his head and nodded at Gene. "None. We think he kept her tied up, strangled her, and then untied her. If she was conscious, that keeps her from fighting back, and keeps any defensive wounds off our assailant."

Lorber looked around the room. When no more questions came he handed the clicker to Luke.

"Any more questions for Doctor Lorber?"

No one spoke. The five county officials seated next to MacLean looked queasy. They were used to dissecting county budgets, not human beings.

Luke gestured at Wolf. "Chief Detective Wolf, you conducted the interviews with the campers nearby on the river, correct?"

Wolf nodded. "My detectives did, yes."

"Would you like to come up to the front and tell us what they said?"

Standing up, Wolf took position next to Luke. "There were three camps within a quarter-mile of where the victim was found. One down river, two up river. All of them within distance of being able to hear something, and perhaps see something, but that would have been on a normal night. Since it was raining they all gave similar stories—they were holed up in their tents until the morning. They saw and heard nothing." He sat back down.

"Thank you Detective Wolf." She bent over her computer and chose a different file on her desktop. Clicking it open, a hokey looking font flashed up on the screen that read, "The Van Gogh Killer."

"All right," Luke said. "We've covered Sally Claypool. Now let's get everyone up to speed with what we have on our Van Gogh Killer."

Clicking her handheld pointer, the next slide of her presentation came up.

It read: Modus Operandi.
1) Strangulation.
2) Semen inside victims. (Non-match in NDIS to date)
3) Lacerations.
4) Tying of victims' wrists and ankles.
5) Abrasions, bruising.
6) Display of corpse.
7) Severed ear.
8) Fentanyl injection.

"You can read the list up here," Luke said, "and see the MO matches closely with Sally Claypool. The strangulation, the lacerations, the tying of the wrists and ankles, abrasions and bruising on the body, the Fentanyl injection, the display of the corpse for the public to see, and most importantly the severed ear—it's all there for Sally Claypool. But," she circled item number two with her laser, "there was no semen inside Sally Claypool, no DNA from our killer. Not the case with our killer down south. He left semen in each of his victims."

She clicked the button and a slide came up that was segmented into eight different squares. Within each square was a head shot of a dead victim on an examiner's table, each with a missing ear, save the first victim who still had both ears.

Groans passed through the room.

"Seven victims in all, but we're including the first victim here," she circled the first square with her laser, "because although the killing did not follow the same MO as the others, she still has both ears, semen with DNA matching the killer was found inside her."

"How was she killed?" Lorber asked.

"Blunt force trauma to the head and chest." Luke clicked the button again and a map came up on screen.

The map was of southwestern Colorado, with the four corners of Colorado, Utah, Arizona and New Mexico borders butting up to form a plus sign in the lower left corner of the screen. There were eight red dots on screen, all contained within the Colorado borders.

"These are the locations the eight bodies were found. As you can see, it's quite a spread of territory the killer covered, but all within Colorado. Silverton, Colorado, was the first. The one with blunt force trauma, and not strangulation. That was Jessica Meinhoff, our number one here." She circled the laser. "It's also important to note that in Silverton, Jessica Meinhoff was not displayed like the others, either. She was found along a hiking trail. Two: Downtown Cortez, Maria Chico.

This was the first body to be displayed. She was found on a neighborhood sidewalk in much the same position as our Sally Claypool. Three: Bayfield, Samantha Winston. Also displayed. Number four ..."

She listed the eight victims and their locations, of which three were found within Durango city limits.

"The timing is over two calendar years, ending at the end of the summer two years ago. The frequency of the kills went up in the end, almost to a frantic pace, with the last three murders occurring in three consecutive months in the summer until," Luke snapped her fingers, "it all came to a stop."

She clicked back to the eight victims and circled the laser on number eight.

The headshot photo was like the others—swollen, closed eyes, black bruising on the neck. Her hair was crow black, her skin pale clay.

"This is Rose Chissie. Our final victim down south, killed right before our killer," she paused and chose a word, "took a break. Rose Chissie grew up on the Ute Mountain reservation, south of Cortez, and then moved up to Durango after high school, where she attended trade school and met a woman named Mary Attakai.

Luke paused for effect.

"Yes. They are related. Mary Attakai is your deputy Jeremy Attakai's little sister." Luke slipped a leg on the edge of the table and sat. "I mentioned the killer got more frantic in the final months of his killings. The amount of time between killings became shorter. The display locations more brazen. One victim was found in the middle of an intersection of the side streets of Durango. And no, there were no witnesses.

"But in the end, it looks like his recklessness caught up to him. Because on August twenty-third, he was staking out a parking lot of a restaurant where our eighth victim, Rose Chissie, worked. Mary Attakai came to pick her up, and our man abducted them both. He incapacitated both of them, drugged them with a needle, put them into his SUV, brought them out in the desert, and began doing his thing with Rose Chissie. Mary woke up and miraculously escaped on foot, eventually making it to the highway, and was picked up by a trucker, who brought her to the hospital.

"She gave law enforcement a description of an overweight, bearded man with long dark hair. But that's all she had."

Wolf's heart pumped harder as he thought about the man near the river. He'd had a dark beard. Long, dark hair.

"She also said that he'd been wearing some sort of mask as he was attacking Rose," Luke continued. "A Native American ritualistic mask. She said he lifted the mask for a second, and she ran away. I said earlier that her escape was miraculous, because she ran straight off the edge of a cliff."

The room let out a collective gasp.

Luke nodded. "Her wounds corroborate her story of tumbling down a tree from top to bottom until she hit the ground. She had multiple contusions, scrapes, bark embedded in her skin, but no broken bones. The hospital found she had fentanyl in her system.

"Her story is she got up and walked out of the valley, all the way to highway 550, where she was picked up by a trucker. With all that happened to her combined with the drugs in her system, we've been taking her description of her assailant with a grain of salt."

"What about the vehicle?" MacLean asked. "Did she have a description of that?"

"Her description of the man's vehicle was a white, midsized SUV. Older than new, she said. The man? Fat. Hairy. But quick."

MacLean cleared his throat. "Excuse me."

"Yes." Luke clasped her hands behind her back.

"But my Deputy Attakai, and check me if I'm wrong, isn't an overweight man with long hair and a beard. In fact, I've seen his photos from La Plata County SD when he worked down south, and he never had long hair and a beard, nor was he ever fat."

"Correct." Luke raised her eyebrows, as if to ask if he was done.

MacLean sat frozen with one hand in the air, then he dropped it.

Pushing off from the table, Luke clicked the clicker and a picture of the dirtiest SUV Wolf had ever seen in his life came onscreen. It was reddish brown from the mud that caked every inch of its surface from the roof to the rubber on the wheels.

"Five days ago a company carrying out a fracking well cleanup project unearthed this south of Durango. They pulled it out with their excavators."

Luke clicked to the next slide, which was a rear perspective of the SUV. The words Ford and Explorer were wiped clean of dirt and the green Colorado license plate had been cleaned to reveal the number.

"The company informed La Plata SD about their find. The department traced the SUV's registration and came up with the name Fred Wilcox. Seen here."

She clicked a button again, and a headshot of a man came up on screen.

Fred Wilcox's hair was a tangled mess, pulled back into a ponytail. The skin of his face was pasty white, the lower half covered in a greasy beard. He had oil pool black eyes that were wide open, like he'd been photographed the moment after somebody told him he had a month to live.

Wolf's first impression was that they were looking at a cold-blooded killer. If you decided there was no humor in the ludicrous facial expression, then all that was left was psychotic murderer. There was no in between.

"Looks like a perfect match for Mary Attakai's description," MacLean said. "Minus a Navajo mask I guess."

Silence descended on the room.

Luke clicked again. Tight, blue carpet filled the screen. It was filthy, stained with maroon and brown, streaks of black and tan. There was a woman's shoe lying in the upper corner of the photo.

"This is the interior of Fred Wilcox's Ford Explorer. This shoe had Rose Chissie's blood on it. We tested the rug in the back of the Explorer and found DNA matching our eighth victim, Rose Chissie. Subsequent testing has matched a different sample of blood to our sixth victim."

"So," MacLean snorted, "Fred Wilcox is the killer. This fat guy with a beard, just like Deputy Attakai's little sister said. So why are you guys so erect over Deputy Attakai being the culprit?"

The room turned and looked at MacLean.

MacLean blinked.

Luke clicked the pointer again, and a picture of a cell phone came up on screen. It had push buttons and a one-square-inch screen, not a small television like the ones most people carried. A dumb phone. A burner phone.

"We found this phone in the center console. It took us a while to clone it and access the data, but when we did we found this was a burner cell purchased in southwest Colorado at a big box retailer. There was one phone number it had called repeatedly, and only one.

"Our techs tried to locate the phone it had been calling but got nothing. The other phone was dark. Not transmitting at all. That was a few days ago. But then we were surprised that the next day we tried again and someone answered. The duration of the call was short, but long enough to locate it. It was transmitting to cell towers here in Rocky Points."

"We triangulated it to a few hundred square meters. A small space, relatively speaking, but not exact by any means. And found the epicenter to be the front of this building."

Once again Luke let silence descend on the room.

"That's when you came into town," Wolf said.

She nodded. "That's when we came into town. We set up surveillance cameras at various points outside your building, and we called it again. But unfortunately there was no answer. And since that moment, since that first call that was answered, it's been shut off."

"And then Sally Claypool was murdered," Wolf said.

Luke nodded. "Before we could coordinate anything with you, Sally Claypool was murdered, and we've been on scramble mode ever since."

"But you heard Sally's mother talk about how she had been dating Deputy Attakai," Wolf said. "And you thought about the phone call coming from the building so you thought it must have been him."

Luke gave a non-committal shrug.

MacLean raised his hand. "I hate to beat a dead horse here, but, you found the truck down in Durango that all but proves the killer was Fred Wilcox, so you came up here and went after Deputy Attakai?"

She said nothing.

"Why would you do that?" he asked. "Why are you in the slightest bit interested in my deputy?"

"Because there was a second killer," Wolf said.

Every head in the room turned toward him.

"What?" MacLean asked.

"There were two cell phones, because there were two killers," Wolf said. "There are missing pieces of the MO, because only one of them killed Sally Claypool—the one who isn't Fred Wilcox, would be my guess. Otherwise, we'd be finding his DNA inside of Sally Claypool. Otherwise, the feds wouldn't be here looking for someone who isn't Fred Wilcox. They wouldn't be arresting Deputy Attakai."

The heads of the room turned back to Luke.

She said nothing, just gave a look to her superior, raised her hand and clicked the button again.

Another slide came onscreen, and another gasp swept across the room.

There were eight squares again, all with different colors of flesh inside each box. But this time they were looking at feet. Left feet.

In all the pictures except the first square, there were red stumps where the big toes should have been.

"Good work, Detective Wolf." Agent Luke stood and paced. "When the FBI were called into southwestern Colorado after the third killing, we were surprised to learn that local law enforcement had been hiding a piece of the signature from the public—a severed left big toe."

Dr. Lorber slapped his knee and leaned forward in his chair, smiling.

"As we're all aware of," Agent Luke said, "Sally Claypool did not have a severed toe. If Fred Wilcox had done it, and he followed the MO of his previous eight victims, then we would have found DNA inside of Sally Claypool. But we didn't."

She set down the laser clicker on the table and held out her hands.

"That's where we're at, folks."

MacLean let out a long sound that sounded like a laugh. "Okay, so let me wrap my brain around this. You find Fred Wilcox's truck buried in the ground four days ago."

"Five," Luke said.

"Whatever. You figure out, from the DNA inside—his and the victims'—that he's the killer … or one of the killers."

"Correct. We found his hair in the driver's seat. We found the DNA of two of the victims, blood and hair, in the back. We then checked his DNA against the database and found it to match the semen found inside—"

"Yeah-yeah-yeah … and you also found a phone, that you called and it dials a number that leads you here. The reason you suspect Deputy Attakai is his past … his sister's past."

"Correct," she said. "His sister was one of the—"

"Yeah-yeah-yeah … so … his sister was a victim, though." MacLean clamped down one eye. "Why would he have kidnapped his sister two years ago along with Rose Chissie. And … what about his alibi that night two years ago? You guys figured out where he was then?"

For the first time Luke looked like she didn't have an answer.

"Aha." MacLean pointed at her. "He has an alibi."

"We don't know," she said. "He won't talk to us. But he wasn't on duty."

"So, you don't think Fred Wilcox had anything to do with this?"

"I didn't say that," Luke shook her head. "We don't know. But there are significant missing pieces of the signature. Like Detective Wolf said, there were two cell phones. They called one another often."

MacLean looked like he wanted to stand up. "But the existence of a second cell phone doesn't exactly point to there being another killer."

"You are correct. But when taken with the missing pieces of the signature, then the two killers theory holds more water."

"Or maybe Fred Wilcox has just gotten smart about his approach," MacLean said. "He didn't leave DNA this time. Or he can't get it up."

"He has a point there," DA White said. "Here's what I want to know. Why bury the truck?"

"He ditched the evidence and came up." Dr. Lorber turned in his seat and talked as if he and DA White were the only two in the room. "I'd say it is Fred Wilcox if I had to bet money. And he's exacting some sort of revenge on Mary Attakai for getting away from him. He comes up here, stalks Mary Attakai's brother for a while, biding his time for the right moment and the right way to get back at him. And then he sees the FBI come into town, makes his move. Kills Attakai's girlfriend, gets his revenge, puts her on display to rub it in your faces." Lorber pointed a long finger at the FBI agent next to him.

MacLean bugged his eyes and stared into the ether. With a shake of his head he said, "So Fred Wilcox gets back at Mary Attakai by killing her older brother's girlfriend? Why?"

"Actually," Lorber said, "you're right, it would make more sense if he made his way straight for his little sister. If it were me, I'd get my revenge for her getting away by taking her out. Finish the job I failed at before."

They looked at Luke.

"We've thought of that and have twenty-four-hour surveillance on Mary Attakai's place in Durango."

"This is making no sense to me," MacLean said. "If we think that—"

ASAC Todd stood with his hands up. "Please! Please … if it all made sense, then we'd be charging a serial killer, or pair of serial killers, right now in court." The handsome special agent scanned his blue gaze across the room like a searchlight. "I assure you we are working on this with all our resources. We have more people working in La Plata county as well. Clearly Detective Wolf here will be a good addition to our team."

"So what's next?" MacLean asked.

Luke cleared her throat and stepped forward. "We've obtained a search warrant for Deputy Attakai's property. Detective Wolf, Special Agent Hannigan, and myself will conduct the search. We'd like help from Dr. Lorber and his team for a forensic sweep of the place. After that, we'll come up with our plan of attack and execute from there."

"And let us know what's happening every step of the way," District Attorney White said.

Luke put on her sarcastic smile, which was probably indistinguishable from the real deal to most of the people in the room, but Wolf had seen it many times before.

"Of course we will," she said.

Chapter 13

"Anything?" Wolf asked, reaching Patterson's desk.

She had his cell phone plugged into her computer and she was looking at a picture of the maroon sedan. "No … not really. The guy was too far away. There's a lot of shake in these pictures, and even if I could correct it the angle's all wrong. I can't get a look at his license plate."

"How about the car? Can you get a make on it?"

She looked up at him. "Looks like a Pontiac Bonneville. I could figure out what year … but then what? The car could be licensed in any state."

"Start looking at the name Fred Wilcox and try and match that car with him."

"Who's Fred Wilcox?" She unhooked his cell phone and gave it back to him.

"A killer."

***

Doubling as an access road for the top of Rocky Points Ski Resort in the summer months, County Road 34 was a well-populated valley at the northern perimeter of the ski resort.

Clusters of condos and townhomes built in the nineteen eighties, with their straight boxy lines and fading blue paint, were strewn up the narrow valley on both sides.

Attakai's place was one of these, an end unit in a row of three townhomes with a decent view of a tract of forest to his north side. It was small,the type of place the Denverites snatched up for seasonal retreats because one could technically ski-in-ski-out. Though one would have to ski *up* the valley for a few hundred yards to the nearest ski lift to "ski-out". But there were shuttles that ran year round, bringing people to the base, and when they were done they could point their skis to the door.

Which meant even though they were small, they pushed north of half a million dollars each. According to department records, Attakai rented his place.

Wolf drove himself, trailing Luke and Hannigan who rode in Luke's Tahoe. Behind Wolf, Dr. Lorber and Gene Fitzgerald followed in the county "meat wagon", as Dr. Lorber referred to it, which was a Ford Econoline Van equipped with all the latest and greatest tools of the medical examiner trade.

He parked in a vacant parking spot and got out into a cool breeze that whistled through pines to the north. It looked like the clouds of yesterday were gone and not coming back, replaced by wind, blue sky, and piercing sun.

Luke and Hannigan were already parked and appraising the place.

Carrying matching aluminum cases, Dr. Lorber and Gene got out of their van and joined the huddle behind Luke's Tahoe.

"Kind of a shithole," Hannigan said.

"I live two buildings down," Dr. Lorber said.

Hannigan raised an eyebrow and looked at him. "Really?"

"Yeah."

"Well I'm sure they're great places." Hannigan took a big breath through his flared nostrils. "It's good to be back in the mountain air. No smog. No crack hobos. Just mountain air. Smell those pines."

Wolf wondered how the man smelled anything, because they were all standing in an eddy filled with the scent of his metrosexual cologne. The special agent's jacket flapped open, revealing his muscled physique through his expensive-looking button up shirt. The tie was held firm by a silver bar tie clip, which matched the platinum chunk of a watch on his left wrist. He had taken the FBI dress code and added a few chapters of his own to it.

Luke gestured at the row of townhomes. "With the dirt under her nails, I'd think we were looking for an outdoor shack, a barn or something with a dirt floor. Where's she gonna get dirt under her nails here? Unless he kept her in the woods."

Dr. Lorber shook his head. "We're south of the Rainbow Creek valley. This isn't the right dirt anyway."

"Could have kept her tied up somewhere else north of Rainbow Creek," Hannigan said.

Luke flipped her sunglasses onto her head and read the warrant. Her cinnamon colored eyes flashed with intelligence, judgment, and calculation. To most men they were intimidating to look at, those eyes, and Wolf was seeing it firsthand again as Dr. Lorber and Gene watched her with anticipation.

And then there was her skin; she was in her late thirties, but she still had the skin elasticity of a woman half her age. But even the great Kristen Luke hadn't eluded time. At the corners of her eyes, she was acquiring some shallow crinkles.

"What?"

"You been in the Caribbean or something?" Wolf asked.

"Yeah, as a matter of fact. Flamingo drug cartel bust in Punta Cana. Then I had a few vacation days lined up, so I read a few books on the beach."

Hannigan raised his eyebrows. "Must be nice, huh?"

"All right," she said. "We're looking for a cell phone. And anything else that suggests deputy Attakai killed Sally Claypool two nights ago. Specifically, we're looking for hemp rope. A sharp knife with her blood on it. A pile of ears in the corner, some toes, and any other anomalies. Doctor Lorber and Gene will be looking for the small stuff—drains, sinks, and the like—and we'll conduct a thorough search of the rest. Let's go."

She marched across the parking lot to a steep set of wooden stairs that led to the front door. "And it was my first vacation in three years. And now I'm up here with you assholes, so I wouldn't be too envious of me."

She fished a keychain out of her pocket and climbed the stairs. "Which one is it?"

Out of male heterosexual reflex, Wolf watched her backside climb a few steps.

Visions of Kristen Luke's naked body swirled in his mind. He and Luke had slept together for many months after they'd met several years ago, eventually breaking off their relationship due to the physical distance between them. She lived in Denver, and he lived two and a half hours away in the mountains. Not only that, it was clear the relationship was a merely physical outlet for both of them, and the commitment they both had to their jobs would never allow either of them to give up and move nearer the other.

Out of the corner of his eye, Wolf caught Hannigan looking at him. The special agent's mouth was curled into a knowing smile.

"What?" Wolf asked.

Hannigan darted to the top of the stairs, the wood creaking under his considerable bulk. Lorber and Gene followed, and Wolf took up the rear.

While Luke and Hannigan fiddled with the lock he thought of Lauren again, and their time in bed yesterday morning. Then he thought of the tear running down her face as she'd given him the "we have to talk" speech.

"What the hell's your problem?" Luke said as he reached the open doorway.

"Nothing."

She eyed him suspiciously and put on a pair of rubber gloves. "You're hiding something." After a few seconds she lost the staring contest and waved him inside. "Age before beauty."

Lorber and Hannigan were already deep inside the darkened interior.

Hannigan stood in the hallway. "The place reeks."

It did reek. Like Jeremy Attakai needed to ditch the shoes lined up inside the doorway and start a strict regimen of athlete's foot treatment.

"Sally Claypool stayed here often? "Hannigan reached the kitchen at the end of the hall and stood with his hands on his hips, appraising the place with clear disgust. "Shithole."

A pizza box was lying on the linoleum kitchen counter, still cracked open and revealing a pile of old crusts. At least thirty empty cans of Bud Light were pushed into a corner on the counter, Attakai's first stage of a recycling effort.

Lorber set his case on the ground and opened it up.

"I'll be in here," Gene said, disappearing into the bedroom off the living room.

A smell came from the refrigerator, or from the trashcan next to it, or both. The place needed a deep clean, and for all the time Sally Claypool supposedly stayed here, Attakai could have used a woman's touch.

Of course, Wolf had seen much, much worse, with the places they'd stepped foot inside throughout the county.

Wolf had to cut the guy some slack. It was a typical single male's abode, and could have been Rachette's on any given day, or Wolf's on any given day pre-Lauren.

"I'm opening this place up." Luke went to the sliding glass door. It took both her hands and a mighty pull to open it. "Place is depressing. What's with you men? It's like scented candles are this mythical thing that only women can purchase at some secret, magical market. And how about cleaning supplies?"

"Hey," Hannigan said, "You've seen my place. Is it anything like this? Hell no."

Wolf watched their banter with interest. Up to this point Special Agent Hannigan had been a Grade-B asshole as far as Wolf could see.

But now that they were alone, they seemed to have an easy brother-sister rapport.

Hannigan walked to the living room and shook his head. "Wouldn't be caught dead."

"Yeah, but you're a homosexual."

Wolf flicked a glance between them. Luke was dead serious and Hannigan didn't bat an eye, he just shrugged his huge shoulders and walked into the bedroom.

They followed inside. Gene was in a small bathroom off the bedroom searching the drain.

The bed was unmade, sheets thrown to one side. The stuffy air held the mustiness of a single man's bedroom, and it didn't take a detective and two special agents to see it spawned from the dirty clothes piled in the corner.

Luke plucked a pair of women's underwear from the pile. "I guess that proves it. She was crazy."

In the other corner sat a television on an old table and the wall to the left had a sliding door closet. A beer-can-turned-tobacco spitter sat on an end table next to the bed.

"He a good deputy?" Luke asked.

They looked at Wolf.

"I don't know. I've never worked with the guy. He was hired by MacLean a couple years ago. He's a hunter. A fisherman." Wolf remembered what Rachette had told him.

Wolf went to a beat up dresser and pulled open the top drawer. Inside there were two pairs of boxer shorts and three pairs of socks. The next drawer had folded clothing. It was unimpressive. Nothing stood out as the belongings of a murderer.

"Just to be clear here, we're thinking he was involved with the rest of the murders down south," Wolf said.

Hannigan began rifling through coat pockets in the closet. "If we find the phone, then that's exactly what we're saying. Why? You don't see it?"

Wolf opened the next drawer. "MacLean was right. Attakai's sister was kidnapped. She escaped Fred Wilcox's clutches. Why would Jeremy be involved with kidnapping his own sister?"

"He wasn't," Luke said. "According to Mary Attakai's report with the La Plata SD, it was Fred Wilcox who kidnapped her and her friend. Not her older brother. But what if Fred wasn't supposed to pick her up that night? Have you thought of that?"

Wolf said nothing.

"What if Fred called Jeremy, you know, after he's picked up the two girls and has them knocked out in the back of his Explorer and he says, 'Hey, I got two girls.'" Luke narrowed her eyes. "And then, maybe Jeremy figures out Fred kidnapped his sister. Maybe …" she stopped talking.

"Maybe what?" Wolf asked.

She shrugged. "I don't know. I'm just saying, there's ways Attakai could be involved here. It's fishy that his sister was the only one who got away."

"With a chopped off toe," Hannigan said under his breath.

"What?"

Hannigan looked at Wolf, and then his partner. "Yeah. Her toe was cut off."

"You never mentioned that in the meeting."

"The end of that meeting was a shit-show. It slipped my mind. That's why we have a set number of people on these task forces, you know. There're too many ideas flying around. And I shouldn't have told anyone anything," she looked at Wolf, "except for you. Someone has loose lips. You see the news this morning talking about the Van Gogh killer? Who leaked that?"

Wolf opened the third drawer and found it empty save a pack of cigarettes.

"No blood in either of the drains in the bathroom," Gene said. "Nor the shower."

Lorber poked his head into the bedroom. "Nothing in the kitchen sink. Anything interesting in here?"

"Just interesting smells, Doctor," Hannigan said.

Lorber tilted his head. "I see a cell phone on the top shelf of the closet."

"What?" Hannigan pulled his hand out of a jacket pocket and got on his toes.

Lorber walked over and reached up with a basketball center's reach, plucking a cell phone off the shelf.

Chapter 14

"Where did you keep her?" Agent Brian Todd's voice was like a vinyl recording coming out of the speaker above Wolf's head.

Deputy Attakai sat motionless, his head in his hands, his elbows on the metal interrogation room table.

"He's not gonna talk," Luke said.

"No shit." Hannigan preened his nails, not bothering to look through the one-way mirror.

"It's over," Agent Todd was saying inside. "Okay, Deputy? Do you understand? We have you now. We know you've been working with Fred Wilcox from the beginning. So I want you to tell me everything. Tell me."

Attakai shook his head in his hands. "We weren't."

"What's that?" Agent Todd leaned forward. "Tell me, Jeremy. Come on. Is this about your sister?"

Attakai shook his head some more.

"It is, isn't it? She wasn't supposed to be taken by Fred that night two years ago. What happened after that? Did you and Fred split up? You guys got together and buried his car and split up the little team you had going down there? And now you're up here ... and ... what happened? You decided to start up again. Why?"

Deputy Attakai leaned back in his chair, revealing a calm face. "I don't know what you're talking about. I don't know why that cell phone was in my house. I've never seen it in my life. That's all I'm going to say."

Agent Todd looked at him with utter disappointment and stood up from his chair. He nodded at the other agent in the room and they walked out.

The door opened. Hannigan stood at attention as his boss entered the observation room.

When he shut the door, Agent Todd turned to the one-way glass and clasped his hands behind his back. "He's lying."

Wolf had watched the interrogation from the beginning. Attakai had said little, which was smart. To say anything in an interrogation, no matter what the circumstances, was as good as a confession of guilt. Words could be twisted. Investigators and lawyers and juries could twist inflections of words. *Anything you say can be used against you in the court of law.*

"What's next?" Luke asked.

Agent Todd turned and ran a hand across his face. "We found the phone at his house so he's ours for now. So we'll keep him and try again later with his lawyer present. In the meantime, I want to get into this guy's past with a fine-tooth comb." He looked at Agent Luke. "We need to talk to Mary Attakai."

"We already did that two years ago," she said.

"So talk to her again."

She looked at her partner and then Wolf. "You ready to take a drive south?"

Chapter 15

Highway 50 traveled west across the high flat lands of the Rockies, meandered up and over steep mountain passes, and dumped onto the western slope. There Wolf followed highway 550 through Ridgway and into the jagged mountains to the south.

Luke drove all of it like she was going for Nascar points, passing every single vehicle she came upon at almost twice the speed limit.

Wolf kept up for a while, following in his own SUV. He had decided to drive himself. Sure, she was a speed-freak, but he trusted Kristen Luke's driving skills enough to ride with her. Hannigan's presence, however, changed the dynamic and he didn't feel like sitting in a back seat for hours, at the mercy of the two agents' schedules and motivations.

And the way they'd been slow leaking information so far had gotten to him. To have his own vehicle felt like his only way to keep hold of some control.

He kept up for the first half hour of the three-and-a-half-hour drive, then decided against dying and eased off the gas.

Instead he enjoyed the drive. He was in country he hadn't visited for years. The mountains here reminded him of those found in Patagonia, South America, with their steep rocky crests that took on all kinds of shapes.

He passed through Ouray, which billed itself "Switzerland of America" because of its location in a narrow head of a valley, surrounded on all sides by steep cliffs. It was a quaint town that he and Sarah had once visited in college, but his destination was twenty-five miles south over Red Mountain Pass.

The section of 550 from Ouray to Silverton was dubbed "The Million Dollar Highway" as it snaked over Red Mountain Pass. It was generally thought to be one of the most dangerous roads in Colorado, with its sharp switchbacks, steep drop-offs, and lack of guardrails, and when Wolf was done with the white-knuckle drive he thought it could use another few million in modern upgrades.

After Red Mountain pass, the road eased down in elevation alongside Mineral Creek, cutting through aspens, and finally dumped out into the bowl valley where Silverton sparkled in the late day sun.

Greene Street, the main thoroughfare that ran through Silverton, was paved and modern feeling, but at the same time felt to be a hundred fifty years ago. The side streets were dirt, the buildings between them squares and rectangles with covered wooden walkways in front just like the pioneer days when miners dug silver out of the surrounding mountains, but with fresh paint jobs of orange, green, red, blue, and yellow—with neon in the windows and motorcycles parked in front.

A row of bicycles lined the wall outside a bar, which was bustling with a happy hour crowd of locals mixed with tourists coming off the steam train in from Durango fifty miles to the south.

Already passing through town, he reached the end of Greene Street within seconds and pulled into the San Juan County Sheriff's building. He was surprised to find his vehicle the only one in the lot besides a beat up Ford Bronco with a San Juan Sheriff's department logo on it.

For a moment he wondered if Luke had skidded off Red Mountain Pass, landing in a bright explosion in the river below, then decided that would be a manner of death too tame for Kristen Luke.

Wolf stepped out and stretched his arms overhead. The scent of beer and fried food wafting up from blocks down saturated the still air, which was rapidly chilling in the fading daylight.

His work boots crunched on gray gravel as he walked around the front of the building. It was thick and solid construction, built from smooth, gray stone with a bell tower jutting up in front. Silverton was the San Juan County seat, the only municipality within the whole county, which said volumes of how rugged and remote the surrounding terrain was.

Climbing the two stone steps, he grabbed hold of a cold piece of metal history and pushed, and a heavy door creaked inwards.

Dust tickled his nose as he walked in, and each footfall on the old wooden floor sent echoing moans through the building.

A scuffed wooden desk sat unoccupied in the entryway underneath a vaulted ceiling.

"Hello?" He called out.

No answer.

There was an open doorway ahead with two desks inside. A topo map hung on the wall between them, marked with pins and notes dangling from thumbtacks.

Modern office phones sat on the desks, but everything else looked from a half century ago—the desks themselves, the wheeled chairs, the turquoise wall, the faded pictures that hung on them.

An old Motorola police dispatch radio sat on a table underneath a warped glass window. A wooden sign hung on the doorjamb said Sheriff Sue Meal.

A call bell sat on the entryway desk so he tapped a finger. The tiny clang pierced the silence.

There was a rustling, and then a toilet flushing deep in the recesses of the building, then running water and a door slamming.

"I'm coming!" A man's voice said deep within the building. "Coming. Coming."

Quick footsteps came closer and a man dressed in jeans and a button up khaki sheriff's department top appeared at the doorway.

Wolf eyed the stripes on his uniform. "Hello, Sergeant."

The man craned his neck and looked past him. "You Wolf?"

"Yep. You Vernon?" Wolf held out a hand.

"Yep." Sergeant Vernon had a champion thumb-wrestler grip. One that was still moist from the bathroom. "I thought the feds were coming, too."

"They are." He wiped his hand on his jeans. "They haven't been here yet?"

Vernon shook his head.

On cue the door clacked and flew open, and Hannigan's bulky figure poured inside followed by Luke on his heels. They both wore sunglasses for the first five or so steps, like they were following some obscure fed protocol on how to enter a building with maximum intimidation.

Luke stepped around Hannigan and thrust out her hand, pulling off her glasses. "Special Agent Luke."

"Hi." Vernon wiped his hand and shook. "Sergeant Vernon."

"This is Special Agent Hannigan."

Hannigan was preoccupied with looking up the staircase and the walkway above.

"Hi." Vernon's boyish brown eyes were taking in every inch of Luke, his breathing going rapid, his face turning red behind his two-day beard.

"You have what we need?" Luke locked on his eyes.

"Yeah. The report? Yeah."

"The Jessica Meinhoff report." A smiled tugged at her lips.

Another man, another piece of putty in Special Agent Kristen Luke's hands. It was a superpower.

"You got it. It's … in here." Vernon waved a hand and walked through the doorway. "Go ahead and follow me."

Luke followed him and then Wolf. Hannigan took up the rear, and it sounded like a rhinoceros was following them through the narrow wooden hallways of the ancient building.

They passed a closed door and Luke made a show of pinching her nose on the way by while Vernon obliviously led them onward.

"In here." Vernon unlocked a doorknob with a cartoon-version of a key on an oversized hoop keychain. Flicking on a light inside, he pushed open the door and held out his hand. "There you go. It's the one on the right."

Luke stood blinking. "What's this?"

The room was six by six feet at most. There was a folding card table with two cardboard file boxes atop them. Both were warped and leaning haphazardly, like they'd been hosed down and then tossed inside the room.

"Last year's flood got to the files. Snowed two feet and then rained two inches on top of that. Freak, thousand-year type of thing. Flooded out the whole basement, so we had to move the files up here."

"And keep them in the same boxes," Luke said under her breath.

"What's that?"

"Nothing." She walked to the box and pulled out a thin manila folder.

"That's it," Vernon said.

"It's the only one in here."

Vernon hitched his jeans up, eyeing them defensively. "Yeah. Never had many files."

Luke peeked inside the other box, clearly out of sheer curiosity, made a face, and came back out of the room.

"Can we look at this in your office?" she asked.

"Yeah, sure." Vernon led them back through the narrow hallway and to the office. He flicked a switch and an overhead yellow light turned the turquoise room green.

Luke slapped down the file and opened it, revealing a stack of water-damaged photographs.

Looking at one in particular proved worthless, because each photo was at least half-damaged by water, but spreading them all out on the desk gave them a clear enough picture.

A grim picture.

Jessica Meinhoff had been a pretty young woman until Fred Wilcox was done with her.

Agent Hannigan looked down at them with a somber look, the muscles of his jaw flexing beneath his smooth facial skin.

"Jessica was twenty-one years old." Sergeant Vernon stood a few paces away keeping his eyes off the photographs. "Had just come home for the summer from her junior year at Colorado Mountain College in Steamboat Springs."

When Vernon stopped talking, Luke looked up at him. "No, keep going."

"Right." Vernon nodded. "Twenty-one. Came home for the summer. She hitched a ride with another guy in town that was also at CMC. They weren't dating or anything, just friends."

Wolf listened to the story and studied the photographs closer. Jessica Meinhoff was naked, tossed in the bushes like a discarded dishrag. Her clothing was ripped and strewn in the grass.

It lacked the symmetry of the other seven victims, the thoughtful, artistic touches.

"… found her while she was hiking with her dog up at Boulder Gulch. It's just right there, you can walk out the front door here and be there in minutes. Anyway, her dog found her body, and she came running and screaming to us. I was just out of the police academy. It was my first year in the department." Vernon's Adam's apple bobbed and his eyes glazed over. "Never seen anything like that, and sure hope I don't ever again."

"I know what you mean," Luke said, studying a photograph closely. "Who did the rape kit?"

"We got help from La Plata County. Guys down in Durango. We don't really have the means."

Luke nodded. "Tell me about your investigation."

"The whole town was crazy for weeks after the killing. You know, like pitch forks and torches out in the middle of the night type stuff.

"We figured out she'd been drinking that night down the street at the Handlebar. She showed up with four men, all around the same age, all transplants from elsewhere who worked at the mountain in the winter."

"The mountain?" Hannigan asked.

"The ski resort up the valley."

Hannigan nodded.

"We questioned all of them, and the patrons at the bar. Everyone had the same story that she left by herself that night. The owner of the bar, the waitresses, the patrons, they all corroborated. Even so, we brought in the four men who came into the bar with her. None of them had any defensive wounds." He shrugged. "We took DNA swabs, and La Plata checked them against the rape kit. No match. We had nothing on them, so we turned our investigation outward. And found shit. Pardon my French."

"Where are these men now?"

Vernon chuckled humorlessly. "They left town. Ran out in the following months, you could say. It didn't matter that they were innocent. I mean, they were my friends … anyway, nobody could ever get what happened to Jessica out of their minds, you know? They kept looking at them like they knew something. Fights would break out. And her freakin' dad. He was stalking them. Pulling them aside on the street, asking questions, basically threatening them."

"Jessica Meinhoff's father?" Wolf asked.

"Yeah. Guy was taking the investigation into his own hands. He was always a drunk, and, well, let's just say that after her death we got calls every other day about Chris Meinhoff. He was in here harassing us once a week too. Asking about DNA tests, whether or not we botched it." Vernon snorted at the memories.

"Where's he now?" Luke asked.

"Drank himself to death a couple winters ago. Found his body down by the river next to two handles of Jim Beam."

They let the silence take over for a beat.

"Anyway, after you guys came in a couple years ago," Vernon pointed at Luke and Hannigan, "with the new DNA evidence from down south, that put us at ease, that's for sure. Up until then, you'd be walking around here and wonder how many times you'd seen the killer that day. Wonder if you'd been having a beer with him that night. We were all on edge. And now, what? He's up in Rocky Points?" Vernon looked at Wolf.

"That's what we're trying to find out," Luke said. "Have you ever heard of a man named Jeremy Attakai?"

Vernon shook his head.

"How about Fred Wilcox?" She produced a pair of photographs from her pocket and showed them to Sergeant Vernon.

He studied them and turned down his mouth. "Hmmm, nope. Can't remember ever seeing these guys around here."

She smiled apologetically. "You've been a big help. Thank you."

Vernon looked like a whipped puppy at the prospect of her ending the conversation. "Yeah. No problem."

"Give Sheriff Sue our regards, and tell her I say hi," she said.

They shook hands and Luke gave him a wink.

Hannigan and Wolf exchanged a glance, Hannigan rolling his eyes as he stepped out of the San Juan County municipal building.

The sky outside had darkened to a deep blue, the final glow behind the western mountains fading like cooling embers of a campfire.

Gathering in the dirt parking lot outside next to the vehicles, Hannigan looked longingly down the street. "Let's get down to Durango. I'm hungry and I need a beer."

Chapter 16

Rachette tried to ignore her, but it was impossible with her incessant talking.

"And she has a guaranteed job when she gets into town." Patterson raised her eyebrows and turned to him.

He slowed to a stop at the stop sign and shook his head. He shouldn't have mentioned his sister. "Julie's a bitch. You don't know her the way I do. She'll do something stupid, then I'll have to clean up her mess."

Patterson gave him a puzzled look. "Are you describing yourself right now?"

"You know what?" Rachette gunned the engine. "Screw you."

"I'm sorry, but come on." She twisted in her seat. "I'm just sick and tired of watching the dance. You watching Charlotte's every move, still drooling over her like you have been since the day you met her. Her trying to make you jealous with an older guy."

"You think she's trying to make me jealous?" he asked. Probably a little too quickly, but he'd been wondering what the hell she was doing with that guy. He was a nerd. Way older than Rachette. The opposite of him in every way. It puzzled him why Charlotte had latched onto Gene so quickly. Now it made sense if she was trying to get back at Rachette.

"Yeah," she said. "I do. I mean, Gene's a nice guy, good-looking, smart—"

"Okay."

Her expression softened. "But she clearly loves you. Don't you value that? Don't you want to patch things up with her?"

He shook his head. "I told you. She doesn't want to hear anything I have to say."

"Well, you hurt her. Badly."

Rachette said nothing.

"Maybe your sister could help. You never know. She comes into town and stays with you, and she could give you some insight as to how to approach it with Munford. This might be a blessing in disguise."

Yeah, right. He knew her mother-in-law was babysitting her son nowadays and Patterson resented it. She'd been in a pissy mood for over a month because of the situation. Patterson was looking for any excuse to get the old lady out of the picture. She must be desperate with pushing such a thinly veiled agenda.

"I know this is hard to believe," Patterson said, "but your sister is a likable person. Which is so, so hard for me to believe."

Rachette pinched his eyebrows together. "Thanks."

"Seriously. She has none of your genetic traits it's …" she widened her eyes. "Wait. Was Julie adopted?"

Rachette gave her a look that said *I'll murder you if you speak again.*

"Is she?"

She didn't get the hint. His partner was too lost in her thoughts to realize the subject was done. Dead. That his sister was dead to him.

It was infuriating how Julie had somehow won these people over with one quick visit two years ago. Now it was childhood all over again. The way she danced and flaunted in front of everyone, while he was left sitting in the corner by himself. Now she wanted to roll into town and start dancing in front of everyone here.

"How the hell did she turn out like she did, and you turned out like you did?" Patterson asked, a shit-eating grin on her face.

He jerked the wheel to the side of the road and slid the SUV to a stop, enveloping them in a cloud of dust. "How the hell did she turn out different? Hmm, well, let's see. Maybe because she didn't get smacked around when dad got drunk. Or when he was pissed off because his son didn't hit a homerun in baseball for three years. Maybe because she used to get hugged by her parents, not punched in the fucking nose!"

Patterson's jaw dropped and she put a hand over her mouth.

Good. Suck on that, he thought.

His breathing was shallow and before he knew it tears ran down his face. "God damn it. Look what you made …" he stopped talking, because the sound of his voice reminded him of being twelve years old again.

"Oh my God, I'm so sorry, Tom. I had no idea."

He wiped his eyes and checked the side view mirror, then turned and looked backwards to hide his face. When that failed he opened the door and stepped out onto the dirt road, slamming the door behind him.

Christ. What was happening to him? This! This is why she needed to stay away. This is why she needed to get her own life in Nebraska, and stay the hell out of his. And especially now.

Patterson sat in the SUV, not bothering to come outside to apologize further. She knew when to leave him alone, he'd give her that.

After a minute he got back inside.

"Rachette …"

Pulling back onto the road, he was taken by a numb calmness that shut Patterson up. He rarely blinked, rarely had a thought. Just drove, and scanned the woods for any sign of Fred Wilcox or the maroon sedan Wolf had taken pictures of.

More futility. They had been driving for hours, taking every single road in town that was passable with the Adrenaline Games crowd, then they had spiraled their way outwards. Searching every road out here was an impossible proposition.

"I'm hungry," he finally said after an hour of wandering the side roads in town for the third time of the day. "So I'm going to stop at Burger Shack."

Her voice cracked, "I'm uh, going to meet Scott and Tommy on Main Street for dinner. You can drop me at third. If you see MacLean, tell him I'm taking a shit or something."

The defiance in her voice was a little off-putting.

"You all right?"

She looked at him and nodded. "Yeah. I just need to spend more time with my family, or I'm not going to have a family anymore."

Main Street was two blocks to the east, so he pulled onto third and made his way there, stopping at the traffic barricade and letting her out.

They exchanged a glance; hers saying "I'm sorry," and his saying, "Whatever. Don't worry about it."

"I'll be back at the station in an hour or so." She closed the door and disappeared into the crowd.

After a quick stop at the Burger Shack drive-through he went to the county building, made his way up to the squad room and ate at his desk, watching the orange light of the sunset fade in the windows.

His thoughts bounced between his father, his kid sister, and his failed attempt at starting a family before it had begun. Every waking thought was a reminder how he was too much of a pussy to even try and be a better man than his father had been.

He'd left her at the altar. That was movie-type stuff.

He pulled out his cell phone. There were three missed calls from his sister today. Five yesterday. There would be more. But he wasn't in the mood to talk to her yet. There was no sense pouring salt in his wounds.

Screw it. He dropped the cell phone on the desk and leaned back, sucking the cool Coca Cola, washing the last of the French fries down his throat.

His stomach was bulging to the point his leather belt was painfully digging against his belly. Taking another sip, he pinched the small roll of fat that billowed over. His gut had definitely grown since the wedding.

"Hey, fat ass, Tammy says you're not answering your desk phone." Deputy Yates appeared at his desk.

Rachette leaned forward and studied his desk phone, then pushed a button, rendering it usable again. "Oh yeah, I had a woman on hold … yesterday."

Deputy Yates waited with raised eyebrows, looking for more explanation that wasn't coming. "She says you have a guy downstairs who needs to talk to a detective."

Rachette sat forward and let out a long burp, pointing out the floor to ceiling windows at the darkening silhouettes of the peaks. "Now?"

Yates shrugged. "You want me to tell him you're busy jerking it?"

"Okay, okay. I'm on my way." He gathered up the remnants of his food, scraped them into the bag and tossed it on the way out of the squad room.

Riding the elevator down to the first floor, he walked to the front reception area of the building and eyed Tammy, who was behind the reception desk and standing with a phone pressed to her ear. She turned to him, said a few words and hung up, like she had been talking to somebody about him. Pointing to the waiting area, she sat down and dug into some task on her computer. Probably ordering a new assault rifle.

Over near the windows there was a detention deputy dressed in full khakis talking to a civilian male. They both turned in his direction at the same time and he noticed it was Deputy Hartman, a grunt from the prison downstairs who talked way too much when he drank.

"Detective Rachette," Deputy Hartman said. "This is Mr. Ellington. He needs to speak to you."

"I need to speak to you," Mr. Ellington said.

Rachette started to smile and smothered it when he saw the dread on the man's face. "Right. Thanks deputy Hartman."

"Detective Rachette will take care of you now, sir." Hartman patted his shoulder and left to the elevator bank.

"My name's Tom," Rachette said shaking the man's beefy hand.

"I'm Bud Ellington."

"What can I help you with, Mr. Ellington?" Rachette asked, eyeing the windows. Patrons streamed by, sipping yellow beers and eating meat in various forms. A group of laughing women passed by, all of them dressed in zip up jackets and tight jeans.

In contrast, Mr. Ellington was dressed like a lumberjack. He wore dirty overalls with a checked red and black shirt underneath. His graying beard reached his chest, rounding out the image. But contrary to the manly rest of him, his eyes were red and moist, like he'd been crying.

"My daughter's missing," Mr. Ellington said.

Rachette pulled his eyebrows together and nodded, like the man had said something mildly interesting, and not butthole-clenching terrifying in the current state of everything that was going on in town.

"Okay," he said. "Please, let's take a seat here."

The huge man followed his prompt and sank into a chair. He removed a trucker hat, revealing a shorn scalp, and began rubbing it with both palms.

Swallowing, Rachette looked out the windows again, willing Patterson to materialize out of the crowd and come walking inside, but there were just more unnamed faces streaming by.

He tried to remember his training in situations like this.

He didn't want to fan the flames of any negativity going through the man's mind, but blowing smoke up his ass would be worse.

"Tell me, when is the last time you talked to her?" he asked.

"Yesterday. Uh, last night."

Rachette nodded. He wanted to tell the man to not worry, that there was a waiting period of twenty-four or thirty-six hours and then he could worry, but he knew that was bullshit. There was no waiting period in the real world. If someone's missing, time is usually of the essence. Especially now. Especially here. "Tell me what happened? Why exactly do you think she's missing?"

"Because she's not answering her phone or her text messages. And this is since last night. She lives in town, in the Rocky Points Condos."

"Wait, is your daughter Lindsay?"

Mr. Ellington's eyes widened. "Yes. Why? What? You know where she is?"

"No ... sorry, I just. I live in the Rocky Points Condos, too. I know her."

Mr. Ellington closed his eyes and despair took over again.

Rachette felt like he'd just swum to a drowning man and dunked his head underwater. "Okay. Listen. Let me have her phone number."

With the monosyllabic tone of a zombie, Mr. Ellington rattled off his daughter's phone number while Rachette fed it into his phone.

Putting it to his ear, he listened to ring. It immediately stopped and went to voicemail. Lindsay Ellington's high-pitched voice came on and told him she wasn't there and to leave a message.

He hung up and stood. "I'll be right back." He walked across the floor, over the terrazzo seal of Sluice-Byron County, to the half-moon reception counter where Tammy sat a foot above him.

She was on the phone, her eyes wide and locked on her computer screen. She held up a finger at Rachette. "I need it right now." She looked at him. "I don't care, give me a location right now."

The intensity of her tone made him realize her words for his benefit. He showed her his phone with Lindsay Ellington's phone number on it and she nodded. She was already trying to locate her phone through the local cell carrier dispatch.

Rachette slowed his breathing and stood coolly with his elbow on the counter, resisting the urge to wring his hands and pace.

The automatic front doors slid open, letting in a blast of music and the scent of corndogs.

He turned his head to look, but it was nobody, just a toddler who had wandered underneath the infrared sensor of the automatic doors outside.

Mr. Ellington was staring at them. His mouth was moving, his eyes going skyward, looking like he was saying a silent prayer.

Rachette turned to Tammy. With clenched teeth, he whispered, "What the hell is going on? Talk to me, Tammy."

She lowered the phone and spoke in a low, controlled tone. "They're locating her phone now. I'm on hold with Summit Wireless, and now they've finally got me … yes? Okay." She pulled a piece of paper off her notepad and jotted something down. "Thank you."

She hung up and handed the paper to Rachette.

It said, 1503 Main Street, Rocky Points. *The Pony Tavern.*

Rachette nodded and pocketed the piece of paper.

The walk back to Mr. Ellington was ten paces at most, but felt like a mile. His legs felt like a separate entity to his body. What the hell was he going to tell this guy?

Chapter 17

Patterson and Yates pulled into the parking lot of the Pony Tavern and parked. Rachette was parked a few spots away milling around the rear of his SUV with a burly looking man.

"There he is," Yates said.

To say Rachette looked relieved to see them was the understatement of the month.

She had gotten the call from Rachette a few minutes ago and had to haul ass back to the station and hitch a ride here with Yates. She had hardly shut the door when Rachette was right next to her, hissing in her ear.

"About time."

"Hey, what's going on? You said Lindsay—"

"This is her father."

"What?"

"Her dad. Lindsay Ellington's dad."

The full situation came into focus, and now Rachette's over-excited tone on the phone made sense.

"Yeah, he followed—"

"You her?" The burly man was right next to them.

"Hello, sir. My name's Detective Heather Patterson."

"Bud Ellington." The man had crossed arms over a barrel chest. He was searching the night beyond them. "They don't have her phone inside."

Patterson glanced over her shoulder, seeing the man was looking at nothing in particular. The trees. The unknown.

Two more vehicles drove into the lot, Gene Fitzgerald in his dirty white Honda Civic followed by Charlotte in her Jeep Cherokee.

Rachette's face dropped at the sight of Munford, and then his eyes narrowed at the sight of Gene. "What the hell are they doing here?"

"They were at the station, too. They're here to help," Patterson said, directing the words at Rachette as much as the missing girl's father.

"Shit … help with what?" Mr. Ellington had a hand on his forehead now and was pacing back and forth.

"Sir," Patterson said. "We'll be right back." She clamped onto Rachette's arm and they walked to Munford and Gene, who were talking with Yates.

"Hey, what's happening?" Munford asked Rachette, looking him directly in the eye.

The words looked like they stunned Rachette, like she had hauled off and punched him rather than asked him a basic question.

"Uh …" Rachette looked at Gene, letting his sentence die.

"Mr. Ellington," Patterson said. "His missing daughter."

"Yeah." Rachette blinked, snapping out of it. "We have a misper. Lindsay Ellington. She's not answering her phone. She came here last night for ladies' night. Her roommate says she never came home. I just called her phone. It goes straight to voicemail."

"But you pinged it?" Patterson asked.

Rachette nodded. "Yeah. The last GPS signal was registered right here."

Patterson eyed Mr. Ellington, who was a few yards away with his own phone pressed to his ear. "Why's he here?"

"He followed me." Rachette got in her face. "What the hell was I supposed to say? 'Sir, I've traced her phone, but I'm not going to tell you where it is. Here, take a seat on this shitty plastic chair while I go look for her. Would you like a soda while you wait?' The guy's …" Rachette lowered his voice and looked over his shoulder. "The guy's a freaking wreck."

Munford stepped up and put a hand on his shoulder. "It's okay."

Rachette closed his eyes and nodded. "Okay. Thanks. Thanks for coming."

"Did you check on the ground?" Patterson asked.

The parking lot was a large, simple square, surrounded by hip-high grass singing with crickets. On the west side, about a stone's throw away, was the Chautauqua River, quietly bubbling in the still night air.

"No, not yet. We were just inside talking to the bartender. She says she was in here last night. I had her pull her credit card slip. Looks like she paid it at 11:22 p.m. The bartender doesn't remember her. Says it was real crowded last night. More Adrenaline Games crowd."

Mr. Ellington pocketed his phone and came over. "What's next? What are you going to do?"

"Sir," Patterson said.

Gene stepped out of the powwow and put a hand on Mr. Ellington's shoulder.

Mr. Ellington looked down at it with an aggressive bulge of his eyes, but Gene was unrelenting, pulling him gently away from Rachette, Munford, Yates, and Patterson.

"Sir, these are deputies with the Sheriff's Department ..." They retreated toward the front door of the Pony Tavern, Gene talking in a soothing voice.

Munford eyed Gene with something akin to awe, and then stepped away from Rachette, leaving Patterson's partner looking like a pathetic dog sitting in the rain.

Patterson punched him in the shoulder. "Let's get moving."

Rachette's department SUV was equipped with two Maglites and Yates's had two as well. Mr. Ellington stood in solemn silence with Gene in the parking lot.

A few minutes in, they joined the search, using the flashlights on their cellphones.

The grass was thick and high, reaching up to Patterson's elbows, or everyone else's waists. The beam of her flashlight swept back and forth, covering just a few feet in front of her. The ground was muddy at the stalks, holding the moisture from rain two days ago.

Fanned out in a straight line, just over an arm's length from one another, the six of them made three passes back and forth.

Patterson saw mice and crickets, but no telltale flash of glass or plastic.

Another pass later Munford raised her hand. "I have something. I have it."

Swimming through the grass, they huddled around Munford.

Illuminated by her flashlight beam sat a shining cell phone screen burrowed in some grass.

"That's it," Mr. Ellington said, bending over.

"Don't touch it," Patterson and Rachette said in unison.

Mr. Ellington ignored them and picked it up. "This is it. Why would it be here?"

He looked at them for answers. They had none.

Chapter 18

Molas Pass climbed out of the west side of Silverton. It was too beautiful in the sunset light to try and keep up with Luke's suicidal driving, so Wolf sat back and enjoyed the Les Paul tune pumping out of the speakers.

He'd cracked a window, letting in the pine and grass scent, but had to roll it up to keep out the cold and the bugs, which were so uniformly splattered on his windshield it looked like the sneeze guard at Rocky Points Ice Creamery on the fourth of July.

The road wound tightly around curves, ascending and descending, and then finally straightened out as it dove down south toward Durango.

Following a green line on the GPS function of his dash mounted laptop, he pulled into a motel called the Pine Bark Inn and parked underneath the covered drive-up.

The motel attendant was a skinny young man with tight clothes and a greasy Mohawk, and his eyes lit up at the mention of Kristen Luke's name. Handing over a key he said, "She said to tell you they're at the restaurant across the street."

Wolf looked out the window.

"Shocker's sports bar," the man said. "Not the other place."

"Thanks. How long ago did they get here?"

"Must have been about fifteen minutes ago?"

Wolf nodded and took the key. "Thanks."

He parked the SUV next to Luke's bug-encrusted Tahoe and went to his room. Unlocking it, he tossed his toiletries bag onto a floral patterned queen sized bed and shut it again, and then made his way across the highway to Shocker's Sports Bar.

The place was decidedly un-shocking. Just another bar—two pool tables, a juke box in the corner, a sparsely populated cluster of tables, a row of booths along the neon adorned windows, and a big screen television above the bar.

"Hey, over here!" Luke called out.

Hannigan and Luke sat at a booth along the windows just digging into a meal. Hannigan had a burger that looked too small in his oversized hands, plus fries, and Luke had a plate of salad with a breast of chicken dropped on top of it.

He slipped in next to Luke, because that was the option that was given to him.

"What took you so long?" she asked.

"Yeah, right. I'm still not sure how I beat you to Silverton."

"Oh, that. We stopped for gas, and this guy had some sort of bathroom emergency."

Hannigan was wiping his hands on his napkin, the burger already gone.

Another skinny kid with tight clothes on came over to the table. "Hi, would you like to see a menu?"

"No, thanks," Wolf said. "I'll just have what he had."

"Okay."

"I'll take another." Hannigan shoved a wad of fries in his mouth.

"Beer?"

The beer in front of Hannigan was halfway finished.

"Burger. And beer."

The kid laughed. Hannigan didn't.

"And to drink for you, sir?"

"I'll have a beer," Wolf said. "Thanks."

The kid recited a novella for their beer list and Wolf took a brown ale from a local brewer.

"So what did you think about Jessica Meinhoff?" Luke asked.

"They found Fred Wilcox's DNA inside her, right?"

Luke nodded.

"I was struck by how sloppy the kill was compared to the other seven victims."

Luke took a bite of salad and pointed with her fork. "And no ear missing. No toe missing. No display of the body. No lashing of the arms and legs. No cuts on her skin. It's like he was a completely different man in Silverton, then he goes down south and becomes this artistic killer."

"I think if there was any doubt he met somebody down here and started killing with them, then it's gone after looking at those pictures," Wolf said.

Luke nodded. "Agreed. The killing in Silverton is night and day from the rest of them. The only thing connecting it at all to the ones down here is Fred Wilcox's DNA."

"Here you go." The waiter put a beer in front of Wolf and Hannigan. "Anything else?"

Hannigan slammed the rest of the beer in his hand and gave it to the waiter.

Wolf took a sip of his beer, savored the cool, bitter ale that had a nutty aftertaste.

"Jesus Christ." Hannigan pulled the beer from his lips in mid sip, sending a spray across the table. "They just got a grand slam? Rockies suck. You know, Cubs are playing tonight." He raised his voice and looked at the bartender.

The bartender smiled and started talking about the Cubs lacking bullpen.

"Anyway," Luke said rolling her eyes. "Three years ago, when we were called in after the second killing down here, we saw the stark difference in the killings, but we didn't know what to make of it."

Wolf's phone buzzed in his pocket. It was Patterson. He held up a finger and pushed his way out of the booth.

"Hello?"

"It's …"

He walked out the front door. "Hello?"

"… hear me?"

"Go ahead."

"We have another missing woman."

The statement was loud and clear, the words hitting as if he'd stepped out onto the highway and gotten plowed by a car. "Shit. Who?"

"Lindsay Ellington. You know her?"

Wolf knew her.

Her father, Bud Ellington, worked at the hardware store full time and was a master carpenter.

Once Wolf had asked him about the best way to go about making a shoe bench. Ellington had asked him questions about the dimensions, the material he was looking for, and then told Wolf he'd get back to him, that he had a great resource on it. Wolf had assumed he was going to come to him with a book, a website link, to help him build the bench, but two days later Ellington had shown up to the department asking for him, and then he brought him out to his truck. In the truck was the finished bench, just as Wolf had described it.

Sitting in the passenger seat of Ellington's truck that day had been Lindsay Ellington. Ellington had beamed with pride as he introduced her.

Wolf struggled to remember her face, but he remembered she was smiling.

"Sir?"

"Yeah, I know her. What happened?"

"Her father came in and said she's been missing since last night."

"Since last night?" Wolf started pacing. "When?"

"Lindsay Ellington signed a credit card slip inside the Pony Tavern last night at 11:22."

"Shit." He put his hand to his forehead and began pacing.

Luke came outside. She walked past him and to the end of the building, talking heatedly into her own cell.

"We found Lindsay's phone in the weeds outside the Pony," Patterson said. "They're interrogating Attakai again," she said, "but …"

"But he's not saying anything again. What about the pictures of the maroon sedan I gave you?"

"It's going slow, especially since MacLean had us out all day, then we were dealing with Lindsay Ellington. I haven't had much time to sit down at the computer. But from what I've done, I'm pretty sure it's a Pontiac Bonneville, either 1994 or 1995. They're basically the same models both years. I can tell you Fred Wilcox doesn't have one, or if he does, it's not registered under his name in the state of Colorado. The last thing he registered was his Ford Explorer, and since then he's gone off the map. I can't find him doing anything in the last two years—no credit card transactions, no cars, no insurance, no nothing."

He watched a pickup truck coast by into the outskirts of Durango. It reminded him of Bud Ellington's truck.

"Sir?"

"Yes. Okay, that's good work. I'm not sure those pictures are going to do us any good anyway."

He thought of the man across the river. The dark beard. The dark long hair. Had it been a coincidence? A guy driving through town, stopping to take a leak, and …

Yeah, and he just happens to match Fred Wilcox's description—a cold blooded killer, right when killings are starting to happen in your town. You need to get your ass back to Rocky Points.

"What are you going to do?" she asked.

Luke was pacing at the far end of the building, talking heatedly into her phone.

"Sir?"

"I don't know yet. Keep me posted and I'll do the same." He hung up and waited for Luke to end her phone call.

A few seconds later she ended her conversation and pocketed her phone. "Bad news."

"Lindsay Ellington." Wolf raised his phone.

Hannigan came outside and put his hands on his hips, stretched his back. "What?"

"They have another missing girl in Rocky Points," Luke said.

Hannigan blinked slowly.

"There's a big problem, however." Luke folded her arms. "She was taken last night. We know this because of a credit card slip signed at the Pony Tavern in Rocky Points, and they just found her phone in the weeds near the tavern parking lot."

"And Attakai was in jail," Wolf said. "But he could still be involved, because he had that cell phone, and we saw the pictures of that Ford Explorer, Fred Wilcox looked to be the abduction guy all along. Patterson and I were discussing the same thing."

Luke stared at him.

"What?"

"And it looks like they might let him out tomorrow morning."

"What?" Hannigan held out his hands. "But he had the cell phone."

"Which his lawyers are now saying the FBI planted in his house. They're threatening to go to the media with the story unless we play ball. It doesn't matter, we'll have surveillance on him."

He looked at his watch: 9:30 p.m., which meant they could be back in Rocky Points by 1 a.m. Maybe earlier if they pushed it.

Luke put a hand on his shoulder. "We need to stay down here."

"What?" He almost got whiplash from looking at her so fast.

"Agent Todd is up there. He's got your entire department, plus twenty agents of ours on their way up from Denver. That's over thirty personnel who are going to be up all night looking for her up there. What good is it going to do for us to drive all night, leaving the case here unattended?"

"The killer is up in Rocky Points," Wolf spoke slowly.

"But the investigation is right here. We don't have any leads up there that amount to anything, and that's why we're here."

"Yes we do."

"Are you thinking about those cell phone photos you took? Fuzzy pictures of a maroon Bonneville? I'm not seeing it."

"I know what I saw. The guy had long black hair. A beard."

She said nothing for a beat. "It's a coincidence, or it's a lead. Either way, they're following up on it. There're going to be those pictures you took on every unit's dash computer. If that car is in Rocky Points and it's findable, they're going to find it."

She narrowed her eyes. "But you know the clues are pointing down here. Why did Attakai have that phone? What does he have to do with this? And there's another thing I just found out."

"And what's that?"

"They checked Attakai's cell phone records for the last few weeks. On the day Sally Claypool showed up dead he called his sister down here in Durango."

"Before you guys brought him in?"

"Yeah." Luke narrowed her eyes. "Why would he call his sister right then?"

He shrugged. "I don't know. Maybe he calls his sister a lot."

"Nope. Todd checked. Not once in the last twelve months." She pointed at the ground. "We have to stay here."

"*We* don't have to do anything. Those are your orders." There was little conviction in his voice.

She put a hand on his shoulder. "We'll go to our task force headquarters tomorrow, meet the guys down here on the case. You can see everything we have. And then we'll go talk to Mary Attakai."

"I paid the tab," Hannigan said. "Let's go get some sleep."

"Yeah." Wolf thought of a woman tied up by her ankles and wrists, sitting in a dark, cold place somewhere north of Rainbow Creek. Digging her nails into the dirt as a sick man slashed her with a knife. He thought of her father. He thought of his deputies working all night. "Right. Sleep."

Chapter 19

Wolf's eyes were puffy feeling. His thoughts slow. He'd slept little the night before, waking in adrenaline-fueled sweats whenever he managed to fall asleep, only to wake up and repeat the process over again a half an hour later.

There was no news on all fronts.

"Used to be covered in mud." The deputy jammed a single sunflower seed in his mouth, a few seconds later spitting out the shell onto the blacktop.

Wolf snapped on his latex glove and reached for the handle of the Ford Explorer. "You mind?"

The deputy stood motionless for a moment. "I don't care, do whatever you want. You're part of the task force now, right? It's been fully processed by the feds. I'm just an evidence clerk. Well, not just an evidence clerk. I've actually been assigned a field training officer …"

Now Wolf understood why Luke and Hannigan had opted to let Wolf go alone to the impound lot at the rear of the La Plata SD headquarters building. The guy wouldn't shut up.

Wolf turned off his ears and pulled on the driver's side door handle of Fred Wilcox's Ford Explorer. It bounced open with little effort.

He paused, staring inside.

Cool air seemed to flow out of the vehicle, despite the early morning heat. Or it could have been that he was more intimate than he wanted to be right now with a sick killer.

It was hard to tell what was normal Fred Wilcox wear and tear and what was the after-effect of being buried for a couple years under the southwestern high desert. The cloth seats were frayed in spots, slashed in others, like he had taken his aggression out on them with a pocketknife. The early morning sun lit up the spider web of cracks in the windshield.

Leaning inside, Wolf dared a breath through his nose and thought he smelled blood, though it was probably impossible after all this time, with all the vehicle had gone through and all the testing chemicals applied by the forensic team. Then again, maybe it was blood.

"… and then I'm going to make detective someday, too. It's always been my dream to …"

The floorboard carpets were dark brown and crusted with mud. He shut the door and opened the rear door. The back seats were folded forward. More room in back for Wilcox to keep his victims.

Leaning inside again, he held his breath this time and studied the carpets. Blood. Clear as day against the otherwise dirty nylon loop material.

Holes in the roof, where an excavator had discovered the vehicle with its jagged metal teeth, were now covered with a blue tarp and the little light that passed through the plastic bathed the inside in icy light.

" … but without no one playing, you just have to practice by yourself. That's the only thing about it."

Wolf shut the door. "Thanks, I'm done."

The deputy blinked, looking like a blabbering demon had just been exorcised from his body. "All done?"

"Yeah, if you could just show me back to the task force room, that would be great."

The deputy smiled. "You got it. Right back this way. Dang, it's already hot today and it's not even eight a.m. They say with climate change there's going to be longer summers and shorter winters, but I think …"

Wolf turned back to the vehicle and gave it one final look. It was dented badly outside, like somebody had raged on it with a sledgehammer.

Keeping a polite smile plastered on his face, Wolf followed the deputy back into the La Plata County SD building. The guy was stalling, trying to walk slower to finish a story, so Wolf slapped him on the shoulder and walked away.

Two right turns later he was alone and had found the small room.

Inside Hannigan was leaning on a desk talking to another FBI agent. He turned with a smile. "How was it? Did you meet Deputy Jergens?"

Wolf nodded.

Hannigan smiled to his FBI colleague.

It was freezing cold in the room and there were no windows. If he didn't know any better, he would have thought it was January. To add to the atmosphere, there were pictures of the victims lying on metal slabs plastered all over the walls. A pen board at the front of the room had half-thoughts scrawled all over it in poor handwriting.

"This is Special Agent Wells," Hannigan said.

Wolf nodded and shook the man's hand.

"Nice vehicle out there, huh?" Wells asked.

"Yeah."

The agent clucked his cheek and sipped his coffee.

"Where's Luke?"

"Right here." She came into the room behind him, bringing in her fresh scent. She must have brought her own soap and shampoo on the trip. "Let's roll."

"I thought we were waiting for Mansor and Wines," Hannigan said.

"We're meeting them at the hole."

"Oh," Agent Wells stood up, "Going to see us a hole, huh?"

"You're staying here," Luke said.

Wells's face dropped and he sat back down.

"We've already seen the hole," Hannigan said.

Luke walked out of the room. "Not all of us."

They got in their vehicles once again and drove—Wolf following behind Hannigan and Luke—south out of town.

They passed signs for Mesa Verde, which was a World Heritage Site that preserved some of the most pristine Ancestral Puebloan archeological sites in the United States, but their destination proved to be a few miles closer.

After a short climb out of the Animas Valley, they turned south off the highway and followed a network of dirt roads that seemed to wander aimlessly. The wellheads and oil containment tanks proved the roads followed the oil deep beneath the surface of the earth to different fracking operations, which, Wolf knew from his friend Nate, ran into the hundreds in this immediate area alone.

Luke stopped numerous times at forks in the road, consulting her telephone or a map, Wolf couldn't tell, until they finally reached a well site that was a pair of containment tanks tucked into a low juniper forest.

They parked and got out, and then they stood in the heat for ten minutes until crackling tires approached up the road.

A Chevy Blazer with turret lights on top wobbled toward them and stopped.

Wolf clamped his eyes shut and held his breath as a cloud of dust hissed over them.

The Blazer doors opened and thumped shut.

"Sorry." The gleaming sheriff's badge was visible through the dust before the man's face. "Doesn't matter how much rain you get out here, always gonna be dusty as hell. Hi there. Sheriff Ron Mansor." He held out a hand to Wolf.

"Detective Wolf." Wolf shook the man's hand. It was puffy and red, like the rest of him. His head was the shape of a saucepan, his deeply wrinkled face shaded by a wide brim cowboy hat.

"This is Deputy Wines," he said pointing behind him.

Deputy Wines tipped his cap, eyeing Luke with a smile.

Mansor nodded at Hannigan and Luke. "I heard what happened up there. And you have another missing girl?" He looked at Wolf.

Wolf nodded.

The sheriff wheezed, and Wolf wondered if the dust was getting to him or if he was having a cardiac event, but the sheriff seemed to think it normal and just walked.

Deputy Wines waved an after-you hand and tucked his thumbs in his duty belt.

The junipers swayed in a light, hair-dryer breeze, their scent mixed with the twisted bones of a long-dead deer alongside the dirt road. Insects hissed and snapped, and a lone hawk screeched while it floated in a lazy circle high above a pair of rusted cylinder oil tanks in the distance.

Sheriff Mansor watched Wolf take in the sights and walked next to him. "All the fracking equipment has been taken off location. The company that dug the truck out of the ground was doing something with the wellhead, but they weren't suckin' it out of the ground, that's for sure. There're hundreds of sites like these around here. Most of them look like this now. Maybe one day the price of oil will go back up, and this place will be rocking and rolling again."

"Or maybe we'll be driving in electric cars," Luke said.

Sheriff Mansor laughed like that was the funniest joke he'd ever heard.

"Just up here," Mansor said. "On the other side of that gray tank."

Deputy Wines took a silent cue and ran ahead of them, disappearing around the nearest oil containment tank.

Wolf could feel the heat coming off the rusted out metal cylinder while he watched Deputy Wines lift some rocks off a blue tarp and snap it away, revealing a dark hole underneath.

"Big hole, huh?" Sheriff Mansor said in between wheezes.

The hole was large enough to comfortably park a 1995 Ford Explorer inside with plenty of room to spare.

"The roof was five, six feet underneath the ground?" Sheriff Mansor asked his deputy.

Deputy Wines silently agreed with him, keeping his solemn gaze at the bottom of the hole.

"Deep," Mansor said.

Luke took off her sunglasses and walked around to the other side. She was in her white blouse, sleeves rolled to the elbows, the wind pushing the fabric against her skin.

Wolf's next thought was involuntary, like a jab to the nose that had gotten through his guard. *What was Lauren doing now?*

He had tried to call her last night and gotten no answer. After he left a voicemail she sent a message that said, "We're okay. We're in Aspen."

It was as if the cell phone in his hand had turned to a block of ice. Of course he'd known they were in Aspen. He wanted to know how they were. What were they doing? How were they holding up?

Maybe that was none of his business anymore. Or maybe it was. He had given their last conversation a lot of thought.

We do *need to talk.*

Is that what she'd said? Without a second's hesitation he'd gone on the defensive and left, probably out of fear of hearing what she wanted to say. He assumed it was going to be a not-you-it's-me speech or some variation to make it seem like it wasn't a not-you-it's-me speech.

"What did you want to talk about at the fair?" Wolf had texted back.

His cell phone had sat silent all night, and now she still hadn't answered. His hurt was quickly giving way to bitterness.

"… the excavation companies in town," Sheriff Mansor was saying.

Wolf looked at Hannigan, because the sheriff was now talking to the agent.

Hannigan's Ray Ban Wayfarers glasses revealed nothing. "You sure?"

Sheriff Mansor squared off with him. "Yeah. An excavator with a three-twenty-B, thirty-six inch, six-tooth bucket."

Hannigan raised a corner of his mouth. "Okay. And what about the excavator that discovered it?"

Mansor pointed at a wall of dirt inside the hole. "Four toothed. The fracking company had a four-toothed. You can see where they stopped digging when they hit the roof of the truck. Then they pulled it out with a chain."

"Okay." Hannigan held up his hands. "So it was a six-toothed excavator."

"I'm sorry," Wolf said. "What are you two talking about?"

Mansor pulled a can of Copenhagen from his back pocket, took a pinch and shoved it in his lip, leaving grains dangling on his chin like black ants were crawling on his face. "We were talking about the two different kinds of buckets that dug in this hole. The original hole was made by a six-toothed bucket. The truck was discovered by a four-toothed bucket the fracking company had."

Wolf eyed the hole in front of them and nodded. Erosion from a recent rain storm, probably two days ago by the looks of it, had done its thing, rounding the edges, and the bottom was a smooth floor where mud had pooled and hardened, but there were places that were clearly stabbed with exactly what the sheriff had said—four-toothed excavator marks and six-toothed.

Mansor spat on the ground and eyed Wolf.

"Who has excavators?" Wolf asked. "Excavation companies? What about construction companies?"

"Some construction companies have them," the sheriff said, "but they usually outsource the dirt moving to excavation companies."

Mansor poked up the brim of his hat. "We've been checking all day yesterday. It's across the board. Depends on the company. Every place we've talked to has paper trails that need to be followed, which is gonna take warrants and time."

"Paper trails? How are you going to do that? You don't know when the Explorer was buried, do you?"

Mansor winked. "Didn't they tell you? The gas tank was filled to the brim, and he had a gas receipt sitting right on the passenger seat for August 21st."

"A little thin," Wolf said. "Just because that's the last time the truck was filled up doesn't mean that's when it was buried."

"True," Agent Hannigan said. "But we also found a newspaper in his truck dated the same as the gas receipt. A Durango Herald, purchased at said gas station."

Wolf gave them a skeptical look.

Luke jumped in. "There was not just a newspaper in his truck. There was a box full of newspapers in his truck. The first of them was dated August 7th, the day after Rose Chissie was discovered in the park. The front page was all about it. A big four page special on the investigation so far. Then he had every day's newspaper until August 21st."

Wolf narrowed his eyes. "So you're saying he was collecting them."

"He became a collector," Hannigan said. "We know that. Every newspaper in that collection had the Van Gogh killer as front-page news. We checked with the Durango Herald, and they had Van Gogh front-page articles for consecutive weeks after August 21st. So why weren't there more newspapers in the back of his truck?"

Wolf nodded. "Because the truck was buried on the 21st ... okay, I'll buy it." He walked around to the other side of the hole. "Why bury the truck in the first place? Why bury the newspaper articles if he was collecting them? Wouldn't he take them?"

Mansor chuckled, then shrugged. "Because he was spooked? Mary Attakai saw his SUV that night, and he wanted to make sure nobody found it so he buried it. There was a lot of DNA and blood inside, which would have tied the killings to him. Have you seen the truck yet?"

"I have." Wolf stared inside the hole. "But Mary Attakai's attack, her escape, happened on August 5th."

Mansor nodded. "Yeah?"

"So he waited sixteen days to bury his vehicle. If he was spooked about Mary Attakai seeing his vehicle, wouldn't he have buried it ... I don't know, on the 6th or 7th? Not wait around for sixteen days and then bury it?"

They stood in silence, contemplating the question.

"Maybe he didn't have a reason to think he was in danger," Luke said. "And then something spooked him sixteen days later. And as for the newspapers, that's sixteen newspapers to carry around with him. If it were me, I'd leave them in the truck. Why carry those things around if you're trying to ditch evidence?"

Mansor spit in the dirt. "Makes sense to me."

Wolf looked around. "You're looking for excavator companies."

"That's right," Mansor said.

"And checking their paperwork?"

"Yes sir."

"I don't think you're going to find anything."

Mansor chuckled humorlessly. "Well I don't know about that."

"Fred Wilcox worked as a janitor at a funeral home," Wolf said.

"Yeah?"

"Where did he live?" Wolf asked.

Luke cleared her throat. "An apartment in town. One bedroom in the basement of another house."

"How much did it cost him?"

"Three hundred a month," she said.

"What did he get paid?"

Luke shrugged. "Probably minimum wage. Somewhere around there."

Wolf nodded. "How much does it cost to rent an excavator? One big enough to put a six-tooth shovel on the end of it?"

"Probably a few thousand at least," Agent Hannigan said with a nod. "I see what you're saying. How the hell did the guy afford to rent out an excavator? You gotta put it on a trailer, hook it to a big diesel, haul it down here. Dig the hole, put the car in, fill up the hole, pay for delivery charges, pay for excavator gas ... we're talking a big bill at the end of all of that. Sure a lot more than a funeral home janitor can afford."

"He could have a history of running big machinery we don't know about," Luke said. "Could have had a friend who loaned it to him. Or someone who helped him."

Wolf nodded. "I think it certainly had to be a friend who loaned it to him, or more exactly, he had a friend who helped him. Think about the explanation he would have to give to a company he hired out of the blue about why he was burying a truck next to a wellhead."

"They wouldn't do it," Hannigan said.

They stared at the hole for a while longer.

"Well I'm gonna keep looking at the excavator companies. Something might jump out." Sheriff Mansor folded his arms over his ample gut.

Wolf stared at the ground for a few moments, trying to connect new information with old. He felt like he was trying to mash together a dozen puzzle pieces with his palm.

Mansor spit again. "I hear you guys are holding Jeremy Attakai in connection."

"He had the cell phone in his apartment," Wolf said.

"Yeah. I know."

Wolf began the walk back to the other side of the hole. "He was dating the victim."

Mansor said nothing.

"His sister was the only one who got away."

"If you want my opinion," Mansor said, "he ain't your guy."

"And why's that?" Luke asked.

"Why's that? Because he was a good man. Went to the police academy in town. Made some bad mistakes at the beginning of his tenure with us, but hell, everyone gets drunk and does stupid stuff. But a cold-blooded killer, cutting off ears and toes? Displaying their bodies like we seen? No way. No …" He glared at them in turn, as if daring a contradiction.

"Do you know where Jeremy Attakai was the night of his sister's abduction?" Wolf asked.

Mansor snorted. "Jeremy? He was … he was at the hospital later that night. When his sister was brought in, we called him and he came in."

"But where was he before that?" Wolf asked.

The sheriff thought about it and shook his head. "I don't know. He … I don't know. He said he was supposed to pick her up that night from work but he didn't. I got the impression he was out drinking. I guess you'd have to ask him. But like I said, he was at the hospital. So I guess he was at home when she showed up there. What are you saying anyway? Mary Attakai said a fat, hairy man attacked her. Fits Fred Wilcox's description. We found her blood and hair in his SUV."

Wolf and Luke exchanged a glance.

"Does he have any history of violence?" Luke asked.

"Attakai?"

Luke nodded. "Yes. Attakai."

"Nope." After another spit he said. "Just a fight during his early years. But like I said, we all get drunk and do stupid stuff."

"What fight?" Hannigan asked.

"Some guy was hitting on his girl, so he took it outside. Got a little too physical and put the guy in the hospital."

"In the hospital for what?" Luke asked.

"Two broken arms."

She whistled. "That's more than a little too physical. Why wasn't this on his record?"

"He was a good kid, I'm telling you. It was a freak accident. He threw the guy down, and the guy landed weird, broke both his arms." Mansor raised both hands and stared at them. "The guy with the broken arms agreed, it was a freak accident."

Luke snorted. "Right. When you were done twisting one of his casts."

Mansor lifted his chin toward the sun and closed his eyes, then stepped to the edge of the hole. "I'm telling you my assessment of Deputy Jeremy Attakai. You can take it or leave it."

"What was his reason for leaving here and moving to Rocky Points?" Wolf asked.

Mansor turned his head and cocked an eyebrow. "I don't know for sure. Back then he said he needed a change … but I have a theory if you want to hear it."

Wolf nodded.

"He was really spooked about his sister when she escaped this guy. For a few weeks after that he requested the night shift. He staked out her house personally, tailed her to work every day, guarded her at lunch, tailed her after work all the way home, then slept outside her house and did it all over again the next day.

"He was a mess. I think he thought he'd let his sister down in the first place. Like I said, I think he was supposed to be the one to pick her up from work. He was putting it all on himself."

"So he left?" Wolf asked. "Goes from protecting her day and night to leaving her high and dry?"

"I think it was his sister who ran him out of town in the end. She couldn't take the smothering anymore." Mansor shrugged with a wheeze. "Of course I don't know for sure. You'd have to ask him. All I know is I saw them fighting once—him and his sister—outside the station. And then he asked for a week off, which I gave him, and he came back a week later with a job up in Rocky Points."

"When did he leave on vacation, exactly?" Wolf asked.

Mansor shrugged. "I don't know. A month after his sister got attacked?"

"I'd like you to check for the exact date when you get back to your office."

"Why's that?"

The truth was Wolf had no answer for that, but something was telling him it was important. "Just to know."

"You really think Attakai's involved in this?" Mansor asked.

"He went north and so did the killings. He had a cell phone that had been communicating to this cell phone found in this hole. His sister was the only one who escaped the killer."

Mansor shook his head.

Wolf pulled out his phone and checked his home screen. There were no missed calls, no received text messages. No news about Lindsay Ellington.

"We were out in full force that night," Mansor was gazing into the past with unblinking eyes. "Mary was unconscious in the hospital and we hadn't gotten a chance to talk to her so we didn't know the whole story. Didn't know Rose Chissie was still out there. Didn't know about the Ford Explorer. But this sick bastard, Wilcox, didn't know that. For all he knew, we had him identified. But he still had the gall to come driving into town with a dead body in the back and dump it in a park next to a schoolyard."

Mansor took off his hat and twisted the brim. "Three kids, aged ten, twelve, and fourteen. They were dressed in church clothes. They found her. Now they gotta live with that image flashing in their mind every single day of their life."

"Attakai could have told him," Hannigan said.

Mansor frowned. "What?"

"Attakai could have told Fred Wilcox that his sister didn't tell you guys anything yet, and he was in the clear to come into town and dump the body."

Mansor turned to them with narrowed eyes. "Deputy Attakai was there when we got called to it. The guy was just as upset as the rest of us.

Way more than the rest of us. You ask me, this Fred Wilcox was a sick bastard, and he's messing with Jeremy right now. It has to be that. Plain and simple. Jeremy's not working *with* him. Wasn't working with him. That kind of sick shit? That's not Jeremy Attakai. I saw the determination in him to find this bastard after his sister crawled out of the desert." Mansor glared at them, as if daring them to contradict him again.

No one did. At least not out loud.

Luke looked at her watch. "We have to go. Mary Attakai's expecting us."

Chapter 20

Highway 160 cut east out of Durango through low hills and slanted plateaus covered in junipers, yucca, and other shrubs that thrived in the oven-like heat outside.

Wolf followed Luke's Tahoe for ten miles and pulled off the highway onto a dirt road that ducked north into the trees toward a line of brown cliffs.

Farm machinery and plastic toys littered a yard in front of a house, but Luke kept driving past it and further into the hills.

Mary Attakai's place was a mile later—a single story doublewide trailer with a deck off the back set on a few acres of scorched lawn. The cliffs back-dropped the property, glaring in the late morning sun.

A few men sipped beer around a smoking grill on the deck. Four women sat on a picnic table on the lawn watching kids play soccer.

Passing a cruiser with the La Plata County Sheriff's Department logo on it, they pulled up to the front of the property. The women stood while the men lowered their beers.

Slotting their vehicles between two oversized pickups and a minivan, Wolf got out into hot air smelling of barbecue smoke and weeds.

"What can I help you folks with?" Two thick and short men with dark skin, hair and eyes came marching around the house. The lead one was talking and looked like he meant the question to be rhetorical.

Luke consulted her notebook and raised her sunglasses to her forehead. "You must be … Hector?"

Agent Hannigan ignored the interaction and gazed at the landscape.

The man folded his arms. "What do you want?"

"We're here to talk to Mary. My name is Special Agent Luke. This is Special Agent Hannigan and Detective Wolf from Sluice-Byron County Sheriff's Department."

"About what?"

"About her brother," Wolf said. "I work with him up in Rocky Points. You know what happened, right? How he's being held in jail right now?"

The man said nothing, just stared at him for a few seconds, until a woman came around the corner.

She was short and squat, like the two men who'd greeted them, but she had kind eyes that matched Jeremy Attakai.

"Mary?" Wolf asked.

The woman wiped her hands on an apron, on it the image of bikini clad breasts of a much thinner woman. "Yeah?"

"I'm Detective David Wolf, with the Sluice-Byron County Sheriff's Department."

Her every movement was strained: a hesitation, a thought, a decision, and an execution. She nodded and tilted her chin back. "Yeah?"

"I talked to you yesterday," Luke said. "About us sitting down for a chat. Could we please—"

"She doesn't have to talk to you," the man said.

"Hector, please," Mary said.

Hector pointed at Luke. "She already told you everything she knows. Back after that guy attacked her. Now you sick bastards want her to talk about it some more? Don't you guys have the first discussion on video? Why don't you go watch that and leave our family alone?"

"We're back again because he's back again," Wolf said.

Mary nodded, flicking a glance at the deputy vehicle parked down the road. "I know. I heard."

"You've heard about your brother being in jail?" Wolf asked.

She nodded.

"You talked to him, didn't you?"

Mary Attakai wore baby blue shorts that hugged tightly on her trunk legs, a huge cell phone jutting out of the rear pocket. Unconsciously, she moved her hand to the phone and touched it, then, as if she realized what she was doing, she dropped her hand and folded her arms.

"We know you've talked to him, Mary," Wolf said. "Right now they're holding your brother in jail because they suspect he might be connected. Don't you want to help him?"

"He called me when you guys found that girl dead by the river," Mary said. "He wanted to make sure I was all right."

Hector turned his head an inch, giving Mary a sidelong glance.

"And are you all right?" Wolf asked.

"Yes." She pointed toward the dirt road. "The sheriff has a guy parked here all the time."

"Mary," Luke said, "yesterday on the phone you said you'd be willing to talk to us."

"Hector's right," Mary said. "I don't have to talk to you. Not anymore."

Luke put up her hands. "We understand it's difficult to talk about. It's painful to remember, but we think he has another girl, and we think you could help."

Tilting her head back, Mary closed her eyes and exhaled. "My God."

"Fuck this," Hector said. "You don't gotta talk."

"What's the problem, Hector?" Hannigan unbuttoned his jacket and took a step forward. "We're not talking to you. So why don't you walk away?"

"Why don't you take your meathead ass and get back in your car and—"

"Enough!" Mary's voice echoed off the cliffs. "Just … come inside. We can talk in the living room."

"Mary—"

"I'll be okay, Hector. Please, go play with the kids."

"I'll come with you." Hector made to follow her, but stopped when Mary turned around.

"I'll be all right." Her eyes widened, and a secret communication shot between them. A warning? A reassurance?

Hector and the other man turned and disappeared around the side of the house.

"Please. Come in."

Mary held an aluminum screen door open for them and they stepped inside into the living room. It looked like a toy store had been hit by a tornado. There were two felt couches configured in an L shape, a beat up wooden coffee table, both of them covered in toys that spilled onto the blue carpet.

Plastic crunched underneath Hannigan's foot. "Sorry," he said, kicking a LEGO piece aside.

Wolf pushed aside a headless doll with his foot.

Mary made no effort to apologize for the state of her house. Her dead gaze said take it or leave it.

A continuous sizzle came from around the corner and bold smells of vegetables sautéing in spices hung in the air. Squealing children and a warm breeze floated in from an open window.

"You okay, Bipa?" Mary gestured to the two couches for them to sit and leaned around the corner.

"Oh yes. I'm fine," a frail voice said.

"No, you can stay in there. I'm just …"

An old woman shuffled around the corner, wiping her hands on a bib that said "Over forty and feeling sexy" in bubble letters. Her hair was long silver, pulled back in a ponytail. Her face was a dried lake, all creases and the same earthen color as Mary's. Her eyes twinkled and her lips stretched into a straight line. "Oh, hello. Who's this?"

"Some people, Bipa. Please. Go back in and we'll be right there."

Bipa eyed Wolf's badge, the stalk of Hannigan's Sig Sauer poking out of his jacket from his shoulder holster, and her face creased even more. "This about that man? The man out in the desert?"

"Bipa!" Mary was hissing now, pushing her out of the room. "Please."

Bipa slapped Mary's hand away. "Woman. Be respectful of your grandmother."

Dropping her hands, Mary stood obediently while the elder berated her with flashing eyes. After a few seconds of thick silence, she left the room.

"Sorry about that," Mary said. "You can take a seat if you want."

Wolf and Luke sagged toward one another as they sat on the over-soft couch. The fabric felt like an old velvet painting of a black lab Wolf's father had hung in the barn when he was a kid.

Hannigan took up the entire other couch.

"Well?" Mary shrugged and looked down at them.

"Please," Luke said, pointing to a chair against the other wall. "Sit down."

Mary did as she was asked. "What do you want?"

"You know what's going on up north," Wolf said. "At the moment, it seems that he's back."

Mary closed her eyes.

"We'd like to talk to you about what happened that night, Mary." Wolf leaned forward. "It might give us a clue, now that things are active again. Something might help."

Mary was blinking rapidly, calculating something. "How do you guys know it's the killer from two years ago?"

"Mary." A voice came from the entryway to the kitchen. Hector was back.

She looked up at her cousin and then at Luke. "Well? How do you know?"

"Okay," Luke said. "The sheriff's office pulled up a vehicle that matches the description you gave on the night of your attack. Inside of it we found Rose's blood, and some hair that matched your DNA profile. It was his truck."

Mary narrowed her eyes. "Okay. And … you think he's back in Rocky Points now?"

Luke shrugged. "We're not sure, Mary. It's complicated, and we can't really talk about the details of the case."

Mary went back to staring at the coffee table. Thinking.

Hector shook his head. "You don't have to talk."

"Hector's right," Luke said. "You don't have to talk. You don't have to tell us about what happened that night again. But … it could help us. Because maybe we'll ask different questions than the men who talked to you back then. And maybe your answers can help us find this guy."

"What's the guy's name?" Mary asked.

Wolf watched Hector's eyes dart to Mary.

"We're not sure," Luke said slowly. "That's part of the investigation, which we can't really talk about."

They sat in silence, listening to sizzling vegetables and squealing children.

"Please," Luke said.

Mary closed her eyes and nodded. Took a breath and started talking.

"I had a late shift at the restaurant, and Jeremy was supposed to come pick me up, but I called him and he was out having beers and was too wasted to come get me. So I called Rose." Mary's eyes started dripping, but she made no effort to wipe them. "So she drove over to get me, and called me when she got there, and I told her I'd be right out, cause I had to do my silverware. She said she was gonna have a smoke so she would see me outside. Said 'Okay, see you when I see you.' Those were the last words she ever said to me."

Hector's eyes turned to sparkling orbs.

"When I came outside, I went to her car. But it was weird, cause she wasn't there. And I remember thinking, 'that's weird', and then something didn't look right. I saw her door wasn't closed all the way. And then I saw the truck next to hers moving real fast back and forth. Like somebody was inside screwing or something. I remember thinking 'What the hell? Is she with some dude getting it on in the truck next to her?' So I walked up and the movement stopped. It was like they saw me coming, or at least that's what I was thinking at the time. I called out Rose's name, and nobody said nothing. And I started getting a weird feeling, so I backed off, and then this guy came charging at me out of the dark.

"He was big and hairy, but real fast. Strong as shit. And he had me in a headlock in like two seconds. I couldn't scream, cause he had a hand over my mouth. And then I remember feeling a sting in the back of my neck, and then ... and then the next thing I know I woke up on the ground, stars all around me." Mary wiped her eyes and looked at Luke. "Then I heard ..."

"Shit," Hector said, covering his mouth. "Why the hell you gotta ask about this?"

They said nothing, just watched Mary's eyelids slide down a fraction of an inch. "I heard him ... with her. And I looked over, and I saw ..." She sucked in a breath, "I saw what he'd done to her. She was limp, eyes open. Bleeding."

Wolf swallowed and glared out at the blue sky through the windows of the doublewide.

"And no, I don't remember what he looks like, if you're going to ask that. He was wearing this mask. Like an ancestral Puebloan mask, and I remember being so tired, so groggy, and wondering if it was all a dream? And then I started coming to. And I felt the pain in my foot."

Mary slipped off her shoe and sock, and then displayed the fleshy stump on her left foot where her big toe had been.

Unconsciously Wolf ran a finger across the web of scar tissue on his own hand.

She slipped back on the sock, and then the shoe, and then she continued. "I sat up, and I remember he said, 'I'll get to you in a bit.' And I remember being so confused. Wondering, is he helping me with something? What's he going to help me with? And then my mind just started working again. Just like that. And I started freaking out. I realized I had no pants on. No underwear. A bleeding foot that hurt with every heartbeat.

"And then I looked at what the guy was doing again. He was having sex with Rose." Mary opened her mouth and nothing came out.

"Then what happened?" Wolf asked quietly, trying to nudge her past the horrific moment.

"I … I got up and ran. And then I fell because of the pain in my foot. And he started yelling at me. 'Stop, bitch! Stop!' And I just ran. I didn't care about the pain no more. I heard his footsteps thumping on the dirt behind me, and then I was falling all of a sudden. I didn't even know, but we were right next to a cliff, and I ran straight off the edge. I remember the wind, and then pine needles, and branches, and twisting and tumbling. It was like a car accident or something …" She said nothing for a few moments and blinked. "And then I remember hitting the ground, and then not being able to suck in a breath.

"And then waking up again." She smiled like she was saying something so absurd it deserved a laugh. "And then I heard him again. 'Yeah bitch. Yeah! Woohoo!' He was yelling over the cliff. I got up, and at that point I was so numb, I just started walking. Nothing even hurt. I just walked, and walked. And then I was out of the trees. And then I followed distant lights, which was highway 550 they told me later." She wiped her eyes and blinked, and she was done crying. "I remember shivering. I remember the road. And then the trucker who picked me up, and then …"

With a shrug Mary turned to them.

"And then you woke up in the hospital?" Luke asked.

Mary nodded.

"And then what?" Wolf asked.

She took a breath. "My brother and his boys … the deputies … were all there the next morning, and I told them what happened. And they said they found Rose in town."

Hector was watching Mary closely. His lips were parted and he was holding his breath while he watched Mary talk.

Waiting for something. For what? Hoping? It looked like a mother watching her child at a school play, willing the child to remember the script.

The thought was like a punch. Was this a well-rehearsed story? If that had been a made up lie, then that had been the best acting he'd ever seen. Which would also make it one of the sickest things he'd ever seen. Nobody makes up a lie like that. So why was Hector in here? Why was he so concerned with what she said?

"Then what?" Wolf asked, looking at Hector as he said it.

Hector met his gaze and looked away.

"Then … my brother and his boys looked for the killer. Never did find him. The trucker showed them where he picked me up, and I went there with them. But I couldn't tell which direction I'd walked to the highway from. Couldn't remember how long I'd been going, or how long I'd been out when the guy took me and Rose. There were a couple different valleys I could have come out of, but I just don't remember."

"And your brother?" Wolf asked.

"What about him?" she asked.

"He protected you after that, right?" Wolf asked.

Mary nodded. "Yes."

"How?" Wolf asked.

"He followed me to work, watched the place during the day, followed me home at night. Slept in his car outside. Or on the couch right here. He thought the guy was coming after me, you know?"

Wolf nodded. "Because you were the only survivor. The only one who'd ever seen this guy and lived."

"Right." Mary's voice was a whisper.

"So … your brother wanted to protect you at all costs. He slept in his car, on the couch. Followed you to work, staked out your work."

"That's what she just said, de-tec-tive," Hector said. "You guys finished yet?"

Wolf held his gaze on Mary. "So why did he move north?"

Mary froze. The sizzling was done in the kitchen, and all that remained was the sounds of the game of soccer out back.

"Why would he protect you for … what? Two weeks? Three weeks?"

Mary said nothing.

"And then just up and move north?"

"He was starting to piss me off," she shrugged. "I told him to get the hell out of here and I didn't want to see him. I might have mentioned that it was all his fault." She stared unblinkingly at Wolf.

Now *that* was a prepared story.

"And why did you talk to your brother the other day? He gets taken in for questioning about the murder of his girlfriend, and he calls you?"

Mary frowned. "Yeah. He knew it was the guy. So he was worried."

Hannigan chuckled to himself.

Mary glared at him. "What?"

A woman with the same hereditary traits as Mary and her cousin came into the room. She locked eyes with Mary and said, "The food is ready, Mary. It's time to come eat now." She stood with her hands on her hips.

Hector pushed off from the wall and walked to the door. Pushing it open, he eyed them expectantly. "Thanks for coming by."

They left, and the door clacked shut after hitting Hannigan's heel on the way out.

Chapter 21

They drove back into downtown Durango in their respective vehicles to Fred Wilcox's only known place of residence.

The front yard was weeds and dirt, and it was at least a hundred degrees in the midday sun.

"Another place fit for a king." Hannigan had his hands on his hips.

"Okay … see you." Luke stepped out of the Tahoe and pocketed her phone. "He's almost here."

An octagon with a lipstick-cone shaped roof, the house in front of them reached two stories tall. At one time, perhaps fifty years ago, it would have been futuristic looking, now nothing could mask its datedness. The light blue paint was flaking off, the concrete of the walkway to the front door was cracked and growing weeds.

The yard clearly had no irrigation system, nor did it look like it was mowed more than once a semester. An empty keg of beer laid on its side next to it a half-gone sleeve of red plastic cups. Just in case it wasn't obvious that college students lived inside, there was a Durango Brewery sticker on the porthole window on the front door.

Crackling tires pulled their gaze to the approaching BMW sedan, which parked in front of Luke's Tahoe. A man stepped out in mid-sentence, having a conversation on the Bluetooth headset jammed in his ear. He was thin and fit, wearing gray slacks. His sleeves were rolled up on tanned arms, a thick watch reflecting the sunlight in golden swirls.

When he reached them he said, "I gotta go," and pushed a button on his earpiece. Lifting his sunglasses, he revealed beady blue eyes and shoved a hand at Luke. "Hello. I'm Kendall. But you can call me Ken."

"Right." Luke shook his hand.

Wolf and Hannigan introduced themselves, never getting eye contact from Ken, who was still laser fixed on the lower half of Luke.

"Here to talk about Freddy Wilcox, eh?" he asked.

"Yeah," Luke said. "We'd like to see his place, if you don't mind."

Ken studied them for a second. "Can I see those badges?"

Luke pulled hers off her belt and held it in front of the man.

He ignored Wolf's and Hannigan's. "You need a warrant to go inside, right?"

"Does he live there anymore?" Luke asked.

"No."

"Who does?"

"Nobody. Changed it to a storage unit after he left for the tenants who live up front." Ken pulled out a piece of gum and shoved it in his mouth.

"Then what's the problem?" She lifted her sunglasses. "How about you just do us a favor and show us the storage unit?"

"Might be a problem to the students who have their stuff in there." Ken broke into a grin, showing off his corn kernel teeth. Chomping his gum, he shook his head, looked Luke up and down again and began walking at a no-nonsense pace. Fishing for a key on a large ring filled with at least fifty of them, he said, "It's around back."

They passed four sides of the octagon.

When they past the keg Ken said, "These college kids." Then he raised his eyebrows at Luke and said, "They pay a pretty penny though."

Luke jammed a gag-me finger in her mouth when he turned around.

They were at 568 10th street in downtown Durango, and the research had shown Fred Wilcox living at 568-½ 10th street, but by the looks of it, it was decidedly less than half a residence. There were two steps down to a sunken doorway. Grass spilled over the crumbling concrete, and a huge cobweb had enveloped the upper half of the door.

"Charming," Luke said.

"Storage units don't have to be charming."

"You remember Mr. Wilcox, do you?" Hannigan asked.

Ken smiled at him. "Well, yeah. What, am I going to forget after two years? Especially after he screwed me over like that."

He kept walking, stepped down the stairs and fished open the door. It yawned open, revealing a dark carpet and tiny kitchenette off to the side. "After you." He smiled and winked at Luke.

Luke hesitated at the top of the stairs. "So, how exactly did Fred Wilcox screw you over?"

Ken looked at Luke, then up to Hannigan and Wolf. "Are you guys putting me on right now? Didn't we already go over this? Oh right, I guess you guys are feds. Feds don't talk with other agencies, is that it?"

Luke frowned. "I'm not following you."

"Like I told that cop before, he just moved out. Disappeared and stopped paying rent. Never said anything to me. Not that he said much to begin with."

"You talked to the police before today?" Luke asked.

"Yeah. Right after he left. They were asking about him."

"The La Plata County Sheriff's office?"

"Yeah. Well, it was a single cop I should say. Called me on the phone, asking about Fred, wanted to come see his property, so I came and met him here. That's when I figured out he'd skipped town on me. Place was all trashed. Had a broken window, glass on the floor. The fat bastard."

"What was the cop's name?" Wolf asked.

Ken thought about it and threw up his hands. "I don't know."

"Deputy Attakai?" Luke asked.

The landlord shook his head. "Seriously. I couldn't remember if you put that gun to my head. But don't get any ideas."

"Did this guy have a badge and a uniform on?" Hannigan asked. He pointed at Wolf. "Or was he dressed like him."

"Had a uniform on and everything." Ken smiled. "You guys are kind of freaking me out right now. Was that a real cop I was talking to? What the hell's going on here?"

Luke stepped down the stairs and made to get by. "Don't worry about it."

Wolf followed her, with Hannigan taking up the rear.

The air inside was hot and stagnant. The electric burners in the kitchenette were blackened with soot. A microwave stood on a countertop, the door of it hanging askew. The space where a refrigerator once stood was empty, with mouse droppings in its place. The air had a vague smell that was hard to put a finger on.

"Smells like boiled ass," Hannigan said.

"Ha. Yeah, well, smells better than when I came in here that first time with the cop. Fred was a pig. So what's the big deal about him, anyway? Cops are after him, he skips town. What is he? A serial murderer or something?"

Wolf chose his words. "What did you and the police officer discuss that day? What was he looking for?"

Ken smiled, let it really settle onto his face. "What's going on here? Seriously." His face dropped. "Can I please see your badge up close?"

Wolf rolled his eyes and plucked his badge from his belt.

Ken bent near and nodded. "Rocky Points. They … shit, that girl got murdered up there. FBI agents? A detective from Rocky Points? Jesus H. mother, are you guys … wait a minute …"

Hannigan slapped a huge hand on the man's shoulder.

Ken flinched and ducked out of the big man's grip.

"Just answer the questions we shoot your way, eh Ken?" Hannigan winked. "What was he looking for? The cop, when he came over that day. Was he searching the house? Was he asking you specific questions? Can you remember? It would really help us out."

Ken back stepped.

"What did he look like?" Hannigan stepped toward him.

"Uh … he was dark haired. Looked like an Indian. You know, feather, not dot."

"And what did he say?"

Ken shook his head. "Can't remember."

"You want to know the truth?" Hannigan said. "The cop was probably a fake."

His face turned white. "What?"

Hannigan nodded. "Serious as a heart attack. But there's nothing to worry about. Unless he told you something that he'll want to keep secret. Maybe he …" the agent made a contemplative face and let his sentence die.

"What?" Ken stepped forward. "Wait, he … he just met me out front like you guys did. We walked back here, to the door, and he made me stay back while he went to the door. Yeah, I remember. The window was busted and the door was unlocked. And then nobody answered. He looked in the windows, I remember he pulled his gun and went in."

Luke squinted. "The window was busted and the door was unlocked? Did it look like somebody had broken in?"

"I guess. But I'm not sure why somebody would break into a shithole like this. There was trash everywhere, dirty clothes. Nothing for anyone to take. I figured he locked himself out and had to break himself back in."

Luke nodded. "What did the cop do when he came in?"

"He searched the place pretty good. Upturned everything." Ken pointed to the single room off the kitchenette. "Searched his bedroom, which is right here."

The bedroom was six by eight feet at most. Dark, no windows. Inside there were boxes and skis and mountain bikes leaning against all of it.

"They use it for storage now." Ken pointed toward a small inset. "I remember the cop searched in there. That was his closet. All I know is, whatever he was looking for, he didn't find it. He left here empty handed and kind of pissed off. I remember that. And I was pissed off too. I had broken glass everywhere. Place was trashed."

Wolf flicked on his cell phone light and ran the beam around the room. It looked normal enough as a storage space, dismal as a dungeon for somewhere to live. Just the kind of place a serial killer would be at home with his tormented thoughts.

He stood still, trying to picture Fred Wilcox living in it—the day to day weirdness that took place, the nightly rituals of a serial killer—and decided it was too disturbing to meditate on. He thought of the picture of Wilcox Luke had shown on the big screen in the situation room—those black hole eyes. If these walls could talk, Wolf wasn't sure he'd want to listen.

"The cop left with nothing?" Wolf asked.

"Yeah, nothing."

"And Fred Wilcox never came back?"

"I don't think so. I called him repeatedly after that. He never answered and looked like he never returned. Never paid any rent again, that's for sure. Just disappeared. I had to get my guys to come in and clean the place out."

Wolf walked to the front door. There was a tall, skinny window right next to it. "This the window you were talking about?"

Ken nodded.

Wolf walked outside into the blazing sun.

Luke and Hannigan were close behind, and a minute later they said their goodbyes to Ken the landlord and walked to their cars.

"I need to eat," Hannigan declared.

Luke looked at her watch. "It's 2:40. I set up a meeting with the funeral home guy at 3. You'll have to wait."

Hannigan's jaw flexed.

Wolf was starting to feel the effects of going non-stop for almost three days and needed food too.

"What'd you guys think about that?" Luke asked.

"I think it was Attakai who came searching the place," Hannigan said. "Said he was dark-skinned, Native American looking. Sounds like Attakai to me."

She looked at Wolf. "What are you thinking?"

He stared into the near distance, seeing none of the parked cars and high trees on the Durango back street. "If Attakai was here, then he knew it was Fred Wilcox who was the killer. That either means he was working with him all along …"

"Or he figured out who the killer was," Luke said.

Wolf nodded.

"That's what I was thinking, too. And what about that broken window?" she asked. "Is that something?"

"Broken windows and unlocked doors usually mean break-in," Hannigan said. "Who did it and why? Those are other questions."

"And for what?" Wolf asked.

Chapter 22

Dispatch do you copy?" Patterson lowered the radio and then raised it again. "Dispatch do you copy?"

The speaker crackled, and then for a split second there was noise—it could have been a woman's voice or a beep—and then it was gone.

"Dispatch, this is unit 14, do you copy?"

No answer.

Rachette blew air through his lips. "Put it down, you aren't going to get anything up here."

Up here was dozens of miles north of Rocky Points in the Cave Creek wilderness area. The dirt road they were on swerved between hills topped by smooth granite outcroppings that looked like sculptures in the mid-day sun.

Few people lived here, and those that did made do without modern amenities such as cell phones, satellite reception, or cable service. Patterson had driven these roads a few times before, but never this far in.

"You know we're going to find him now." Rachette smiled, turning a corner too fast.

She hung up the radio and grabbed the ceiling bar as they bounced through a pothole. Pulling out her cell phone, she checked her reception again.

"Just relax," he said.

Patterson ignored him and checked the laptop. "Nothing."

"Oh damn, we can't post a selfie when we're up here?"

She slid him a look.

"That's why we like working up here in the Rocky Mountains, right? The remoteness. How do you think they did it twenty years ago?" He looked at her seriously. "You ever made a traffic stop without radio?"

"I have, and I didn't like it."

They turned a corner and the narrow valley widened to an open meadow surrounded by dense forest. It was like the sky had opened up, and she watched as the screen of the laptop flickered.

"There, we have contact."

"Well, good. I was about to shit myself."

She took out her phone and checked the reception. There was one bar, but it also had an X next to it, which was never a sign of reliable cell service.

"Seriously you have to …" He straightened in his seat so fast his head almost hit the ceiling. The SUV drifted sideways as Rachette skidded to a stop.

"What?" She followed his gaze out the windshield and saw it immediately. A sedan parked in front of a single story house at the edge of the woods, the sun gleaming off the maroon paint job.

"You-are-shitting-me." Rachette leaned forward. "That's it, right?"

Patterson had the photos on her phone but she already memorized them. The dent in the right rear bumper. The chrome strip around the lower part of the car scraped at the front. "That's it."

Rachette picked up the radio and put it to his lips. "Dispatch, do you copy?"

No answer.

"What's your phone say?"

She lifted her screen. "No service. It had a bar a few seconds ago." She twisted in her seat. "Back up a few."

"He's outside."

She turned back to the windshield.

A man, *the* man, was walking out of his house and making for the rear of his car, stopping at the trunk and opening it.

He was just as Wolf had described him: long black hair, burly beard that was on the ratty-looking side of the spectrum. He wore a dirty white tee shirt and dirty jeans. Just like Wolf had told her, he was overweight, but not heavy.

"That him?" Rachette had his gun on the steering wheel, pointed out the windshield.

She nodded, her hands and feet starting to tingle. Her heart was bumping inside her ribs and she realized she was holding her breath.

"That him?" Rachette asked, this time almost yelling at her.

"Yeah. That's … the guy fits Wolf's description, and that's the car for sure."

"It's Wilcox, right? That's him."

"Looks like it."

A cloud of dust from Rachette's stop had passed them and was floating across the meadow, straight for the car and the man, who now had his head was down in the trunk. He appeared again and slammed it, making way for the driver's side door.

"He's leaving." Rachette whispered as if the guy could hear them.

Opening his door, the man gave them a double take and paused—one foot in, one foot out of his car.

Even through the dust, Patterson could see the surprise on Wilcox's face before he sat down and shut the door.

Was it Wilcox? She thought Wilcox was fat. In his driver's license photo, he looked fat, with a thick neck and shoulders. If it was him, he'd definitely lost some weight, which was possible. The photo had been taken six years ago.

"He's just driving away." Rachette let off the gas and eased forward.

There was a dirt clearing in front of the house, and the maroon sedan swung around in a half-circle and bounced its way toward the dirt road.

The side windows were tinted, so it was impossible to see what Wilcox was doing or where he was looking.

The sedan came to a complete stop at the dirt road, and then without much hesitation it swung in their direction and started driving.

Her heart raced faster. The world tunneled down to the glared windshield coming at them.

"What do we do?" Rachette asked. "I'm gonna block him."

She nodded. "Yeah. We have to. Do it!"

She hit the turret lights button and leaned back into the seat.

Rachette put his gun on his lap and gunned the engine, cranked the wheel to the right and skidded to a halt so they were a perpendicular, blocking most of the road with Rachette's side facing the oncoming car.

Rachette popped his door and exited.

Patterson pulled on the handle and tried to jump out but was stuck. *Seatbelt!*

Unbuckling herself, she got out, slammed the door, pulled her gun and leaned on the hood.

As she did this she was vaguely aware of the sound of a revving engine, and then when she looked she realized the sedan was barreling at them.

Rachette stood with raised gun shouting, "Sheriff's department!"

It kept coming.

"Sheriff's department! Stop! Right now stop!"

The vehicle swung to the driver's right, their left, and hugged the side of the road. She almost yelled shoot, but it was clear Wilcox meant to miss them completely.

The sedan's engine sputtered loud, dust kicking up behind it, the loose parts of the beat up vehicle rattling like an oncoming train.

Rachette fired once, then twice. His aim was low, aiming toward the tires, she realized.

Risky. If he popped the tires Wilcox might careen right into him.

The man ducked out of sight behind the windshield, diving toward the passenger seat. The sedan followed the driver's movement, jerking to the side and careening off the road.

It left the ground for a moment as it leapt off the shoulder and down into the drainage depression.

Engine roaring, with a loud squeak, the front of the car bounced upward out of the trench. Its momentum slowed by half as a spray of earth shot forward and the bumper ripped off. Bouncing back to its wheels, it coasted forward and slammed into a pine tree, coming to a stop.

"Go!" Patterson knew the crash would have stunned the driver and they had precious few seconds to get a jump on him.

Rachette looked like he was already thinking the same thing as he took off at a full sprint.

When they got there the engine sputtered and died, and a blast of steam hissed out of the hood.

Guns drawn and aimed at the driver's side door, they swung to the front of the car to get a clear view inside. The windshield had a crater in it where the man's head must have connected. The glass was still in place but in a million pieces, looking like bludgeoned ice.

Rachette opened the door and aimed with an isosceles stance. "Freeze!"

The guy froze because he had no choice. Slumped over the center console, the man's face was down and covered with his long hair. The back of his neck was exposed, revealing a rivulet of blood trickling down his skin.

"Unnngh." The man stirred.

Rachette holstered his gun. "Cover me." He shuffled into the open door and pulled the man upright, searching for weapons. "Clear. Help me."

They leaned the man out of the vehicle and yanked him free, dragging him to some shade alongside the road.

The man was rocking side to side, making noises like he was having a nightmare.

"Damn, he's hurt bad," Rachette said.

She stepped over the man and cuffed his hands behind his back.

After another fit of grunting, the guy seemed to go into a deep sleep.

"Is he dead?" Rachette stepped back.

She reached down and dug her fingers into his sweaty beard, feeling for a pulse. It was pumping fast and strong. "He's okay."

They stood and looked at each other.

"Well, we found him." Rachette stared down, then turned to follow Patterson's gaze.

"He was looking in the trunk," she said.

Rachette stepped over and popped the trunk lever inside the driver's door.

It swung up and bounced with a squeak.

She walked to the rear, dread filling every cell in her body in anticipation of what they might find.

It was filled with dirty clothing. Men's clothing. Three empty plastic bags from the grocery store. A set of jumper cables and a lot of dirt.

Rachette appeared next to her. "I'm not seeing anything out of the ordinary."

"We have to check the house." She turned to look up the road. "He might have Lindsay Ellington in there."

Rachette nodded. "We can't just leave him here."

They looked down.

Rachette dug his hands in the man's armpits and wrestled him into a seated position. "I thought he was supposed to weigh two-forty something."

She grabbed the man's ankles and lifted, and they carried him to their SUV.

He was no more than a hundred eighty pounds. His arms and legs were thin, as he was carrying most of his weight in his gut.

"Yeah. I was thinking the same thing," she said. "He either lost a lot of weight or this isn't our guy."

They opened the back door of the SUV and wrestled him into a lying position on the back seat.

"Check his pockets," Rachette said, stepping back.

She glared at him. "Like I enjoy digging in strange men's pants for things? How about you do the honors."

He rolled his eyes and ducked back into the SUV, rifling the man's pockets. "Nothing in the front pockets … here." He produced a wallet and opened it. His eyebrows came together when he looked.

"Who is it?"

Rachette gave her the wallet.

The driver's license picture looked like a different man altogether. She bent inside and compared it to the man's face, realizing it was just the lack of hair and beard in the driver's license that threw her off. "Jim Brewer?"

"Definitely not our guy."

"Not Fred Wilcox," she said. "So why was he watching the crime scene?"

Rachette put his hands on his hips. "Jesus. The guy was probably just taking a leak on the side of the road and Wolf saw him."

She thought about it and shook her head. "Wolf said there were three news vans and this guy was watching them and looking down at the crime scene. Not taking a leak." She set down the wallet on the seat and eyed the house again. "And why was he driving like that? He was trying to get away from us."

Rachette shook his head.

"We have to check the house."

"All right," Rachette nodded. "Shut the door. Let's go."

They climbed back in and drove.

Jim Brewer smelled awful in the back seat, like chopped onions that had been sitting around for a week.

Rolling down the windows all the way, Patterson stuck her face in the wind as they pulled into the man's driveway and parked.

Music came from inside the house, rattling windows covered from the inside by blankets.

She pulled her gun and Rachette came next to her and did the same.

Stepping up onto a four-foot slab of cracked concrete, she knocked five times with the side of her fist and stepped back.

They waited with guns raised halfway.

The music went silent and a finger appeared at the edge of the blanket, pulling it aside. An eyeball appeared and disappeared, then the blanket dropped back into place.

"Sheriff's department!" Patterson said. "Please open up!"

For a few seconds nothing happened, and then a voice came from the other side of the door. "Sheriff's department?"

"Yes ma'am! Please open up!"

The one drawback of being a detective was that sometimes people didn't recognize them as law enforcement. Their badges were prominent on their belts, but not in a high stress situation like this one. The SUV was dark gray and unmarked. They wore jeans and button up shirts, so for all this woman inside knew, Rachette and Patterson were two crazy people pounding on her door and wielding guns.

It was a real possibility that that was why Jim Brewer had been driving so offensively. Had he seen them as cops or as crazy people attacking him with guns?

The door cracked open. "Please don't shoot me!"

"We're not going to shoot," Rachette said, "as long as you come out with your hands where we can see them above your head."

Two open hands came out of the doorway first, followed by a skin-and-bones woman in her late thirties. Or forties. She was clearly an addict and the drugs had aged her at an unknown rate.

"What's going on?" The woman squinted and put a hand over her eyes. "What do you want?"

Rachette gave Patterson a glance, his eyes saying, *What now*?

Patterson lowered her weapon and stepped forward. "Ma'am, we have probable cause to believe you and your … husband?"

The woman frowned. "Husband?"

"That you and your husband may have kidnapped a woman."

"Kidnapped?" Her eyes went wide. "We kidnapped a woman?"

Rachette pointed his finger. "You kidnapped a woman?"

"Please step off the porch, ma'am." Patterson ushered the woman off the concrete onto the dirt.

The woman was barefoot. "Ow. No, we didn't kidnap anybody. Did not. I didn't say—"

Rachette grabbed the woman's arm and led her toward the rear of their SUV. "Please step over here, ma'am."

Patterson pushed on the front door of the house and aimed her weapon. It took a second for her eyes to adjust from the bright afternoon sun to the cave-like interior. "My God."

"What?" Rachette ran up and stopped next to her. "Jesus Christ."

They stood dumbfounded inside the doorway. For years they had entered other peoples' houses and for years Patterson had been amazed at how far some people could let their houses go without cleaning a lick. She refused to step foot in Rachette's apartment for that very reason. But this place …

"This is the dirtiest place I've ever seen in my life," Rachette said. He slapped her on the back and walked back into the sunlight. "I searched his pants. Have fun. I'll be out here with … what was your name, ma'am?"

She took a breath and stepped inside, her Glock leading the way. It was hard to keep her focus forward. She kicked aside a Styrofoam cup, an empty can of Pringles, what looked like a muddy pillowcase—God, she hoped that was mud—and then stepped onto a stack of junk mail, which slid underneath her boot.

There were dozens of black trash bags strewn around the room, all of them looking like a bear had ripped into them and all of them with actual trash spilling out. It was like she was strolling through the county dump.

She took to shuffling forward, kicking aside things as they blocked her progress. Twice she saw mice skitter away in her peripheral vision.

Though she dreaded it, she stepped into the kitchen, and it was worse than she could have imagined. A cloud of flies had taken over the place, dining on the leftover food on the stacks and stacks of dishes that filled the sink and every square inch of the tiny kitchen counter.

She turned and left the kitchen. Entering a hallway, she had to climb around pieces of furniture to reach two bedrooms. One was a nest of dirty sheets on top of a concave mattress surrounded by clothing and more trash, and the other housed a huge pile of boxes and junk.

"Anyone here?"

There was no answer, save the buzzing flies in the kitchen down the hall.

A door at the end of the hallway was blocked by a bag of trash and an ironing board.

She breathed into the sleeve of her shirt a few times and held her breath.

Moving the debris out of the way, she opened the door and found a pitch-black space. It was hot inside. She pulled the flashlight off her belt and flicked it on.

It was a garage with a different category of junk stacked floor to ceiling in it—three washer and dryer sets that were rusty and dented, a wheelbarrow, a car with no tires sitting directly on the ground.

If these two people were kidnappers, they had no place to keep their victims in this house. How they lived here was beyond her.

With eyes watering and her lungs convulsing for air she refused to give them, she zigzagged her way through the hallway, back through the living room and back out the door.

"Anything?" Rachette asked as she exploded out of the house.

She put her hands on her knees and sucked in a deep breath, then coughed. Putting her hands on her head, she walked away and faced the meadow, drinking in the view of the swaying grass and trees. The blue sky.

"That bad, huh?" he asked.

She turned on her heel, searching the property for outlying buildings. There were none.

"This is Sheila Johnson," Rachette said. "She's a friend of Jim Brewer."

Sheila was standing at ease now, her hands by her side. "You just missed Jim," she said. "He left to get Cokes a few minutes ago."

"He went to go get Cokes," Rachette said.

Patterson turned her head and looked at the still smoking maroon sedan across the meadow. It was tucked in the shade, but clearly visible next to the road. She eyed their SUV and saw no movement inside the rear windows. Jim Brewer was still out cold in the back seat.

"Well." Rachette stretched his hands over his head. "We appreciate your cooperation. We're going to be leaving now."

"Good." Sheila Johnson stepped gingerly across the ground and disappeared into the house. A second later the door slammed shut.

Patterson put a hand on her forehead.

"I think we'd better move," Rachette said climbing back into the SUV.

Patterson sucked in a breath through her nose, filling every last bronchiole of her lungs with clean air, then climbed inside the passenger seat.

Chapter 23

Wolf, Luke, and Hannigan left Fred Wilcox's last known place of residence and drove eleven blocks north to Buntley Mortuary, Fred Wilcox's last known place of employment.

Buntley Mortuary was a brown and white Victorian house tucked amid old trees. Old bushes and trees trimmed in rounded geometric shapes bulged through a wrought iron fence that surrounded the place. The lawn was dark green and lush, manicured with fresh mow lines.

A man waited for them outside the gate. He was thin and tall, standing ramrod straight with the posture of a younger man, but his face looked like he was pushing seventy years old. His eyes were blue, the corners of them turned down, making him look perpetually concerned. Probably a genetic trait that made his family successful at their chosen profession of undertakers, Wolf thought.

"Mr. Buntley?" Luke asked, shaking his hand.

"Yes, and you must be Special Agent Luke. You're even lovelier than your voice on the phone." The man's voice was quiet, well-oiled machinery.

Wolf and Hannigan stepped up and shook the man's long hand and let Luke do her thing.

"We need to ask you a few questions about one of your former employees," Luke said. "A man named Fred Wilcox?"

Terrence's eyes changed, concern showing a sliver of fear. "What about him?"

"We're looking for him," Wolf said. "Have you talked to him?"

"Not for years. Two years." Terrence turned to the gate. "Listen, can we go inside? I need to check on a few things now that I'm here."

Great, Wolf thought. If there was one thing creepier than a morgue, it was a funeral home. Twice he'd had to watch his mother shop for caskets, to bury his father and brother. Setting foot inside places like these brought him back to a bad place and time.

Terrence inserted a key into a slot in the wall and the gate swung open with an electric buzz.

They followed him up a cobblestone driveway, and then up some concrete stairs to a hand-carved white painted door that opened silently.

Compared to the heat outside it was cold inside. The air had a formalin smell.

The entry room had vacuum-striped green carpet that looked like a golf course fairway. It was silent, as one would expect a funeral home during closing hours would be. Light spilled in a stained glass window, painting a shiny show-casket with color.

"Please, make yourselves comfortable if you like." The undertaker pointed at a row of cloth and wood seats and went to a computer that perched on a wooden desk.

"Uh, no thanks," Luke said. "We understand Fred Wilcox worked here full time. Is that correct?"

Terrence studied a piece of mail and ran a finger through his hair, which was so full and gray it drew suspicion. "He was our janitor."

Wolf took a few steps and got a view into the interior of the home. It was unlike many of the Victorian homes Wolf had seen before. Rather than a choppy design with many rooms, the interior had been blown out, and there was a large room with a vaulted ceiling. There were more caskets on display set at a diagonal, like parked merchandise at a used car lot.

"Those are our caskets for sale," Terrence said to Wolf, following his eyes. "Around back is where we do the embalming or the cremation, depending on what the deceased next of kin want."

Nodding politely, Wolf turned to a rack of brochures standing next to the stained glass window and picked one up. It said, "Have You Considered Donating Your Loved One's Remains to Science and Education?"

"Ah," Terrence walked around his desk toward Wolf. "That's an interesting program we do with the university. People can earn credit toward the cost of their funeral services by loaning their remains to science for a short period."

Wolf put down the brochure like it was diseased. Despite the cool air, Wolf was beginning to sweat.

"Can you tell us about how Fred Wilcox left the job?" Luke asked. "Was it on good terms?"

"Most certainly not." Terrence snarled his lip. "He just stopped coming one day."

"Do you know what exact day that was?" Wolf asked.

Mr. Buntley chewed his lower lip. "No."

"Can't you check in the computer?" Wolf asked.

"Oh, I wouldn't know where to begin with that." He chuckled. "I … remember it was August, though, because I remember we had to hire another driver. It was a big fiasco. I was out of town. The exact date, though? I could get back to you on that tomorrow when my daughter comes in to work. She's the HR person."

"You said you had to hire another driver? Was he your driver?" Wolf asked.

"Yes."

"I thought he was your janitor?" Hannigan asked.

"Yes. He was. He was our van driver as well."

Hannigan blinked. "What does a van driver do?"

"He was in charge of pickups. Deceased pickups. He brought them from the hospital, county morgue, accident sites, or wherever, to here."

"Did he work with other employees?" Luke asked.

"No. He was solitary most of the time."

Time alone with dead bodies. Fred Wilcox definitely followed his passion.

Luke looked at nothing in particular and nodded, clearly thinking along the same lines as Wolf. Hannigan had stopped his own reading of a brochure and was looking over his shoulder.

"What's the matter? Did I say something wrong?" Terrence smiled self-consciously.

"Did anyone come speak to you after Fred Wilcox left?" Luke asked. "Like, a police officer?"

He pulled down his lips and looked to the ceiling. "No. Not that I can remember. But I'll ask my daughter about that, too. If it were August, I would have been fishing for most of the month. That's my fishing month."

"Could you please call your daughter and ask her?" Luke asked.

"Right now?"

She nodded.

"Well, yes, I suppose." Buntley walked to the desk and picked up a phone. Dialing, he waited for a minute and then left a quiet voicemail to his daughter. "She wasn't there. I'm sorry."

Luke nodded and handed him a card. "Please, if you could check with your daughter tomorrow and let us know what she says, it would be much appreciated. Please ask her when exactly Fred Wilcox left, and then if someone, a police officer, came and talked to her about him."

Studying the card in his hand, Terrence nodded, new concern etching his features. "Yes. Of course. Ask when Fred left, and then if a cop came asking about him. I will, special agent."

Satisfied with his response, Luke looked at Hannigan and Wolf.

Wolf was the first out the door.

When they were outside the gates of the place Hannigan turned to them and raised his sunglasses. "I'm going to say this one more time, then I'm going to start pulling off heads. We need to eat."

"Don't have to convince me," Wolf said. His stomach felt like it was trying to digest itself.

Luke's and Hannigan's phones chimed at the same time.

"Message says call immediately ..." Luke tapped her phone screen and put it to her ear. "Luke here ... yes ... what?"

Wolf's phone started vibrating. It was Patterson.

"I meant it about eating." Hannigan folded his arms and leaned against the brick wall.

"Hello?"

"Hey, it's me." It sounded like Patterson was in the car. "Hey, we found the maroon sedan from your pictures."

He turned and looked at Luke. She was talking excitedly, clearly getting the same news from her own source.

"Yeah? And what about the guy driving it?"

"It's not Fred Wilcox."

He waited for her to continue.

"It's his cousin, though."

"His cousin?"

"Yeah. The feds are interrogating him at the hospital right now. Rachette and I just left and are on our way back to the station."

"Tell him where it was," Rachette said in the background.

"What? Oh, yeah it was in Cave Creek. We found him in Cave Creek."

"He's in the hospital? What happened?"

"We blocked the road and he careened off into a ditch. Hit his head on the windshield. He's conscious now and talking to the feds."

"And what's he saying?" Wolf asked.

"We don't know. Surprise-surprise, they pushed us out of there."

Luke was pacing now, eyeing Wolf as she listened to her own phone.

"Okay, nice work. I have to go." Wolf hung up.

"… all right," Luke said. "Sounds like it. Okay, see you soon." She hung up. "That was Todd. I guess you heard your deputies picked up a guy named Jim Brewer, apparently the same man you saw at the crime scene. He's Fred Wilcox's cousin."

"A cousin living outside of Rocky Points?" Hannigan asked. "How the hell did we miss that?"

"Brewer is Wilcox's second cousin on his mother's side. What can I say, we missed him."

"What's he saying?" Wolf asked.

She shrugged. "They're still talking to him right now. But apparently he mentioned something about an investigator coming to talk to him a few years ago about his cousin, Freddie."

Wolf pulled his eyebrows together. "An investigator? Attakai?"

"I told Todd about Attakai visiting Wilcox's landlord," Luke said.

Wolf stared at his SUV. "I'm heading back."

"You're heading back?"

"Yes." Wolf walked over and climbed inside.

"Wait a minute." Luke stepped inside his door and blocked it from closing. "What about down here?"

"What about down here? We've seen the truck, we've seen the hole, we've heard Mary Attakai's story, we've seen where Wilcox slept and worked … Lindsay Ellington is in trouble up there. There's nothing else for us here right now."

"And what happens if this interview with the cousin points us back here again? Then what?"

"Then we'll turn around and drive back here." Wolf pushed the starter button.

"There are more interviews we could do. We could look into excavators … look into …" She looked at her watch.

Wolf's dashboard clock said 2:26. He could get back to Rocky Points before sundown.

"Shit." She looked over the roof at Hannigan. "We're going too."

"Great." Hannigan's voice climbed a register. "We can go to Disneyland, in reverse, I don't care. As long as we stop at the nearest drive-thru on the way."

Chapter 24

"Why were you at the river where Sally Claypool was found?"

"I was curious, I guess."

"Why were you curious?"

Jim Brewer's head was centered in the television screen. His head was wrapped in gauze, a small red splotch seeping through white fabric on his forehead.

At the bottom right of the display, Agent Todd leaned in and out of the camera shot, his legs crossing and uncrossing, his hands gesturing emphatically as he interrogated the man.

"It's kind of a long story."

"I have all day." Todd laughed genuinely.

Brewer eyed his interrogator warily, and then cracked a smile that looked like it pained him. "Couple years ago a PI came over to my house asking about my cousin."

"Was this private investigator a man?"

Brewer nodded.

"Could you please use words for the sake of this video recording?"

Brewer looked at the camera. "Yeah. Sorry. Yes, it was a man investigator."

"Do you remember his name?"

He scoffed. "No."

"Do you remember what he looked like?"

"I don't know. White guy. Normal looking, I guess. Like you."

Todd chuckled softly off-screen. "Okay. And what color hair?"

Brewer shrugged. "Dark? Like you? I don't know. I think he had a hat on. A ball cap."

"Tall? Short?"

"Normal."

Todd paused. "What did he want to know?"

"He asked if I'd seen my cousin, Fred. I said, 'No.' Then he asked if anyone else had come over asking about him. I said 'no.' The guy seemed like he didn't believe me. I remember he was all staring me down like I was lying."

"Did he tell you why he was looking for him?"

"Yeah. He talked about that Van Gogh dude down in Durango who was killing girls and cutting off their ears, and then he said they suspected my cousin might be the guy."

Todd paused. "This man said your cousin Fred was the suspected killer?"

"Yep."

"And … what did you think about that?"

Brewer shrugged. "I believed it."

"You believed it?"

"Yeah. Not really a stretch, thinking of Freddie as a serial murderer. Guy was always a scary bastard."

"Can you explain?"

Brewer closed his eyes. "Where to start? Shit … there was the stray dog. When I was a kid I went with my family up to visit them up in Vernal."

"Vernal?"

"Yeah. Vernal, Utah. Anyway, we went to visit them, and you know, I was out hanging with Fred every day while our parents did their thing drinkin' in the back yard. The kid never talked. Just led me around and showed me weird stuff. Dead birds. Dead snakes. Just a bunch of dead stuff. And then, they had these dogs roaming around that would beg behind grocery stores and stuff, and he called one over, pretending like he was going to feed it, and then he hit it with a big ol' rock right in the head.

"The dog got away, but not before my cousin went after him with more rocks. He was snarling like *he* was the feral dog. And he didn't laugh or smile about it afterwards, I remember that was the craziest thing. He was just angry that he didn't get what he wanted, which was apparently to kill the crap out of this dog. Then I realized he'd been showing me stuff he'd been killing himself all day. Hell, I ran back to momma after that. Never left my mom's side on that trip again."

The recording went silent for a moment while Brewer contemplated.

"And that incident when you were a kid was enough to convince you your cousin was the Van Gogh killer?"

Brewer shrugged. "Then there was the time he came with his family and visited us. He was older then, and when he left a few days later there was a lot of dead stuff on our property that wasn't there before. Squirrels, rabbits, chipmunks. Guy was like the grim reaper. I'm telling you, you'd have to meet him to know he was a sick son of a bitch that was going to be a serial killer when he grew up. Yeah. I believed it."

Agent Todd cleared his throat. "I'm still a little confused here, Mr. Brewer. Sorry. So please explain to me, because of this private investigator visit two years ago, you decided to come see the crime scene?"

Brewer shot a hard glare at Todd. "Well, yeah. I talked to this PI two years ago. He comes in talking about how my cousin might be this Van Gogh Killer, cutting off women's ears and putting them on display like that. And then I was watching the news that morning when that girl here was found killed, and the next day they were saying on the news her ear was chopped off, and I put the two together. My cousin was at it again. I was freakin' out, to be honest. Thought he might really come visit me. So, I don't know, I was just driving up on the scene, you know? Checking it out, like you said. I wasn't looking for anything in particular. Just looking.

"Ever since I saw that on the news, I've been staying with my friend up in Cave Creek. I didn't want my cousin coming to look for me. That's where them cops picked me up—at my friend's, Sheila's."

"Those two cops," Todd said, "were with the sheriff's department. That's another point I'm a little confused about. Why did you drive at them with your car?"

"What? I was driving around their car, not at them. They got out and aimed their guns at me. I was just trying to self-defend myself. Get the hell out of there."

Todd said nothing for a few moments. "When Sally Claypool's body—"

"Sally who?"

"The woman who was killed. The crime scene you went to go see?"

"Oh, right."

Another pause. "Why didn't you tell law enforcement about your suspicions about your cousin being the killer at that point?"

Brewer blinked. "Why would I do that? You guys sent some guy to talk to *me* about it. I figured you were already looking for him. Haven't you been looking for my cousin for years?" He smiled like agent Todd was a moron.

"You said it was a private investigator who came and talked to you," Todd said.

"Yeah." Brewer looked confused for a second, then pointed toward Todd. "Like you guys. Plain clothes. Not like a cop uniform."

"Did he show you a badge?"

"No. It was like a certificate or something. A piece of paper." Brewer stared deadpan for a few seconds. "Why?"

ASAC Todd walked to the television and pressed the stop button on the DVR. "Guy's dumb as a sack of dirt. That's the last of his intelligible answers."

Wolf, Luke, Hannigan, and MacLean straightened in their chairs.

MacLean stood and walked back around his desk. He was a silhouette in front of a neon-orange window, the tail end clouds of a rainstorm glowing from the sun dipping below the peaks. Picking up a manila folder, he opened it and read. "Jim Brewer—lives on Third Street in town." He looked at Luke. "You guys ever talk to him?"

Luke shook her head. "We were concentrated down south. And he's a second-cousin. There was no reason for us to come up here looking for him."

"Obviously somebody was on a trail which led to the guy," Wolf said.

"Yeah. Attakai," Hannigan said.

"Attakai? MacLean asked.

Wolf told MacLean about Attakai showing up at Fred Wilcox's place weeks after the Mary Attakai and Rose Chissie attack.

MacLean stood with a solid line creased into his forehead. "So Attakai knew the identity of the killer, right after the attack on his sister."

Wolf nodded.

"And he told nobody?" MacLean looked at Luke.

Luke shook her head.

"And then Attakai came up here," MacLean said. "And then I hired his ass, and he was hiding this information the whole time. He was up here looking for a serial killer and he didn't tell us." MacLean stood and went to the window. He turned around with narrowed eyes. "But Jim Brewer just said that PI was a white guy. Attakai's dark skinned, dark hair. Kind of tough to describe Attakai as a white guy."

Luke snorted. "Yeah. Jim Brewer also thinks Magnum P.I. worked for the federal government."

MacLean petted his mustache.

Wolf walked to the window and looked outside. A single pickup truck passed by below, stopping at the four-way stop sign before accelerating up Main.

The Adrenaline Games had been erased from Rocky Points memory a full five days before the official end of the games had originally been scheduled to end. The town had cancelled the event out of respect for the Claypools and Ellingtons, but the event had officially been over before that because everyone had left.

MacLean looked at his watch. "It's time."

***

The squad room was more packed than Wolf had ever seen it. Wolf took a seat in the middle of the room next to Luke while Hannigan walked to the front to talk to ASAC Todd.

At the front of the room Rachette was telling an animated story to Yates and a couple other smiling deputies, turning an imaginary steering wheel and pointing his finger like a gun.

Patterson was next to Munford a few rows away, Dr. Lorber and Gene a few rows from them. On the other side of the room DA White sat next to his assistant, who was leaning into his ear.

There were all of the elected officials from the prior meeting and then some, including Margaret Hitchens, who faced the front of the room with a blank stare.

Wolf counted nineteen men and women seated in a cluster at the front of the room—more FBI agents up from Denver.

"All right everyone! Listen up!" MacLean stood at the front of the room and held up his hands. "Sit down and shut up!"

The room did.

"Lindsay Ellington." He clicked a laser pointer and a picture of Lindsay Ellington came up on the screen. She had brown hair past her shoulders. Her smile was tight-lipped, her blue eyes berating the person behind the camera for taking the photo.

"Twenty-two years old. This was a photo taken last year, and the most recent we could get. She's not into social media, but from accounts from her father and roommate, her hair is much shorter. Above her shoulders."

"Same color?" Somebody asked.

"Yes. Same color." MacLean pushed another button and a map came up on screen. It was zoned with dotted lines, within each zone was a number. "Deputies and special agents, you have been given a slip of paper with a number on it on the way into the room. Has everyone got a number?"

MacLean looked around the room.

Every deputy and agent in the room nodded, some of them holding up their slip of paper.

"Good. I'm going to adjourn this meeting within the next few minutes." He gestured to the windows. Outside the light was fading fast. "It's already getting dark. When this meeting is over, I want you to pair up with the person with the same number. Need to trade numbers with somebody? Fine. Do it, I don't care. That's your partner for the night."

Wolf held his piece of paper out. Luke had the same number.

"Each number corresponds to a zone up here. We have the same map in the packet of paper you will need to pick up on the way out of the room. Not too hard to figure out—find your zone on the map, patrol it and find Lindsay Ellington within it. Keep vigilant. Keep alert." He looked around the room, as if searching for something to say, and the he settled for a single nod. "Let's go."

The room exploded into movement.

Chapter 25

The glow of Wolf's phone lit up the cab interior like he'd switched on the sun. There were no messages. No missed calls.

"So you broke up with Lauren, eh?" Luke asked.

Wolf hit the side button on his phone, submerging the interior of the SUV into darkness again. "I never told you we broke up."

"I'm an FBI agent." Luke said. "I can read people."

"Right." He nodded. "Patterson told you?"

"She might have said something. She lets me in on the gossip. Speaking of, we haven't talked about how that dipshit Rachette didn't show up at the wedding. I'm glad I ignored that invite."

"Yeah … it wasn't something fun to endure live. Especially being part of the ceremony. Still, he's a good kid."

She made a sound like a sputtering hose. "Right."

Wolf lowered his eyelids and looked past the floating reflection of the FM radio into the night. They drew zone three, which put them on the northern outskirts of town. There was one road in their zone—highway 734—and they'd been driving up and down their section for an hour and a half and decided staying put for a few minutes made as much sense as driving a four-mile groove in the pavement.

An almost-full moon hung over the eastern peaks, spraying the oak trees lining the Chautauqua with light, deepening the inky shadows at their base. The river glimmered, its low roar filling the cab through Luke's open window.

She had one black-socked foot on the dash and leaned against her door looking at him. "So what happened with Lauren?"

"Does it look like I want to talk about this?"

"No. But I know you, and you're kind of clueless when it comes to women. So I figured I'd lend my services."

He raised his eyebrows. "Now who's thinking highly of themselves?"

"Come on, what happened?"

Wolf watched a car pass by, its headlights' aura shrinking in the side view mirror.

"Okay, fine," Luke said. "Don't get it off your chest. Has she called? Obviously not or you wouldn't be checking your phone every three seconds."

"What about you?" Wolf asked. "I recognized Special Agent Brian Todd's name the first time I met him. Then he referred to you by your first name, which got me thinking. Then I realized he was from Chicago. I did some talking to Patterson, too. Your ex-husband is your new boss?"

She stared into the night.

"What's the matter? Don't want to talk about it?" Wolf leaned his head back with a satisfied exhale.

"He used to screw hookers." She said. "Yep. Used to travel to DC a lot, and apparently he had an affinity for young Latino women while he was there."

Wolf sat frozen, trying to choose a response.

"I'm okay to talk about it." She shrugged. "I am over the guy. Didn't take me long to realize there're much better guys out there."

Wolf eyed her.

She stared at the river.

"And now he's your boss."

"Yep. And not only that, I got passed over for ASAC so this hooker screwing dickhead can take the job."

"That's …"

"Yeah. Not exactly how I wanted things to end up in Denver," she said. "Anyway. I have my options open."

"What, you quitting the bureau?"

She smiled. "No. Hell no. I've worked too hard to get where I am to start fresh. I'm just looking elsewhere, where they'll appreciate a beautiful, strong woman who can kick some serious butt."

"That a girl."

"Don't patronize me."

He smiled and checked the mirrors. The highway was empty to the rear. "I'm not checking my phone every three seconds."

"I know, but for not checking every three minutes you're very defensive about it."

He leaned his head back again and they sat in silence for a minute.

"Probably not feeling any better about it, huh?" she asked.

"About what?"

"About Lauren. Not talking about it like that. Just letting it build up inside, like a … I don't know, a pot full of steam. The lid's rattling, the pressure's building."

He rolled his eyes and started speaking in a monotone voice. "We were doing fine—I don't know what happened—she gave me the 'we have to talk' speech—I could read between the lines. There, you happy?"

Luke pulled her foot off the dash and tucked it underneath her. Turning toward him she said, "She told you that you guys had to talk? So … then what?"

He shrugged. "I left."

She blinked. "Check me if I'm wrong, here. But if somebody says they want to talk, that usually means they want to talk about something. If you didn't give her a chance to say what she wanted to say, then …"

"It was the 'We have to talk' speech. You'd have to know the context of things that happened that day for my actions to make sense."

"And what happened? Fill me in on the context."

He watched a saucer shaped glowing cloud slide toward the moon.

With a defeated exhale he said, "Nothing out of the ordinary. We woke up, we were fine. And then later … she was distant. Cold. And now she's avoiding my calls and not answering any texts."

"What day was this?"

"Two days ago."

"The day Sally Claypool's body was found?"

Wolf nodded. "Yeah. I guess it's not really rocket science, huh?"

"Yeah, but why would she be distant and cold because of that? She knows that's your job."

"You know her history. Her ex-husband killed her father and beat her within an inch of her life. Then Ella's kidnapping. She was spooked and left town."

Luke leaned back. "So there you go. It's not you. It's the situation."

"But that wasn't it."

Luke straightened again. Her eyes were shimmering, her face smooth. The top of her shirt was open revealing the skin of her upper breast painted in moonlight.

"That wasn't it?" she asked.

"I know. I sound like a head case. But I saw the look in her eyes. She was breaking up with me, not leaving town. She would have said, 'I'm leaving town because of this,' and then there wouldn't have been a 'we need to talk' speech at all. I can read people too, you know."

Luke nodded. "Okay. So what else happened that morning? You guys have some trouble in the sack?"

He rolled his eyes. "No."

"Maybe she senses that you don't want to be a father all over again."

For a second Wolf pulled his eyebrows together, took in a breath to respond, and then let it out.

I wish you were my daddy.

Ella's words echoed in Wolf's head.

Ella … Jesus.

Lauren's response.

She had been so bent out of shape at her daughter's innocent question. What had Lauren done? She had gone to the stove and put her head down, cracked some eggs. And then he got the Sally Claypool call.

Blinking, he realized he had blanked out.

Luke was studying him, a hint of a smile on her lips. "Do you?"

"Do I what?"

"Want to be a father again?"

"I …" Wolf stopped himself. He was glad it was dark to hide the heat rising in his face.

Luke watched him, her eyes narrowing.

"I just …" He almost climbed out of the car. Almost got out and walked away to the river's edge. And why? Why was he so upset? "I was in the army when Jack was her age." It came out of his mouth without him even thinking about it.

"Ella's age?"

Wolf looked into the side view again.

She leaned back and gazed out her window. "I get it. You're older now. You already had a kid. Jack's in college now, you're done with all that BS. But even if you decided you wanted to be a dad again, like you said, you were gone when Jack was Ella's age. So you think you might not be good enough, because you don't have any experience to draw back on. Cause, being in our profession, shit, we both know that having a bad father can screw up a kid. Especially a girl. That can put her on the stripper pole. Out on the corner selling herself for the next fix." She clucked her tongue and looked at Wolf.

Wolf blinked. "Thank you. Kristen."

"You're welcome. I gotta pee." She leaned over and fished her shoes off the floorboards.

He squinted when the cab light blazed to life, and then the door thumped and her crunching footsteps receded toward the river.

For a full minute Wolf sat motionless.

I wish you were my daddy.

Ella … Jesus.

Taking out his cell phone, he tapped the screen and it glowed in his hand. He stared at Lauren's name and phone number.

"So was I right?" Luke appeared at the window with her head poked inside.

Wolf darkened his phone and pocketed it. "About what?"

She climbed in and slammed the door. "I should charge money for this."

Wolf twisted the cap off his water bottle and took a sip. "Yeah. Maybe quitting the bureau is something you should consider. Maybe you could quit right now."

"Aw, but then you'd be so bored."

They sat in silence for another few minutes, letting the sober reality of the situation grip their hearts again.

The radio scratched. "All units status report."

Luke plucked the radio off his dash.

"Unit one, nothing."

"Unit two …"

The teams rattled off different versions of the same news.

"Unit seven, nothing," Luke said and put down the radio.

"I say we do another few laps," he said.

"Agreed."

"Then we need to take some shifts to get some sleep."

She closed her eyes and sighed. "Oh, man do I ever agree."

Wolf started the engine.

Chapter 26

"Hey!" Something hard connected with Wolf's shoulder.

He cracked his eyes, snapping out of a dreamless sleep. His right arm was numb, twisted and shoved into the crevice between the seat and the passenger door. A stream of drool hung off his chin.

The engine roared and the SUV lurched forward with scraping tires.

Straightening, he finally came back to the moment. They were parked along the river after a long night. He checked the dash clock. 5:38 am. The sky outside was cobalt blue with a golden glow to the east. A mist hung over the river. "What's going on?"

"They found her."

Wolf looked at her. If her tone had been ambivalent, then her hard expression was clear as the water flowing in the Chautauqua.

"Where?" he asked.

He realized the radio was blasting out a constant chatter, but Luke had turned it down. He turned it up and got all the answers he needed.

***

Wolf stood at the edge of Wildflower Park, a three-acre expanse of manicured grass in the center of town surrounded by aspens and pines, and stared at the fluttering tarp covering Lindsay Ellington's corpse.

"Don't they have any decency?" Somebody asked behind him.

They were referring to the two news helicopters thumping overhead. They'd arrived just as Wolf and Luke had, and for ten minutes they'd been swirling and dipping in the sky, changing positions as the situation on the ground changed.

Right now an FBI team clad in white forensic suits was out there, rushing to erect a pop tent, while the rest of them stood back to maintain crime scene integrity.

"Shit," Luke said for the fifteenth time in the last five minutes.

Another SBCSD vehicle came up the road, its engine screaming, its turret lights flashing. With chirping tires it stopped and Rachette and Patterson came spilling out.

They saw Wolf and Luke and came over.

No words were necessary.

"Wish we could shoot those assholes." Rachette eyed the choppers.

"Excuse me." An FBI agent was unrolling yellow crime scene tape. "Step back a few paces, please?"

They did, and when they turned around Wolf saw the line of civilians that had gathered on the road. They were dressed in bathrobes and fleeces, holding onto one another as the scene unfolded.

"See if they saw anything, then get them away," Wolf said.

Rachette and Patterson nodded at one another and jogged toward them.

Wolf watched the terror on their faces. One woman started wailing, a damn of tears breaking and streaming down her face.

"Who called it in?" Wolf asked.

Luke looked around. "It was Unit 8."

Wolf turned to the group of SBCSD uniforms gathered behind him. "Who called it in?"

They all shook their heads.

"We did." A group of FBI agents stood a few feet away. One of them raised his hand.

"Special Agent Shecter," Luke said. "This is Detective Wolf."

"Tell me what happened?"

Shecter shook his head and swallowed. "We'd passed by here a few times. And then … the last time we noticed her."

"You didn't see anyone?"

"No, sir."

Wolf eyed the street. There were cars and trucks and SUVs parked on both sides in front of low houses. They were on third street, three blocks off of Main. The gleaming glass of the county building poked through the trees in the distance.

"Brazen son of a bitch," Luke said.

A black Tahoe came squealing around the corner and parked. ASAC Todd and Hannigan climbed out, approaching at a brisk jog.

Luke broke off and approached her superior.

The crime scene tape bounced and twisted on the wind. The pop tent was up and the side-panels zipped on. Camera flashes lit up a doorway that had been pulled open like curtains. Inside white suits bent over bare flesh.

A black BMW SUV came speeding up the street and through a four-way stop without slowing.

A group of civilians on the sidewalk pulled their horror-filled gazes from the scene to watch District Attorney White park and get out of his car.

White was dressed in jeans and a fleece, a Boston ball cap pulled low on his head. He walked up, pausing to scan the crowd of gathered law enforcement. He saw Wolf, kept scanning. Apparently finding nobody better, the DA locked eyes with him and marched over.

"What do we have?"

"Lindsay Ellington," he said.

"I know we have Lindsay Ellington." He looked at the tent, and then back at Wolf. Grabbing his jacket, the DA pulled him away. "Come here."

Wolf twisted his arm, yanking his jacket out of the DA's grip.

White ignored him and kept walking further. After a dozen paces he stopped and turned. "What the hell happened down in Durango?"

Wolf took his time joining the DA. "We learned some things."

"Learned some things?" White snorted and smiled. "What things?"

It was a good question. "I learned that I need to spend some time with Deputy Attakai to get more answers."

"That's what you learned? Well that's not going to happen. His lawyers are threatening to press charges against us and the Bureau if we continue along that route."

"Where was he last night?" Wolf asked.

"Feds had surveillance on him. So I assume he was sitting at home." White stared at him. "You can't talk to him. So, what else you got?"

Wolf sucked in a deep breath and eyed the crime scene. He flexed his hands and cracked his knuckles.

White stepped in front of him, his face close. "I'm not sure why MacLean is so attached to you. I'm beginning to think you must have something on him and that's why you still have a job. Because frankly I'm not seeing it."

Wolf leaned closer. "I wouldn't expect a man of your intelligence to see much. Now get away from me."

White flinched, shutting his eyes and stepping back. A mock-flinch. Checking his Rolex, he said, "You'd better figure out what you learned in one hour. We need to know which direction to steer this thing."

Another engine revved as it approached. More chirping tires.

MacLean climbed out of his SUV and walked toward them.

Wolf left them to talk.

"What was that?" Luke asked under her breath.

"Nothing."

For the next thirty minutes Wolf and Luke helped Rachette and Patterson question the civilians that were now gathered a block away. Each person had a similar version of events from the night before—they were vigilant and aware of their surroundings. Some insisted they were scared and had trouble sleeping. But when it came down to it, none of them had seen or heard anything.

Wolf now stood next to the crime scene tape in a state somewhere between contemplation and deep sleep. There were no lights in the park. Tall trees surrounded it. Most of it would have been submerged in moonlight shadow for most of the night. No wonder no one had seen anything.

If the killer had parked on the road, he would have had to drive up with headlights on. Open and close a car door. Neighbors could have seen him.

Wolf studied the trees. A person could have parked another block away and brought Lindsay through the trees.

"Rachette! Patterson!"

They came over.

He pointed. "He could have parked over there and walked through the trees."

They nodded and took off in a jog.

Dr. Lorber came out of the tent and made his way toward Wolf. Ducking under the crime scene tape he stood next to Wolf and looked around.

"Same everything," the tall ME said in a low voice. "Severed ear. Rope burns on her wrists and ankles. Cuts on her skin. She's only been dead a few hours. Looks like she was strangled where she is. Nobody saw anything?"

Wolf shook his head.

Lorber stretched his neck.

"Nothing left by the killer?" he asked.

Lorber shook his head. "No. Not that it looks like. Guy's wearing latex gloves while he's doing it."

"Syringe mark?" Wolf asked.

"Yep. Same place. Back of the neck." Lorber looked up like a fly was attacking him. "Don't those things ever re-fuel?"

They stood in silence a few more moments and Lorber ducked back under the tape. "Well. See you in a bit."

Luke came up next to him and Wolf relayed what Lorber had told him.

A few minutes later MacLean appeared next to them. "What the hell was that earlier?"

"What?"

"With White?"

Wolf shrugged.

"Listen," MacLean pointed at Luke and Wolf. "We need to go over everything you three found out in Durango. We're no longer giving this investigation over to the fed task force. We're changing direction on this. So," the sheriff tapped his watch, "Two hours."

When MacLean left Luke rolled her eyes. "Another God damned meeting."

Wolf stared at nothing. "Yep."

"Hey," she held up her cell phone. "So I got an email ten minutes ago from Esther Buntley."

"Esther Buntley?"

"Terrence Buntley's daughter? The funeral home guy?"

"Yeah."

"She says a guy came in and talked to her about Wilcox right after Wilcox quit the job." She raised the phone and read from the screen. "A man with the La Plata County Sheriff's Department came in and asked about Fred Wilcox's employment history and current whereabouts. I don't remember his name or the exact date, but it was right after Fred stopped coming into work. The sheriff's deputy was dark skinned and dark eyed."

Luke lowered the phone. "Sounds like Attakai if you ask me."

Wolf said nothing.

"Hey, you hear me?"

"Yeah."

She walked away. "There's coffee over here if you want it."

Wolf ignored her, staring at nothing with unblinking eyes.

A few minutes later Luke appeared again, slurping coffee through a lid. "So, I've been—"

"You have the keys?" He turned and held his hand out.

"What? Oh, yeah." She fished his SUV keys out and handed them over. "Sorry, forgot."

He walked away.

"Where are you going?"

"I have to go home."

She stepped quickly behind him. "Home? Are you kidding?"

"Jet's been alone for two days."

"Didn't you get somebody to take care of him?"

He nodded, still walking. "I need to get some stuff, too. I'll see you at the meeting later."

He climbed into his SUV and drove.

***

"Where the hell is he going?" Hannigan asked.

Luke watched Wolf drive away. He rolled through the stop sign and pointed the unmarked vehicle toward Main Street, and then he gunned the engine and disappeared into the town below.

She looked at her partner and narrowed her eyes.

"What?" he asked.

"We have to go."

Chapter 27

Wolf raised his Bushnell binoculars and studied the interior of the vehicle again. Two men with loosened ties. Two tired men who'd been there all night. They were chatting with bored expressions.

He leaned against the trunk of a pine tree. The scent of sap and pine needles filled his nose. A woodpecker flitted between the trees and landed on a branch, his head cocking to the side to study the strange looking animal visiting his territory.

The bird took wing and flew out into the clearing, keeping low to the ground, and then he disappeared inside the copse of trees on the other side of the ski slope that dumped out at the rear of the condominium building.

Wolf backtracked into the woods again, keeping the Caprice Classic out of sight behind the trunk of the pine tree. If he couldn't see it, they couldn't see him. Sound enough logic for Wolf.

Making his way back into the forest, he moved down slope, jogging quickly between the trees until the end-unit condo blocked his view of the FBI vehicle.

Satisfied, he walked straight toward the building.

A man was sipping coffee on his back porch and looked up from his newspaper.

"Top of the morning," Wolf said with a wink.

The man blinked and set down his coffee, eyeing Wolf's gun and badge on his belt. "Morning."

The next condo's windows were covered inside with tightly drawn drapes. Probably weekend warriors back down in Denver.

He walked to the last one and climbed up onto the wooden deck. The built-in pine bench creaked as he torqued his body over. When he stepped his weight made the nails in the weathered wood squeal.

The blinds inside the windows were twisted open revealing a flickering TV inside. The drapes on the other side of the sliding glass window were drawn, beyond the glass a light glowed inside the kitchen.

He walked straight up to the door and knocked with two knuckles—*knock, knock, knock, knock*—then he turned to the rear and hiked up his pants, like it was a normal thing he was there and he could wait patiently while the occupant opened up.

When he heard footsteps within he turned around.

Deputy Jeremy Attakai was inside staring out with wide eyes. He wore boxer shorts and a tee shirt and held his police issue Glock.

Wolf widened his eyes and raised his hands, then lowered them and smiled easily. Hooking his thumbs on his belt, he stared down at the door handle, his blank stare radiating total expectation that the door would be opened for him any second.

"What do you want?" Attakai's voice was muffled.

Wolf heard it loud and clear, but he pretended to hear nothing.

Attakai knocked on the glass with the side of the barrel. "What. Do. You. Want?"

Wolf gave him an icy stare. "Open up, deputy. I have some news."

Wolf knew every man and woman in the department, but after the county merger a few years ago and new hires, like Deputy Attakai, there were a lot more of them. And since the creation of his detective squad, he'd been spending most of his time with a lot less of them, which meant he had more colleagues, but not necessarily more friends and allies. Attakai had been friends with Barker. Attakai was no ally.

Attakai flicked the lock and pulled the door open a few inches, keeping his gun at his far side. "What do you want?"

"You heard about Lindsay Ellington?"

Attakai nodded. "Yeah. I just saw it on the news. So what? It had nothing to do with—"

Wolf gripped both hands on the door and pulled as hard as he could. The door slammed to the hilt and shattered. Wolf was inside before the first shards of glass hit the floor.

Attakai stumbled backward against a chair and raised his gun. "Stop!"

Wolf raised his hands just inside the door. The glass continued to splash onto the floor and the deck outside. "I figured it out, deputy."

"What? What the fuck are you doing? You broke my door."

"Where is he?"

"I could shoot you right now!" Attakai's teeth were bared.

There was a frantic knock on the front door. "FBI! Open up!" It was a female agent's voice.

Attakai leaned to the hallway and looked.

Wolf sidestepped out of aim's way and lunged for the gun. Taking it out of the deputy's hands in one motion, he ejected the magazine, the chambered round, and threw them all out the back door.

Attakai watched the hardware clatter off the deck and into the grass. He closed his gaping mouth and leaned against the wall. His chin tilted back, reminding Wolf of his cousin Hector when he'd made the same defiant gesture.

"Get the hell out of here," Attakai said.

"They found Lindsay Ellington this morning."

"I know. And I didn't do nothing. Why don't you ask them? They were outside watching me all night. I didn't do anything."

The knocking on the front door became pounding. "Open up!" Now it was a male's voice.

Attakai eyed Wolf's holstered gun. "Help!"

The door rattled.

"Where's Fred?" Wolf asked.

Attakai made a sour face. "You punks don't get it. I'm not working with that freak. Those feds planted that phone at my house. I've never seen that thing in my life."

"I believe you've never seen the phone. But I don't believe you about Fred. So I'll ask you again. Once. Where's Fred?"

Attakai's defiance wavered. "What the hell are you talking about?"

Footsteps were thumping past the kitchen windows, rounding the back of the condo.

For a moment Attakai looked scared, and then the next moment he ducked and dove at Wolf, wrapping his arms around Wolf's thighs, digging his shoulder into his groin.

Wolf put his right hand over his gun and kneed Attakai in the face at the same time he was pulled into the man's two-leg wrestling take down. Attakai's face jerked up and to the side as Wolf connected a skull-jarring blow, but Wolf was still caught in the man's grasp and fell backward into the kitchen table, his back slamming onto the wood.

The table gave way under their combined weight crashing down, and for an instant the bottom dropped out of his stomach, and then they slammed onto the ground in a heap.

His breath was pushed out of his lungs and more broken glass rained down. Wolf felt a shard bounce off his forehead and the warm flow of blood running into his hair.

Attakai got to his knees and threw wild punches down onto his head.

Wolf pushed Attakai away with his left arm. His right arm was occupied with keeping his gun in his holster so he jammed his head forward, connecting his forehead with Attakai's mouth and nose.

Attakai grunted in pain, his lower face painted in blood from Wolf's wound and the blood gushing from his nose.

The deck outside rumbled and Hannigan came barreling through the door, and just like that Attakai was off of Wolf and sailing through the air with flailing limbs.

"Wolf! What's happening?" Luke came in after her partner, her eyes wide. "What are you doing?"

Wolf ignored her and got up. Blood flowed into his right eye.

Attakai was wiping blood from his lip safely behind Hannigan's bulky frame, which left Wolf little choice but to go through Hannigan.

Hannigan's eyes popped wide. "What are you do—"

Wolf pushed the FBI agent with all his strength, sending him toppling backwards over Attakai into the hallway. Before the tumbling mass of body parts was through hitting the ground, Wolf grabbed

Attakai by the shirt, pulling him hard toward him. Attakai's shirt fabric ripped as Wolf reeled him over.

With lightning speed, before Hannigan had a chance to interfere, Wolf clamped a sleeper hold onto Attakai's neck. "Where is he?"

"Wolf!" Luke had her hand on her gun, unsure whether or not to pull it. "Who? Who are you talking about?"

Attakai's face was bright red and trending blue. Wolf had a grip and there was no letting go.

Hannigan got to his feet, his face twisted into a controlled rage that had Wolf glad there was a body between him and the agent. "Let him go."

"No. Where is he?"

Luke bent over Wolf. "Explain yourself!"

Wolf just tightened his grip. He thought of Sally Claypool, her mother, he thought of Lindsay Ellington and the life that could have been, snuffed out by a monster. He thought about Bud Ellington, and the unshakeable depression that would settle onto the man for the rest of his life.

Wolf tightened his grip some more.

"O-kay." It was two noises coming out of Attakai's mouth rather than a word.

"Okay what?" Wolf asked, easing up on his hold.

Attakai sucked in a breath that whistled in his throat. "I'll tell you."

"You'll show us." Wolf clamped harder again.

Luke and Hannigan were frozen now.

"O-kay."

Chapter 28

The MD 530's skids touched the ground and the turbine's whine lowered in pitch as the pilot powered it down. When they stepped out it was like stepping onto a sizzling frying pan, the desert even hotter than Wolf remembered it being the day before.

"Over here," Hannigan said, grabbing a fistful of Deputy Attakai's sleeve and pulling him.

Attakai stumbled forward and planted his handcuffed hands on the dirt, eating a cloud of dust in the process.

With a yank, Hannigan pulled him back up, and it was like a particularly nasty toddler pulling a stuffed animal out of a toy chest.

"Easy, fella," Luke said.

Hannigan grunted. The big agent's upper lip was fat and split in two from the scuffle inside Attakai's house, making him look like he had a severe overbite, which made him look like a less-intelligent oaf version of himself, which was apparently pissing him off.

ASAC Brian Todd materialized from the dust cloud with four agents in tow, behind that another two powering-down helicopters and even more agents climbing out.

Sheriff Mansor was inside the well site clearing standing next to his Chevy Blazer, his sidekick, Deputy Wines, dutifully standing by his side.

Mansor walked toward them and met them halfway. "Howdy," he said, gesturing to a yellow excavator in the distance. "Got us a digger."

Sheriff Mansor looked on his former deputy with pity in his eyes.

ASAC Todd stood between them, swiveling his head to take in the landscape. "Where to?"

Attakai nodded. "Next to the other hole."

Todd raised an eyebrow behind his mirrored sunglasses and pointed. "After you."

They followed Attakai around the tanks until he stopped about twenty feet short of the hole that had contained Fred Wilcox's Ford Explorer.

"It was there," he pointed a few degrees to the left of the hole. "I had the excavator here. I dug a few feet over from the bigger hole. You can see the lower ground where it settled."

It was obvious now that Attakai had pointed it out.

Sheriff Mansor whistled and the excavator rumbled to life.

Minutes later the machine's teeth were breaking the ground while the group of men and women in suit and uniforms watched. A team of three FBI agents was suited up in white forensic outfits, their hands clad in latex, their gear ready for action at their feet.

It was agonizingly slow going, and Wolf's neck and arms were browning under the sun while his armpits dripped like a leaky pipe.

Though Attakai estimated his original hole being at ten feet deep and as narrow as a single bucket scoop, they scooped a four-bucket-wide swath of dirt, digging down inch by inch, all the while allowing the forensic team to inspect before continuing after every pass.

Watching the project progress on a geologic time scale, Wolf stood alone in the shade of a juniper tree.

ASAC Todd walked over and joined him. Saying nothing, he squinted and looked out into the bright daylight, his eyes landing on Luke.

Agent Luke stood next to the hole, her short-sleeved blouse unbuttoned to air herself out.

"Hot as shit," Todd said.

Wolf raised an eyebrow.

"This place," the assistant special agent in charge said. "Gotta be a hundred and twenty right here in the shade."

It was an exaggeration, but wearing the dark suit and tie Todd was wearing, Wolf believed the man was standing in a vat of his own sweat.

Once again Agent Todd's eyes landed on Luke. "She's told me a lot about you. How you're a good investigator."

I heard you hire hookers.

"Not the most orthodox with your approach. Not the most … politically sensitive. You're lucky you're not in jail right now with that stunt you pulled at Attakai's place."

Wolf watched the boom arm of the excavator bend and contract.

"Anyway. You ever think about joining the FBI?"

Wolf looked at him, wondering what the question meant. "No."

"Why not?"

"Like you said, I'm not the most politically sensitive."

Todd laughed. "A politically sensitive response to that question."

Wolf gave the agent a sidelong glance, feeling like he was suddenly being vetted.

"How did you know?" Todd asked.

"About this?"

Todd nodded.

"Since the beginning it didn't make sense that Attakai moved north and left his sister down here. He went for weeks guarding her night and day, and then he left. He would have only left if she were out of harm's way. And then we talked to Wilcox's landlord and his former employer. They both talked about a cop matching Attakai's description coming in to talk to them shortly after Wilcox disappeared."

Todd nodded. "Ah. And how would Attakai have known Wilcox's identity as the killer unless they ... met one another."

Wolf nodded.

"And then there was his sister's behavior. His cousin's."

"You think they're in on it?"

Wolf shrugged.

"Well ... you could have come to me with this. You know that."

Wolf nodded. "Right."

"Stop!" A forensic unit member climbed out of the hole with his hands up.

The excavator shut down, plunging the desert into silence for the first time in over an hour.

"Okay, let's get him out!" Todd marched out into the blazing sun.

The team of white uniforms picked up their shovels and gear and entered the chasm.

Wolf and the rest of them gathered at the edge of the hole.

It was fast going from then on, their quarry materializing from the blackened earth.

First there was a checked red and black shirt, then jeans, and then the shape and orientation of a buried man. He was lying on his back, feet facing to the ramped edge of the excavator hole.

Next to be unveiled by the forensics crew was a tuft of long black hair, and then a discolored, leathery face. The skeletal smile of teeth. A twist of skin and cartilage where the nose had been and empty eye sockets. Black, scruffy, facial hair.

It looked like the insects had feasted on most of the flesh, but the destruction of the clothing was something else. At first glance it looked chewed, torn by animals, but Wolf saw it was bullet holes.

"Wow," Luke said. "Really did a number on him."

As more and more dirt was cleared away, they got a look at the extent of the damage.

Wolf started at the feet of the corpse and scanned his way up. The shoes looked to have been pierced by bullets. The jeans at the knees were ripped and the fabric dark black. The crotch, the elbows, the shoulders, the center of the forehead; they had all been pierced by bullets.

ASAC Todd nodded to Sheriff Mansor. "Bring him into your station please."

Deputy Attakai sat alone in the shade of Sheriff Mansor's truck. Hands still handcuffed and in his lap, head lolled to the side, the man leaned against a tire and slept like a baby.

Chapter 29

"Every day I watched her. I was outside her house. I was on her couch at night. I slept outside on the back porch a couple times."

Wolf sipped his coffee and put it back on the table.

The lawyer had arrived in time for the interrogation and had been spouting legalese threats for the last hour. The threats were harsh, and most of them involved Wolf ending up in jail, but something in Jeremy Attakai had clicked and he was taking a different approach than advised by his legal counsel.

Wolf had seen similar behavior before. The man wanted the truth out of his head, no matter what the repercussions that might come later from what he told them. He wanted approval and support from his peers. But apparently he wanted approval and support from Wolf and

Mansor, because he insisted that he would talk only if they were in the interrogation room with him.

"I thought he'd be coming after her, you know?" Attakai said. "Mary's daughter was three. Her son was one-year-old. My sister had two freaking kids and this psycho had taken her. And now she could ID his ride. Who knew what that psycho was thinking? She was the only one who ever escaped him."

Deputy Attakai looked at Wolf for reassurance.

Wolf gave it with a nod.

"Then one day, like three weeks after the whole thing, she called me freaking out. I was at work. I had to be." The deputy looked at his former boss. "It was that well fight. Remember that?"

Mansor nodded.

Wolf had no idea what the man was talking about, but he let it go.

"I left her unguarded for one freaking day and the guy jumped on the opportunity. I left her and the next thing she knew that guy was trailing her into town from her house. It was a white SUV and she could see the guy inside. He was big, hairy, tailing her ass with every turn she took." Attakai stared through the table. "Must have been so close to us that whole time the way he swooped in like that.

"Obviously she was freaking out so she called me. But I was down south and at first I was like, 'Go to the cops, now!' But then I knew the guy would just stop following her if she did that. Then we'd be back looking for his ass.

"Then I told her to read off his license plate number to me. But the guy didn't have one on the front of his car. So I was, you know, going through ideas in my head. Wondering how the hell we could get this guy. So," Attakai shrugged and leaned back in his chair. "I came up with an idea. I talked her to me. She'd been on those roads a few times and knew her way around, so I went to that old well and hid my car in the trees and waited, and the guy kept following her, and we led his ass into my ambush."

Wolf narrowed his eyes, thinking about the maze of dirt roads in that area. "How did you *talk her* to you?"

Attakai shrugged again. "We stayed on the phone together. I told her which turns to take, which forks. She led him right to me. She stopped when I told her to, and he did, too. He got out, and he was … he was freaking crazy, man. He was laughing and shit, saying 'I got you now!' stuff like that. Anyway, I got *him*. I came out of the trees, and I pointed my gun, and he … started walking at Mary, and so I shot him."

Attakai scratched his head. "And I went crazy. Man, Rose was family to us. You know that? She was … I dated her for a while when I first met her. I loved her. Even got in a fight once because of her. Broke some dude's arms over that girl.

"And this motherfucker, lying on the ground bleeding out his arm, started laughing again and talking about her." Attakai locked eyes with Wolf. "He was talking about her pussy. How it felt right after he killed her."

Wolf swallowed.

"So I shot the guy in the legs. Then the dick." Attakai stretched his mouth at the memory. "Then I shoved my foot on him, made him straighten out, while I shot him in the elbows. The shoulders. I was trying to make him pay. I wanted him to feel the pain and the hurt." Attakai shook his head. "That guy was sick, though. Not just like, sicko killer … he was an animal. Like, his eyes. They were these dead, animal eyes."

They sat in silence for a moment, watching Attakai relive the events in his head.

Lights blinked on the two cameras mounted in the corners of the room above the mirrored wall.

"Why did you bury him?" Mansor asked, more than a little accusation in his tone. "Why not tell anyone? There were families out there with dead daughters. They had a right to know, son."

Attakai closed his eyes and two streams of tears shot down his cheeks. "I wanted to. But I knew I'd crossed a line with shooting him that many times. I knew with my fight, with breaking that dude's arms and then this," he looked at his former boss, "I knew you would have lost confidence in me, sir. You told me to not screw up again. You said I was at two strikes, one for each of that guy's arms. But this was way more than strike three."

Mansor said nothing, just stared at his former deputy with half-closed eyes.

"That wasn't self-defense." Attakai wiped his tears and sniffed. "I killed the hell out of that guy. Made him suffer." He clenched his teeth when he said the word suffer. "And you know what? I'd do it over again in a second."

They sat in silence for a few moments.

"All right," Wolf said. "So you killed him. You buried him. And so you went looking into his life."

Attakai nodded.

"Why?"

"I don't know. I guess I was … I just wanted to make sure it was him, you know? The killer."

Wolf tapped a finger on the table. "But you said when Fred got out of the car, he was talking about Rose. That's what set you off and made you kill him by shooting him in the arms, the legs, the crotch …"

Attakai's eyes bounced around the room, then landed on Wolf. "The guy got what he deserved."

"I agree with you a hundred percent on that one," Wolf said. "Personally I wouldn't have had the patience and would have started with two shots to the head."

"Damn right."

"But … are you saying there was doubt as to whether or not it was him?" Wolf asked. "Is that why you started looking into him?"

Attakai spread his palms on the table and stared at a spot between them. "I was maybe a little in doubt. I started second-guessing myself. Wondering if my sister was wrong and I might have heard what I wanted to hear … or something. If my rage hadn't clouded my mind, you know?"

"We found Rose and your sister's DNA inside his truck when we pulled it out of the ground," Mansor said. "It was him all right."

Attakai closed his eyes, looking genuinely relieved to hear the news.

Attakai's eyes popped open. "But there's another guy. I never knew there was another guy."

"What did you find out about Wilcox back then?" Wolf asked.

"Shit, not much. I found his name and address on his car registration and insurance cards. I checked records, got the name of the landlord and had him meet me at his house. Got my way inside his place.

"Place was a real sty. Smelled like complete shit. I'm telling you, he was like an animal. I searched the whole place, and came up with nothing. I was expecting to open a drawer, lift a filthy piece of clothing, and find a pile of ears and toes. Except there wasn't anything like that. No collection. No bloody knife. No nothing."

"What about a broken window?" Wolf asked.

Attakai searched his mind nodded. "Yeah. There was. Why?"

Wolf ignored the question. "You visited his house. Then what else did you do?"

"I figured out from the landlord he worked at the funeral home. So I went and talked to them. I wanted to check his belongings. Try and find the toes and ears. But it's not like the guy had an office or something. Just a closet in the back and a van he drove around. Neither of them had much of anything inside."

"Why were you searching for toes and ears if you were going to keep him in the ground and not tell anyone anyway?" Wolf asked.

Attakai seemed thrown by the question. After a swallow he said, "I was second-guessing myself, like I said."

Wolf nodded.

Mansor cleared his throat. "What about the cell phone we found inside his buried car? Why didn't you take that?"

"I never saw a cell phone."

"We found it in the center console," Mansor said. "Didn't you check the center console?"

Attakai nodded. "I remember seeing it. I just left it … I was so screwed up that day. After I shot him, I wasn't thinking straight. I just wanted to bury the body, get the guy in the ground and out of sight."

"What else?" Wolf asked.

"What else what?"

"Did you find out about him? What else did you do?"

Attakai thought about it for a second then shook his head. "Nothing."

They sat in silence for a beat.

"Then what?" Wolf asked.

"Why did you leave?" Mansor asked. "Why did you quit the department and go up north?"

Attakai said nothing, just exhaled heavily.

"Shame?" Wolf asked. "Is that it?"

Attakai's eyes flashed. "Why?"

"Because you got your revenge but you never told the families of the victims about it. You never told them they could rest easy because you got the guy. You just kept your mouth shut about it and moved north. You got to bury the past and start over with a new life. They didn't." Wolf watched him wilt in his chair. "Is that it?"

"Yeah, well there's another guy out there anyway, right?" Attakai shrugged. "There's another killer. I was wrong thinking I took care of the problem."

"Doesn't mean you're off the hook, son." Mansor pursed his lips and shook his head.

The gesture from his former boss seemed to devastate Jeremy Attakai to the core. Tears streamed down his face again. "I know … shit … I know. I told my sister to keep it a secret. I told her to not tell anyone." His eyes pleaded before his words came out. "She didn't do anything wrong. It was all me."

"And your cousin Hector?" Wolf asked. "Did he help you dig the hole?"

Attakai shook his head. "No. No, that's not right. He didn't have anything to do with it. I called Hector down and he drove my sister back. He didn't even know what happened."

Mansor narrowed one eye. "That's three people with three cars. Yours, your sister's, and Hector's. If Hector came down and picked up your sister, how did you get her car out, and yours? And how did you get an excavator in?"

Attakai's eyes volleyed back and forth.

"Doesn't Hector work for La Plata Construction Services?" Mansor's voice was quiet. "Didn't he also work for them two years ago?"

Attakai stared at the table.

Mansor put a palm on the table, as if to steady the deputy's world. "Come on, son. It's time to fess up to all this. To lie more is only going to make things worse."

Attakai looked at Mansor. "Sir, I buried the body and the truck by myself. Isn't that a perfect enough explanation?"

"No, son. I'm sorry. It's not."

Chapter 30

"So the second killer suspected Fred Wilcox was dead? Is that what we're saying?" ASAC Todd paced the front of the small task force room in the La Plata County Sheriff's Office headquarters.

The pen board behind him had a new phrase written in Hannigan's chicken scratch: *Fred is dead.* Lindsay Ellington's picture was tacked to the wall as the ninth victim. Otherwise, the place hadn't changed in their day of absence.

Luke sat next to Wolf bundled in a zipped up hooded sweatshirt that was seven sizes too big for her—a gift from Deputy Wines.

Turning up the heat ten degrees would have been a better gift. Wolf, Mansor, Wines, Agents Todd, Hannigan, Shecter, and Wells all sat or stood with folded arms, trying to retain body heat against the industrial air conditioner jetting out of the ceiling vents.

"Yeah, he knew Fred was dead." Hannigan leaned against the wall at the side of the room. "That's why he broke into Fred's place. Think about it. He knows Wilcox might have something that connects the two of them. Like a burner cell phone. Or a stack of ears or—"

"Toes," Wolf said.

Hannigan blinked, trying to regain his train of thought. "Yeah, or toes."

"Not *or* toes," Wolf said, the edginess of his voice coming without him even trying. ""We have half of the signature missing on Sally Claypool and Lindsay Ellington's bodies. They both have severed ears, but no severed toes. Why? Because Fred Wilcox was the severed toe guy and he's been dead this whole time. Mary Attakai's description of her assailant, her one assailant, was Fred Wilcox. She came out of the desert with a missing toe. Fred was the toe guy."

"Okay, I'm sorry." Hannigan loomed over his shoulder. "Why don't you stand up and take the floor then."

Wolf shrugged.

"No. Why don't you tell us what you've been thinking over here with your blank stare at the wall."

They sat in silence listening to the vent pour crystallized air from above.

"If you ask me," Agent Shecter said, "it still looked like Attakai was hiding something in there."

"You still think he's the second guy?" Hannigan walked to the front of the room. "He was under surveillance the whole night last night."

"Yeah, and Wolf snuck up on him undetected," Shecter said. "Not that big of a stretch that he could have done the same thing."

Todd shook his head. "I don't see it. It's miles back into town from Attakai's house. His car was parked in the garage out front. He didn't leave last night. It's not him."

"Well …" Shecter let his thought go unfinished and shifted in his seat.

"We've gotten everything wrong from the beginning," Wolf said. "We have to start there."

They looked at Wolf.

He pointed at the pictures on the walls of the women's faces, all with missing ears.

"Step one: Fred Wilcox is a janitor up at Colorado Mountain College in Steamboat Springs, where he notices Jessica Meinhoff—a student there at the time. He follows Jessica Meinhoff down to Silverton. Rapes and kills her. He moves on, goes south and gets a job at the Buntley Funeral Home. Once there he meets a second person."

"I wouldn't call it meet," Luke said. "I'd say he teamed up with another person and started killing. That's not just somebody he meets at the coffee shop. Maybe it's somebody from his past."

Hannigan nodded. "Or it's somebody who saw what Fred Wilcox was. Somebody who was already a cold-blooded killer and spotted another cold-blooded killer."

Wolf put two fingers up. "Step two: He teams up with another killer and they start killing in a very methodical way. They contributed differently to the killings. Fred Wilcox was the rapist. That was his MO. And, like we just said, he took toes as his trophy.

"From the looks of it, the other guy was responsible for the rest of it—the tying up, the slashing, the severed ear, the strangulation and the display match across all nine victims."

"Right," Luke said.

"So …" Wolf leaned forward and put his head in his hands. He lined up his thoughts. "What kind of a guy is he? It's safe to say killer two was a smarter man than Fred. Or at least more concerned with getting away with it. Whereas, Fred Wilcox was an animal by all accounts and didn't care about anything but the destruction and the sexual release."

"Killer two was a tamer." Agent Todd said with narrowed eyes. "A … harnesser …"

"A parasite," Hannigan said.

"I'd classify the relationship more as commensalism," Agent Shecter said. "That's where one organism receives benefits while the other receives no benefit nor harm. Fred Wilcox was the one who receives no harm or benefit. He's just a reckless killer, out to get women. The second killer latches onto him and gets his rocks off."

Agent Hannigan raised his eyebrows. "Whatever."

Wolf cleared his throat. "Back then Fred Wilcox was a killer, going about his life, rolling into town with a murder under his belt forty miles north. And like Hannigan said, the other man would have had to know him prior or would have had to recognize that Wilcox was a killer."

"Our bio paints Wilcox as a supreme loner up until this point," Luke said. "He had no friends in Steamboat Springs before he left. Every person we talked to at the university was unaware the guy even existed, except for his boss. And his boss was like the rest of the people who knew him—freaked out by him and kept his distance."

Wolf nodded. "If he didn't know the person beforehand, then maybe it was somebody who witnessed one of his murders?" He leaned forward and put his elbows on his knees. "Maybe somebody caught him in the act of doing something with the dead bodies he was transporting back and forth in that van?"

Hannigan pointed at Wolf and snapped his fingers. "Somebody who also has a job working with dead bodies all day. Like that Lurch-looking boss of his. We know what Wilcox was capable of doing with a corpse. Maybe Lurch caught him doing his thing after hours."

"Terrence Buntley?" Luke asked.

"Yeah. Lurch."

She pulled her eyebrows together. "We talked to him in Durango the night before Lindsay Ellington's murder. That means he would have had to keep Lindsay either with him here, which means he transported her all the way down here, or, he kept her somewhere in Rocky Points and drove all the way back up to kill her after we talked to him."

Agent Todd lowered his coffee from his lips. "They found more of the matching dirt under Lindsay Ellington's nails. If Terrence Buntley did it, then he kept his victims up in Rocky Points."

Luke shook her head slowly. "I didn't get that vibe from him."

"From a guy that puts makeup on dead people for a living?" Hannigan asked. "I'll tell you what, from my point of view, there was no other vibe coming off that guy but serial-killer."

They sat in silence for a beat, and then everyone's eyes slid to Agent Todd.

He took a long slurp of coffee and nodded. "Easy enough to check the guy's alibi for the rest of last night, when he would have had to drive up to Rocky Points to finish ... the deal with Lindsay Ellington. Let's check his whereabouts for Sally Claypool's dates as well.

Hannigan was nodding, looking like a shot of optimism was coursing through his veins and making him fidgety for action.

"We'll check him ... but keep talking," Agent Todd said to Wolf.

Wolf crossed a leg, got his thoughts back in order. "Going by what we learned from Mary Attakai's police report and the DNA found in the back of the Explorer, it looks like Fred was in charge of picking up the women. Abducting them."

Luke nodded. "Wilcox abducts them and calls his partner. Tells him it's a go. They meet with the victim. Fred gets his turn, killer two gets his turn. They take their prize and they leave. Then they put her on display."

Agent Todd shook his head. "If Attakai's not our guy, that means someone else is. So why plant the cell phone at Attakai's house? He's trying to frame him? As much as I don't like this Attakai prick, it's not him."

"Because the killer wanted to draw us to Attakai," Wolf said.

They turned and looked at Wolf.

"The second killer wanted this exact scenario. He wanted us to expose the truth about Attakai. To bring him to justice for what he did to Fred Wilcox. For burying his partner out in the oil fields."

They sat listening to the howl of the air vents.

"What I don't get is why Attakai goes north," Agent Toulouse said. "And then the killings happen up there, too?"

"The killer went north to Attakai," Wolf said. "Not the other way around. Attakai killed Fred Wilcox, and from that moment forward he knew his sister was safe. Or so he thought. It's like I said in the interrogation room, he was running north to get away from the truth he had to live with down here—that he dispatched of the killer and kept it secret from the victims' families. People who would have slept better with that knowledge."

Luke nodded. "Knowledge that would have come at a price for Attakai. He would have been reprimanded, probably thrown in jail. He was afraid of telling the truth, and so he moved north to get away from the constant reminder."

Hannigan mock spat on the ground. "Despicable. Meanwhile, now his sister's in trouble. His cousin Hector. He should have manned up back then. Now they're all screwed. What a pussy."

Sheriff Mansor cleared his throat but said nothing.

"No offense, Sheriff."

"Wait a minute," Agent Shecter said, "So if the killer followed Attakai up north, why didn't he just kill Attakai for revenge, like two years ago?"

"Why didn't the killer cut off his victim's pinkie toes?" Hannigan asked. "It's not academic trying to figure these guys out. It's more abstract art, less math class."

Class.

Academic.

The two words jolted something inside of Wolf—a thought sent whirring in circles in his mind that was moving too fast to catch.

Hannigan pushed off the wall and it was like a rhino waking up from a sedative. "I got it."

Todd moved away, giving the big agent space as he paced the front of the room.

"We know Attakai's not our guy, right?" Hannigan left little space for an answer. "We've established that. Yes … think about it. It's this Lurch-Bunter guy."

"Buntley," Luke said.

"The landlord got a visit from Attakai, and he wondered what was going on. It was two years ago, but it was still pretty fresh in the guy's mind. This guy Buntley? He told us he never knew about Attakai visiting his own place of business? After his janitor disappears and the cops come in looking for him, he doesn't remember?"

"Yeah—"

"Wait, shut up," Hannigan said.

Luke raised her eyebrows.

"And come on, who else would have been in a perfect position to see Fred Wilcox's sick tendencies? He saw his janitor playing with dead bodies. Maybe he had security cameras set up, saw some footage of Fred.

"So he approaches Fred, and tells him, no, you're not in trouble, in fact, I embrace your sickness. I have it too." Hannigan put his fists together. "They form a bond. They become partners. The business owner is the smart, careful guy who covers his bases. The janitor is the wild animal who he can throw a leash around and follow on his hunts."

Hannigan stopped and put out his arms. His jacket opened, revealing pectoral muscles flexing and relaxing underneath his shirt. His eyes were unfocused and unblinking, until they snapped to Wolf. "So?"

"I say we need to check his alibis."

The big agent looked at his boss, then the sheriff. "You gonna get a warrant? Or just sip coffee like a pansy? Sir."

Agent Todd rolled his eyes and set down his cup.

Chapter 31

"And so we're back to square one?" Dr. Lorber asked.

Patterson had been thinking the same thing.

MacLean held up his hands, calming the growing murmur in the situation room. "They found Fred Wilcox's body. That's what I just told you."

Most of the people in the room, if not all, had already known that for an hour before this emergency squad meeting. It had been slow coming, but the news had already filtered through the department of what Wolf did at Attakai's place and that Attakai had confessed to killing Fred Wilcox two years ago, leading them to the dead body down in Durango.

Which meant they had been looking for a dead guy for days.

It had been Patterson herself that had pulled the info out of Luke via phone call, and Rachette who started the rumor wildfire.

She and Luke had always been close, ever since the gorgeous FBI agent had come out for drinks with Wolf that night years ago. It had only taken one beer to learn they had a lot in common. Both of them growing up with multiple brothers, they'd quickly become the sisters they'd both never had.

Luke had made Patterson promise to tell no one about the Fred Wilcox news. The problem was, Rachette had overheard the conversation.

MacLean paced at the front of the room, petting his silver mustache. "I'm not going to sugar-coat it, people. We're more confused than when we started. We thought we were looking for Fred Wilcox and his partner, who we thought might be deputy Attakai. Now we know it wasn't Attakai and Fred Wilcox was dead this whole time. Which means we're looking for somebody else, and I can't tell you who that somebody is." MacLean turned his back to the room. "Damn it!"

His outburst echoed through the auditorium.

The murmuring began again, and then swelled into full-blown conversations. MacLean seemed resigned to let it play out.

"Square one?" Rachette said, leaning close to Patterson's ear. "More like square zero. We know less than day one, when we rolled up with those fed dickheads sitting in their Escalades."

"Tahoes," Patterson said, raising her hand. "Sir?"

MacLean stewed in his thoughts.

"Sir!"

"What?"

"So what are we going to do?" she asked, trying to keep any judgment out of her voice.

The man was putting his head in the sand and she was yanking it out. She knew what the Sheriff was feeling. They all felt it. The news of Lindsay Ellington this morning had been a devastating blow. And now, knowing they had put all their efforts into looking for a dead man, it was like a bomb had gone off at the pity party.

MacLean stared at Patterson, and she watched the despair turn into embarrassment, then turn into determination.

"All right, everyone, pipe down!" MacLean raised his hands. "We might not have a clue who this killer is, but we're going to have to do something about it. The only thing we can fight with at this point is presence. Which means I want everyone everywhere, at all times."

Glances shot back and forth across the room like ricocheting bullets.

"I know, I know. We've been going hard for days now."

"With the Adrenaline Games?" Rachette said under his breath. "More like weeks."

"But …" MacLean's eyes watered and his mustache quivered.

It was a sight that brought instant tears to Patterson's eyes. She knew what he was going to say, and she was tired and already emotional about not being able to see Tommy enough the last month.

"What are we going to tell that next father?" MacLean's voice wavered. "Huh? I for one … I sure don't want to have to go through that again."

The room went silent. The sidelong glances became shameful dropping of heads.

"Let's get out there and protect our people."

MacLean turned around and everyone stood up, funneling up the stairs.

Patterson stood, wiping her eyes while at the same time stifling a yawn. She waited for an ill-timed, inappropriate, quip from Rachette that never came, so she turned to her partner to see if he was okay.

The sight of him sent shivers down her spine.

Rachette's eyes were wide, searching the room, his chest heaving, clearly apprehensive about something.

"What?" she asked.

"Where's Charlotte?"

Chapter 32

The two older men inside the lobby of the funeral home backed away from the group of agents storming the place.

"Mr. Buntley," Hannigan held up a warrant, "Sorry, gentlemen, this is probably not a good time to be … well, I know it's not a good time for you … Luke? Will you please talk to these two gentlemen outside?"

Luke herded the two men outside, whispering apologies.

"What in the name of Moses is going on?" Buntley asked.

Hannigan stepped past him, handing over the warrant without looking at the funeral home owner. "We need to talk, Mr. Buntley. And we also need to search this place for a few knickknacks you might have on hand."

Buntley looked from the piece of paper to Hannigan, and then back again. "What are you looking for exactly, Agent …"

"Hannigan. Sir, where you were when Fred Wilcox failed to show up for work that day three summers ago."

Luke came back inside.

Wolf made his way to the edge of the lobby, getting a clear view inside the casket showroom.

"I told you I was fishing. I always fish in August."

A slender woman with the same eyes as Terrence Buntley came walking through the casket room to the front. "Dad? What's going on?"

"Oh, hi honey. This is my daughter, Esther. Esther, this is some FBI hooligan accusing me of … what exactly are you accusing me of, sir?"

"You fish in August?" Hannigan asked, ignoring the funeral director's daughter altogether. "You simply leave work, go to wherever it is you go, and fish, and come back a month later?"

"That is exactly what I do."

Wolf saw the conviction in Mr. Buntley's eyes and the straightened posture of his daughter and knew this was not going to follow Hannigan's plan. To avoid watching the ensuing train wreck, Wolf turned to the rack of brochures and flicked through them.

"And on that particular day, Agent Hannigan, I was probably standing in the Kenai River, reeling in myself a ten pound Coho salmon. And in case you don't know, the Kenai River is in central Alaska."

The building went silent.

"And I'm sure you can verify that for us?"

"You can ask my daughter here."

Esther nodded.

"But in case you want to check further, I'd suggest calling the Kenai River Red Forest Lodge. Ask for Sam Gables. He knows me, he knows that I always go fishing at that time, because I'm always fishing with him, at his lodge in Alaska."

"Yeah, I get the point," Hannigan said.

Wolf picked up the brochure from the day before.

"We'll do that," Hannigan continued, his voice sounding now more dying animal than intimidating FBI agent. "Right. Now, if you don't mind, we'd like to ask you some questions about—"

"I do mind. And you'll have to talk to my lawyer, whom I'm calling right now."

"How does this work exactly?" Wolf raised the brochure and turned around.

Mr. Buntley was picking up his desk phone. "What? Oh … we talked about that yesterday, didn't we? I'm sorry, I need to make a phone call."

"If someone decides they'll donate their bodies to science and they are transported up to the university, then who takes the bodies?"

Mr. Buntley was asking for his lawyer in the phone.

Esther cleared her throat.

"Don't answer him, my dear," Buntley said.

"Sir, we're barking up the wrong tree here," Wolf said. "We've made a mistake and we're willing to admit it now. But if you'd please just answer a few questions about your procedure here, I think it will shed light on the situation."

Buntley lowered the phone. "I don't even know what that situation is, Mr. …"

"Wolf."

"Mr. Wolf," the funeral director lowered the phone and looked at the suited agents, "this is highly disruptive to my business. I am holding those two men's mother in the back of my building, and you stormed in and—"

Wolf held up his hands. "I know, and we'll leave."

"The hell we will," Hannigan said.

Luke put a hand on her partner's tree-trunk arm.

"One question. Did Fred Wilcox take the bodies from here up to the university?"

Buntley blinked. "Yes. He did."

"And who would he deal with up there?"

"The professor of forensic science. They have a small morgue room at the university where they do the classes."

Luke shot a glance at Wolf.

"Thank you."

Chapter 33

"I don't know." At first reaction, Patterson chuckled at the absurdity of Rachette's question. And then she was breathing fast and searching the room.

"She was at the crime scene. Wasn't she?" Rachette asked. "Wasn't she?"

"Yes. Yeah." Patterson searched her memory. "I saw her by the road. She was pushing back civilians with you guys and Yates, and—"

"Yates!"

Rachette's scream turned every head that was moving up the aisle, including Deputy Yates's.

"Get down here!"

Yates frowned, then made his way against the flow of traffic to the front of the room.

"You seen Munford?"

"Uh, yeah. I saw earlier." He made a show of looking around the room. "I guess I haven't seen her in a while. Why?"

The concern on Rachette's face was contagious. Dr. Lorber and Gene came over.

"What's happening?" Lorber asked.

"We're looking for Munford."

Gene's face dropped. "What do you mean?"

"I mean, she's not here. Have you seen her?" The question seemed to pain Rachette. Like he wanted to ask, *"Were you two out screwing somewhere?"* but didn't have the guts.

"No. I mean ... not since the crime scene. We were working ... and then ..." Gene looked to Lorber. "Have you seen her?"

Lorber's face turned white.

"Have you called her?" Gene asked.

Rachette already had his phone out and pressed to his ear. They stood in silence and watched.

"Shit. Twice no answer. Goes straight to voicemail like her phone is off."

"What's going on?" MacLean broke into their circle. "Get your butts up and out of here."

"Sir, we're looking for Deputy Munford," Lorber said.

"Then let's stand around and talk about it some more, why don't you? Come on, let's move."

"No." Lorber raised his eyebrows. "We're looking for Charlotte Munford. She wasn't in the meeting. And Rachette just called her. Her phone is off."

MacLean looked at them in turn and closed his eyes. "Oh, hell."

Rachette was staring at Patterson. It was more than just staring; he was trying to say something with his eyes.

"What?"

"I need to talk to you."

Patterson blinked. "Okay."

"Up at my desk. Now." Rachette bounded the stairs three at a time, crashing through two deputies at the door to the squad room.

She jogged after him.

Rachette was bent over his desk, fiddling with his computer mouse.

"What?" she asked.

"I need your help," he looked over his shoulder and stood up. "Wait …"

"What's going on?" Lorber asked, coming up fast behind Patterson.

Gene and Yates were right behind him.

MacLean came up last in line and completely out of breath. "What's going on?"

Rachette stood up and faced them, clearly preoccupied with the uninvited audience.

"What's going on?" Lorber asked.

Eyes dropping to the floor, Rachette's face went red as he turned back to his computer screen.

"Come on, why'd you call me up here? We don't have time for charades."

"Yeah, Lassie. Speak," Yates said. "What do you have, girl?"

"Nothing. Never mind." Rachette aimlessly toggled his mouse.

She looked at the screen and saw nothing out of the ordinary, that is, if one considered a picture of Tom Cruise hanging from a helicopter skid as a desktop background image nothing out of the ordinary.

"Whatever's going on, I want to know." MacLean backed away. "I'll be in my office. Find her."

They stared at Rachette's unmoving back for another beat and huddled into a circle.

Lorber slapped Patterson's shoulder. "Why don't you check the women's bathrooms. I'll go down and get Tammy to page her over the speakers. Gene, head down to the parking lot and check for her car."

"I'll check the street out front for her car," Yates said. "She's got that Volkswagen, right?"

"Golf."

They turned to Rachette.

"What?"

"She drives a Volkswagen Golf. Twenty-eleven. Glacier blue metallic." Rachette leaned over and touched his computer mouse again.

"Right." Lorber looked at Rachette. "We'll convene back here ASAP."

Lorber, Gene, and Yates took off running out of the room.

"What the hell is your problem?" Patterson asked.

Rachette watched them leave. His brain was working overtime, Patterson could see that much, but what he was thinking was anyone's guess.

"Nothing," he said, this time with more conviction. "Let's see where her car is."

She frowned and turned to check the bathrooms. "Okay, have it your way. I'll be right back."

Patterson checked the two women's bathrooms on the third floor and found them both empty.

While she was checking the second floor Tammy's voice came over the loud speakers mounted in the ceiling tiles of the entire building. "Deputy Munford, please report to the squad room immediately. Deputy Charlotte Munford, please report to the squad room now."

Ten minutes later she was done searching every women's bathroom in the building and completely out of breath when she reached the squad room again.

Lorber, Gene, Yates, and Rachette looked like they were banking on her news.

"Nothing."

"Shit," Rachette said. "Her car's in the lot outside. Which means she's near. She's probably just down the street getting coffee or something. Hell, my phone is almost dead. I bet her phone just ran out of juice. We've been working days straight. She forgot to charge her phone."

Lorber swallowed, nodded. He wanted to believe the innocuous explanation.

Rachette stared at Patterson. "What?"

"I just ..." she walked to Munford's desk and opened the top drawer, then lifted a white wire that was threaded through a hole in the back of the drawer. "She charges her phone every chance she can get."

"That's on a normal day. The last few days have been anything but normal." Rachette's chin lifted, daring her to speak.

She nodded. Said nothing.

"If she's not out there," Lorber said, "we'll make a plan from there."

"Let's go." Rachette turned and ran.

Chapter 34

Fort Lewis College sat atop a mesa overlooking the Animas River Valley and Durango. Tan rectangular sandstone slabs of varying sizes adorned the buildings resembling the ancestral Puebloan architecture of the Four Corners area.

It was the same architect who created this college that created CU's campus in Boulder, he knew, because he'd been on a tour on this very campus last fall with Jack.

In the end Jack had chosen Boulder's geology program, along with a much heftier student loan to live with after graduation. But that was his choice.

Wolf had been more impressed with the area down here. The college may have been considered second rate compared to CU Boulder, but the view from this campus, with the snow-veined La Plata mountains back-dropping the buildings, the gentle hum of Durango in the valley below—he could have enjoyed college life in this part of Colorado.

"Which way?" Luke stretched her arms overhead and shut the Tahoe door.

"Left." It was Hannigan's first word since they'd left the funeral home.

She looked left, then right. "You sure?"

He held up his phone in his beefy hand. "Biology building. Left, then it's the fourth building on the right. Looks like that huge one sticking up."

"After you."

Hannigan walked. Wolf and Luke followed.

Dark clouds obscured the sun and a mild breeze blew through the sandstone buildings, carrying the scent of industrial chemicals of some sort. Grinding and buzzing came from an open door of a building that said *Economics* on a tan sign. Campus was empty except for a smattering of construction projects.

They reached the biology building and encountered a locked door.

"Damn it." Luke fished out her phone and dialed a number. "Hi, Professor Jones? … yes … we're outside now … I'm not sure which side. Which side are we on?"

Wolf got his bearings. "The west."

"Okay … meet you there." She hung up. "Of course he's on the east side."

They walked around the building and met a man standing in a doorway. He wore thick, petri-dish glasses, a button up checked shirt tucked into green cargo shorts and Birkenstocks over wool socks. His hair was silver and all curls, like the sky in a Van Gogh painting.

"I'm professor Jones."

They did a round of handshakes and followed him into the cool building.

Fort Lewis had been founded in 1911 according to the sign upon entering campus, and just like any other university Wolf had ever been in, it looked over a hundred years old inside—with lots of stone and dense wood, worn out but still standing strong.

"Please, this way." He steered them into an office. Four open textbooks were in an array on the large desk in the center of the room, papers strewn around it. "I'm sorry, I know the office is a mess by some standards."

Luke nodded and appraised the room, looking like she was thinking *any standards*. "We just wanted to talk a bit. You said on the phone that the professor who teaches the forensic science course is gone?"

Professor Jones took off his glasses and his eyes shrank by fifty percent. "He's gone for summer break. He'll be back in just over a week, just like the rest of us. I'm here because, well, I didn't have anything better to do." His face was deadpan.

"And what is this professor's name?"

They hung on Professor Jones's next words.

"Professor Tindal."

They exchanged glances. Hannigan turned to look out the window, clearly hunger and frustration winning the battle inside the big man.

Has he always taught the class?" she asked.

"No." The professor's answer was immediate. "Only for the last two years."

Old framed drawings of Y-sliced, pinned-open animals with their innards exposed—a frog, a lizard, a mammal rodent of some kind—adorned the walls.

"We're talking about the class that dissects human cadavers, correct?" she asked.

"Yes. The Forensic Instrumental and Cadaver labs. Of course, that's only when the cadavers are available. We don't have a high population area surrounding us like other universities, which means some semesters we go without too many specimens."

Wolf studied a few framed pictures of faculty lined up in front of various places in the surrounding wilderness.

Wolf held his breath as he looked at a face staring back at him from the second picture. Vertigo overtook him for a second as the truth coalesced.

"And who taught the class two years ago?"

Chapter 35

They bounded down the steps of the county building, Patterson taking three steps to every one of Lorber's long strides. Reaching the first floor, they sprinted through the afternoon light splashing on the lobby floor.

"What's happening?" Tammy stood up from the reception desk.

"We're looking for Charlotte," Patterson said.

Outside Rachette took a left, followed by Yates and Lorber. Gene hesitated, then took a right and looked over his shoulder.

"Should we split up?" he asked. "Someone's gotta go this way, right?"

Patterson watched the other three men continue south toward the shops of Main Street. To the north there were fewer shops—boutiques, a hardware store, a title insurance company. Nothing that screamed a good hangout spot for Charlotte Munford.

"I'll go this way," Gene said, turning and jogging.

Patterson followed after him. "Wait, I'll come with."

"Meet back here in twenty minutes!" Lorber called over his shoulder.

"Okay!" She and Gene fell into stride.

Gene had his aluminum forensic case with him and it slapped against his leg with every stride.

Despite her short legs, she had to slow to keep next to him and he looked like he had to struggle to keep up.

They crossed the street and ran past the storefront windows of Forest Toad Furniture, then past the narrow hardware store. Patterson had always wondered how it stayed in business in this day and age.

Slowing down, she shook her head. "No, wait. If she's at a shop she's not going to be this way." She pointed where the shops ended and houses began.

Gene took a knee to catch his breath, setting his case on the ground.

"And I guarantee she's not inside the natural stone showroom shopping for kitchen tiles."

The other side of the road was a sidewalk and pine trees beyond it. Beyond that, a row of houses peeked out through the forest.

"Hey!" Gene took off up first-street at impressive speed. "Hey!"

Patterson followed after him at a jog. Something had really lit a fire under him. "What?"

Gene pointed up the street, like he was running after a taxi in downtown New York City, but the only thing in front of him was a desolate city block lined with pines, a few cars, and old oaks.

Her heart was racing at his sudden enthusiasm. What was he doing? Chasing after somebody? "Do you see her?"

Jogging after him, she plucked her radio from her belt, pushed the button, and then realized Gene didn't have one on him.

"What are you running after?" she called.

Gene stopped at the next block at the mouth of a dirt alley and put his hands on his knees. He stood and pointed into the alley. "There," he said between labored breaths.

"There, what?"

She realized he was standing next to his own white Honda Civic. Hopelessly out of breath, he looked like he might puke.

Turning on the gas, she sprinted to him and stopped. The alley had a cat that was looking back at them with wide eyes.

"What were you running after?"

With teeth bared, he pointed at his aluminum case, which was sitting on the ground with the lid open. "In there." He pointed back up the alley next.

"Gene, start making sense."

She looked inside and adrenaline blasted through her entire body, a chemical wave that pulsed across her skin and knocked her vision off-kilter.

Inside was gray padded felt, like the inside of a watchcase her father used to have in his armoire in Aspen. Only there were no glimmering watches inside this case. Instead there was a row of black, vague-shaped objects held in place by quilting pins. Only the two furthest to the right were skin colored.

Like a butterfly collection, he was carrying around ears.

There was a pull on her belt and then something flew through the air, landed on the rocky earth with a metallic thud and skittered to a stop.

She clutched at her empty paddle holster, and then turned to Gene and—

The blow brushed her in the side of the neck, but she'd been spinning already so he missed.

He was so close.

He came at her with the side of his fist and she countered with a forearm block.

As he pulled his hand back, something raked across her skin. Hot, searing pain.

He had a syringe in his closed fist, and it was already coming back at her.

She kicked him in the midsection with the ball of her foot, missing his crotch. But it was more a move to push off and get some space, anyway. To get her bearings.

His element of surprise was gone. Now she was ready. She lined up a series of devastating blows in her mind, thrust angles into joints for maximum pain and destruction.

She stepped over the aluminum case to get into a better position.

A case of ears for God's sake. It dawned on her that she couldn't remember a time the guy was without it. At work. In the station. At karate class.

The thought slowed her for a second. So did the realization that he was taking a different fight stance than he'd ever learned in class, and that his mouth was curled into a sickening smile.

Move.

She came at him fast, a high-pitched scream coming from her lungs as she feigned leading with a right punch, and then stomp kicked into the side of his forward knee.

Gene side-stepped with lightning speed and lunged in, closing the distance between them to nothing.

She blocked his first punch. It was too slow.

But it was a feint of his own.

Shit.

Before the one syllable thought formed in her mind, she was hit with three shots to the face. Devastating—two fists then one elbow—shots to her face.

Staggering back, she fluttered her eyes, darkness creeping in around the edges of her vision.

There was a thump on her arm.

She twisted and brought her hand up to block and slapped his arm away.

The stinging sensation was buried deep within the pain of the blow, but it was there.

"Gotcha," he said with a tittering laugh.

She put her hand over her arm, pulled it off and saw nothing out of the ordinary, but there was definitely something rushing through her veins. Her entire arm went hot, then tingled. Warmth expanded across her chest.

Fentanyl.

How long would she remain upright?

She decided every second considering the question was time wasted. Baring her teeth, she put her guard up and came at him again.

This time she was all offense, hitting his groin with a hard knee, which buckled him forward, and then she landed a rising elbow, which sent him reeling backward into his car. Then she stomped the side of his knee, connecting true this time. Two punches to his face—one on his cheek and the other smashing his nose.

"Ah!" he cried, dropping the syringe onto the ground.

As he bent down, a reaction to the pain in his knee undoubtedly singing a chorus in his entire body, she went for the throat. For Tommy, who was not going to grow up without a mother. The man was going to die. Right here. Right now.

Curling her hand into a rock hard fist, she took aim and punched with all the force she could muster.

And missed.

Completely missed. The world was spinning. She struggled to keep her feet underneath her, and then realized the reason why she couldn't stand up straight was because she was already falling.

Her head connected with the ground with a thud.

Gene was over her now, pointing his finger and saying something that sounded like they were both underwater. Her breathing was slow. No. It had stopped completely.

And she felt fine.

Her vision pixelated, like she was watching a nineteen eighties video game instead of a man wrestling with her. If Gene Fitzgerald was hurting her right now, she was feeling none of it. That wasn't quite accurate. She just didn't care.

"Come on," he said, slapping her in the face. "Let's go."

"Uhhh," she said.

Another tittering laugh.

She was up in the air now, cradled in his arms. And then … she saw Munford in the trunk. And then she was lying on top of her, the heat of her flesh underneath her, and then there was darkness.

Chapter 36

"Gene Fitzgerald," Wolf said, answering Luke's question.

"That's right," Professor Jones said, "Dr. Fitzgerald. You know him?"

Luke snatched the picture from Wolf's hand. "What? Lorber's new ME's assistant?"

"Let me see that," Hannigan said, taking his own turn with the picture. "Which guy?"

Wolf left the room dialing his phone.

It rang all the way until Patterson's voicemail. Then he dialed Rachette's number, which also went to voicemail.

"Shit." He dialed MacLean.

"You think it's him?" Luke asked jogging after him down the hall.

"Yeah, I do."

She and Hannigan caught up to him.

His phone beeped in his ear. He was getting another call from Rachette. Pressing the button, he heard MacLean's voice get cut off.

"Hello?"

"What's up?" Pounding footsteps accompanied Rachette's heavy breathing.

"It's Gene."

There was a pause and the footsteps came to a halt. "What did you say?"

"Gene Fitzgerald is the killer."

"It's Gene?" Rachette's voice cracked.

"That's what I said. Can you hear me?"

Rachette hung up.

***

Rachette pressed the call end button and turned to look the way they'd came. Gene and Patterson were nowhere in sight.

"What's going on? Who was that?" Lorber put his hands on his knees and bared his teeth as he struggled for breath.

"That was Wolf. He says it was Gene. Shit." He cursed himself for not dialing Patterson sooner. Something told him every second counted.

"Wait, wait, wait," Lorber bent down to get to Rachette's eye level. "He said it was Gene? My Gene? Fitzgerald?"

He dialed Patterson and listened to the electronic trill. Once, twice … six rings. Then voicemail. "Shit."

"Answer me!"

"Yeah, he said Gene Fitzgerald!"

Yates was across the street and rushed over at full sprint. "What's going on?"

"How is that possible? He was ... a professor ... oh God." Lorber put a hand over his mouth.

"He duped you, and now he has Charlotte, and Patterson's not answering her phone."

Lorber took off at a sprint back toward the county building, hand planting on the hood and leaping over a car that was pulling off a side street onto Main.

"Wait!"

Lorber heard nothing, just kept running at the speed of an Olympic long-distance runner, looking like a man on stilts.

"What the hell is going on?" Yates's face was red, his eyes bulging.

Damn it. There was hope, he thought, marveling at Lorber's pace. He could catch Patterson and Gene, and they could take him down. Bring him in.

But why was Patterson not answering? The guy had drugs. Fentanyl. Had he drugged Patterson?

"Hey!"

Rachette blinked. "It's Gene Fitzgerald. He's the killer."

Yates's mouth dropped. "Are you kidding? How in the ..."

"Let's go." Rachette took off at a full run.

The world was his breath, the pounding of his feet reverberating into his head, bouncing images of frightened people moving aside, burning lungs, aching legs.

I'm coming Charlotte.

I'm coming Patterson.

He repeated the chant in his brain. There was no way he was letting down Charlotte again. No way the two most important women in his life were going to suffer. And he meant it. For once, he knew he was going to come through for them. And then he was going to pump so much lead into Gene's body his corpse was going to be a health hazard for a thousand years.

Lorber was blocks ahead now, past the county building and looking side to side up and down 1st street. His arms were up in the air as he twirled in a circle.

That was where Gene's car had been parked. Rachette knew the white Honda well.

A few seconds later, Rachette was at the spot Lorber had been, who was now a block ahead of him, checking up and down Center Avenue.

Rachette squinted and got the right angle around the trees, and saw Gene's Honda was gone.

"Hey!" he used the full power of his lungs.

The few people that were out in public, still braving existence in Rocky Points, were all stopped and staring at the commotion now. Tammy was outside the building with her hands on her hips.

"Lorber!" he tried again. The man would be struggling to hear over the sound of his own breath. "Come back!"

He waved. Lorber finally saw, relented, and jogged back toward him.

"What? You find them?" Lorber asked.

"No. But I can."

Lorber's lungs sounded like a kazoo as he rested his hands on his knees. His eyes were rented in pain, his lips peeled back. "How?"

"Are you good with computers?"

Lorber stood up, putting his hands on his sides, his elbows flaring out like metal road gates they had up the county roads at high altitude. The tall man looked into his eyes, and recognized there was hope that hinged on his answer. "I'm the best."

Chapter 37

"It's not working." Lorber shook his head and clicked the mouse again.

"I know it's not working," Rachette said. "I could have told you that. That's why you're here fixing the damn thing so it works and we can find them."

Damn it. Of course his computer was hopelessly broken. The thing probably had a virus. He was such a computer klutz. Once he'd sent a cock-and-balls joke to everyone in the entire department.

"Did you check the internet connection?" Yates asked.

"You want me to get the IT department up here?" MacLean was pacing on the other side of the computer.

"No," Lorber said. "I got it. Jesus, Rachette, when's the last time you installed an update on this thing?"

Rachette leaned over his shoulder. "Updates?"

"Just … never mind. They're installing."

"Is that gonna fix it or not?" MacLean asked. "I can get the IT guys up here."

"I'll work circles around your IT guys. No. Do not call the IT … here. Shit, more updates."

Lorber leaned back, his gaze never leaving the computer screen. His chest pumped up and down just as fast as the rest of them. They were all in a dark place for their own reasons.

Lorber had hired the man, for God's sake.

But Rachette had left Charlotte at the altar. And now … he wondered if she was tied up in a dirt cellar. He wondered if she was dead.

He twisted and pushed his way past Yates. "Shit!"

The outburst failed to make him feel any better. A few paces back and forth, and he pushed his way back to his desk.

It was like a CIA torture device watching the progress bar flicker and grow from left to right. Right now it was only a third of the way across and looked to be stuck.

How long had it been since Gene and Patterson had split off from them out front? He checked his watch and calculated about twenty minutes.

"There." Yates pointed at the screen.

The progress bar leapt to the right, stopping just short of all the way.

They sucked in a breath.

"Come on, baby." Lorber rubbed the side of the computer monitor.

"Is it going to work with the updates? Will it have the information?" MacLean looked at him. "Did you have it on today?"

Rachette nodded.

Lorber was watching his reaction, then put his elbows on the desk and leaned toward the monitor. "We'll see."

"We'll see?"

"I said, we'll see!"

They sat in silence, watching the computer think for a few more seconds, and then the update loaded. A series of windows appeared, progress bars sliding left to right, then disappeared.

Ping!

The sound echoed through the squad room.

"Okay, done." Lorber clicked the mouse. Then clicked again.

"Up there." Rachette pointed at the screen. "That's the route map option."

"Yeah, I know." Lorber ignored him, clicked at a different place. He was searching the history or something.

Rachette turned around and walked away. It was no use watching.

"There, there, there, there!" Lorber shoved his seat back into Yates, buckling the deputy on top of him. "Look, there. It's showing in real time. He's on County 17 …"

"We have to move," MacLean said.

"I'm going." Rachette was studying the map, tracing his finger along the route. "Up 734, left on 23 … right on 17 … where's he going? There's not gonna be cell service up there."

"What's going on?" A group of three FBI agents came striding into the squad room, a man with a black-haired buzz cut leading the way.

MacLean cut them off. "We found the killer. He's an employee of the county ME's office, and he has two of our deputies with him."

The lead agent frowned, stepped around him and looked over Lorber's shoulder. "Who?"

"A man named Gene Fitzgerald," Lorber said, looking like he was wanting to spit.

"You have a GPS device on him?"

Lorber leaned back, looking up at Rachette. "Our deputy's ex-fiancé was dating the man. He suspected there was something wrong with him and put a GPS transponder on his car yesterday. We're tracking it now."

The agent pointed at the screen. "What's this second blinking dot? It looks like it's parked here, at the building outside."

Lorber lowered his eyes and scratched his head.

The agent looked at Rachette.

He swallowed, thought of something to say, then decided on the truth for time- saving purposes. "It's my fiancé's car."

The agent blinked, looked back to his other two agents.

They were both eyeing him. The woman agent had her eyes scrunched up, obviously thinking how much of a scumbag he was.

"Where are they now?" Rachette asked. "We need to move. We're already twenty minutes behind."

"We need to know where they're going before we move," Lorber said. "Go up there and your radio's gonna crap out halfway up. Your phone's not going to work."

The agent looked at MacLean. "We have a bird on the roof, one at the airstrip. The radios won't be affected. And, no offense, but I recommend you give this operation over to us. We have much more training in this sort of thing."

"Whoa, no way." Rachette wagged his finger, making sure to make eye contact with all three of them. "That's my fiancé up there, and that's my partner up there. No way I'm not going along."

"I thought it was ex-fiancé," the female agent said.

He stared her down.

"He's going," MacLean said. "And I'm in, too."

The three agents exchanged glances. It turned out the woman agent seemed to hold more clout than the others, because when she nodded, the black-haired buzz cut guy said, "Okay, let's go."

Chapter 38

Wolf stretched his neck to see out the front of the bubble window of the helicopter cockpit.

"There!" Luke pointed.

The pilot nodded and kept his current bearing.

Sunlight gleamed off the rain-soaked ground below. The sky to the east was like looking into a tunnel, with bands of rain bending northward, splashing against the mountains while cloud to ground lightning flickered every few seconds.

Wolf gripped his knees with white knuckles. But it was not the threat of getting struck by a million volts of electricity and plummeting into a mountain that concerned him.

"There they are." They all saw the scene below without the aid of a tour guide. Luke was talking for something to do. Her eyes were wide, her knee bouncing.

A square log cabin was perched on a gentle slope above tree-line, beneath it a brown road wound up the mountain, ending at the cabin.

A group of SBCSD and FBI vehicles, some still arriving on scene after making the long drive from the bottom of the valley, were parked haphazardly around the building.

Another helicopter was hovering a few feet above the treeless mountain and rising fast—an orange helicopter with yellow stripes, the words Flight for Life on the tail. The pilot started talking into his microphone and swung the helicopter to the right to avoid it.

Two black FBI MDs were already parked on the flat part of the slope below with their rotors stopped—the helicopters Todd, Shecter, and Wells had arrived in from Durango.

Hannigan pointed at the ground. "Try and get over there."

The pilot ignored him, swinging further away from the ascending helicopter.

Among the vehicles below was a white Honda Civic parked in front of the cabin. From their high vantage point they could see inside the empty trunk, which was popped open along with all four of the vehicle's doors.

A few paces from the vehicle, nearer the cabin, stood a group of FBI jackets. A few paces from them sat a rectangular heat blanket, beneath it an unmistakable shape.

"Shit," Luke said, the word sounding like a blast of static in Wolf's earphones.

As the helicopter circled around and halted its forward momentum, Wolf caught sight of a group of agents clustered around the mouth of a hole in the mountain, halfway up the scree-covered slope behind the cabin.

Wolf looked back to the silver heat blanket and his heart clenched and stopped for what seemed like ten seconds.

"Who ..." Luke's question died in her throat.

Wolf willed her to shut up. To not complete the question, because then someone might have the answer and say it.

We have a woman DOA.

That was what they'd heard from ASAC Todd fifteen minutes ago when he and the other agents landed. Since that tidbit of information there had been radio silence. Since that information there had been anything but radio silence inside Wolf's head.

The instant the skids hit the ground, Wolf was out of the cockpit and running. Luke's footfalls were right behind him.

Through watering eyes, Wolf's world turned into the bouncing vision of the silver blanket. There was the pounding of his heels connecting with the ground reverberating up into his brain. His breath catching in his throat, whistling with each inhale.

"Hey!" MacLean waved his hands in Wolf's peripheral. "Hey!"

An FBI agent turned and held up his hands.

Wolf tacked to avoid him and kept running.

"Wait!" MacLean's voice was close now. "They're fine! They're both okay!"

The words were like a brick wall. He skidded to a stop and looked at the sheriff, wondering what kind of sick joke the man was playing. How could someone be so careless with the words that were coming out of his mouth at such a time.

"Who's under there?" Wolf pointed, his voice cracking.

"I don't know." MacLean grabbed him by the arm and pulled him back from the blanket. "I don't know. But Patterson and Munford were just airlifted down. They were injected with Fentanyl, so the EMTs put em' both on an IV cocktail. Patterson's okay, but Munford's worse off."

Wolf blinked. "They're both okay?"

"Yes."

The FBI agent who had tried to block Wolf said, "The blonde, uh, Charlotte Munford had low vitals, but she was stable."

"We heard on the way up that there was a woman DOA." Wolf stared at the heat blanket, vaguely aware of the tears flowing down his cheeks now.

Luke shook her head and walked to the blanket. Kicking aside two rocks she lifted the crinkling fabric, exposing a naked woman beneath.

The woman was on her side, her hair pulled into a tight ponytail, her eyes open and staring at the ground next to her.

"Recognize her?" Luke asked.

Wolf nodded. "Lucretia Smith."

"A local?"

"No." MacLean said, giving the body a double-take. "That's her?"

"That's who?" Luke asked.

"A journalist." MacLean bent nearer. "You're right. I didn't recognize her without all that makeup …"

Wolf slid his gaze up the mountain toward the FBI agents surrounding the mine entrance. "What are they doing?"

"When we flew in, he was down here pulling the girls out of the trunk. He saw us and ran into the cabin, and then he came back out with a handgun and started shooting up at us. He made his way to that mine entrance and disappeared inside." MacLean shook his head. "Rachette flipped out when he saw Charlotte. He ran up and disappeared in there after him."

Wolf looked at his watch. "How long ago was that?"

"Shoot … Twenty minutes? I guess twenty-five now."

"Did anyone else go in?"

"No. It's not stable."

Wolf began jogging up the slope.

Luke appeared next to him, matching him stride for stride.

It was slow going, straight up the mountain at over twelve thousand feet elevation. His lungs pumped and he tasted copper on the back of his tongue. His legs knotted.

They passed agent Hannigan on the way up, who had his hands on his knees, striving to pull air into his lungs.

ASAC Todd, agent Shecter, Wells, and another agent Wolf didn't recognize were watching them approach from above, not seeming too concerned with the opening in the mountain.

When Luke and Wolf got there, Wells was arguing with Shecter. Agent Shecter pointed at a crossbeam that had cracked down the middle at some point during the last hundred years. "… and I'm telling you, we're all going to be buried alive."

Todd nodded at Wolf, ignoring the argument. "You heard about your deputy going in here?"

"Yes," Wolf said between breaths.

ASAC Todd got on his hands and knees and climbed inside the tunnel a few feet, pointing a flashlight inside. He crawled out backwards and shook his head. "I just saw two rocks fall off the roof of that tunnel."

"Does Rachette have his radio?" Wolf asked.

Agent Shecter held up his own radio. "Been trying him. Radio doesn't penetrate through rock, only works line of sight, and apparently he's out of line of sight."

"Every crossbeam is cracked, split, or missing altogether in there," Agent Todd said. "I'm not sending anyone in. There must be other entrances. Let's fan out and find them. Our perp's not going to go in here without knowing he's coming out some other hole. So let's find that, instead."

Wolf held out his hand toward Agent Todd's flashlight. "I'm going in here."

Todd shook his head. "I can't let you do that."

"The guy's not stable."

"Which guy? Your deputy or Gene Fitzgerald?" Agent Todd asked.

Wolf looked at him. "Both. What I'm saying is, the guy might not be fleeing. He might be …" Wolf grabbed the flashlight from Todd's hand and pressed the button. "I'm not asking. Let me have that radio."

Agent Shecter hesitated, looking at his boss. Todd nodded and the agent handed it over.

"I'm coming with you," Luke said. "Who's got a flashlight for me?"

"No," Wolf said. "You're not. Agent Todd's right. There are certainly other exits, some of these mines up here have dozens. We need to cover them. We can't let this guy sneak out."

Luke stared him down, her jaw shooting forward a touch. "Then why are you going in?"

"My detective might be in trouble."

She looked defiant for another few seconds, and then Agent Todd put a hand on her shoulder.

She shrugged it away like it was diseased. "Be careful in there. And make yourself known if you come out somewhere else."

"I'll be the guy yelling *don't shoot*."

"Wait a minute," Todd said. "This is stupid. You're not going in there. You already have two injured deputies flying down to the hospital on that chopper. We have another of your deputies recklessly going in, and now you're being reckless. I'm in charge here, and I'm saying …"

Wolf pointed his flashlight beam and ducked inside the hole. The sound of Agent Todd's rambling was smothered by the yards of solid rock between them.

"All right, your funeral," Todd said poking his head inside. Then a few seconds later he added, "be careful."

Wolf listened to their shouts and retreating footsteps, then turned back to the darkness.

The beam of light penetrated a few yards in, and then bounced back at him on a stream of dust cascading from the ceiling.

Stepping toward it, he blew a jet of air out of his mouth, parting the curtain of dust for an instant, giving him a view a few more yards into the hole. There were just more jagged walls. More sagging, rotten wood clinging to a brittle ceiling.

He put the radio to his lips and pushed the button. "Rachette, you copy?"

The stream of dust grew, and then there was a steady hiss of sand, followed by a chest-compressing thump somewhere behind him.

"Shit."

Pointing the beam up, he saw a rock drop from the ceiling directly above him and lunged to the side to avoid it. Stumbling, he slammed his shoulder into a wooden beam, sending the cross beam it was attached to crashing to the ground.

The first rock hit him in the lower back.

Chapter 39

Kristen Luke's blood was boiling. Why exactly, was tough to put a finger on.

Humiliation. That was it.

She had insisted on staying by Wolf's side and he had stiff-armed her. Worse yet, right in front of Brian and two of his Chicago transplant cronies.

Her ex-husband had tried to play it off, but she had seen the satisfied gleam in his eye for that split second. Agent Brian Todd knew her. Knew her very well. He had a knack for reading people's thoughts and intentions through the most trivial of their actions. Besides, the guy knew her and Wolf's history.

The stones of the scree slope clanked and slid underneath her, and she bent at the waist to stop from falling. She already felt the four men behind her watching her back. Maybe even giving each other sly, knowing smiles. Falling on her ass would be all she needed.

She heard a rumble and froze. Looking down, she wondered if she was going to start sliding at any second.

The men behind her froze too, their eyes wide.

"Look!" Brian pointed back at the entrance to the mine.

"Oh …" Luke clawed her way back across the slope, watching the hole as rocks trickled over the mouth of it. "What the …"

There was more rolling thunder coming from deep within the earth, and then dust belched out of the hole like rocket exhaust.

"No." Luke was unaware of how many times she repeated the word.

"What is that?" MacLean yelled from the cabin below. "What just happened? Was that the hole?"

They were running back up the slope, and then they were hiking, lungs burning, and then they were stopping out of exhaustion and staring at the still-rumbling hole.

There was hissing and clacking and scraping, and then the silence took over.

"Get up here!" Brian yelled at the top of his lungs.

People below scrambled into action, yelling at one another and running toward them.

They look like little ants, Luke thought. And against the amount of rubble she just heard fall within that cave, they would be as effective as ants moving the weight of the mountain off of Wolf.

Sickening thoughts flooded her mind. She thought of Wolf compressed under rock, his last breath being squeezed out.

Staring at the mouth of the hole, she waited for a dusty man to emerge. But nobody came.

"We have to get in there," she said.

Scrambling, they made their way back to the hole. Brian took a flashlight and bent inside. Luke followed close and ran into his back when he stopped.

There was nowhere to go. No more than ten feet inside a wall of rock smoldered with dust.

"Shit. That's a lot of …" Brian let his sentence die.

Luke walked up and moved a rock, and the rock above it moved, which sent the much larger rock above it tumbling toward them.

"Back out." Brian grabbed her by the waist and pulled. "Now!"

Out of harm's way, they stared at the hole.

"What are we going to do?" She felt like she was about to hyperventilate. There was no way Wolf was dead. He would make it. He would have been past that point in the cave by now.

But mine shafts don't just collapse. They stand on the verge of collapsing until something triggers it.

"The plan stays the same," Brian said. "We find another entrance. There's no way we get through that wall of rock."

Footfalls and strained breathing came closer as the others came from below to join them.

"Stop!" Brian held up a hand and cocked his head.

She had heard it, too.

Pop. Pop. Pop-pop.

The sound of gunfire echoed and rolled through the air.

Four, five, six shots. Then it stopped.

"It came from over there."

Over there was the direction of the scree slope they'd been scrambling down minutes earlier. Beyond the slope was a rise, and then sky. The gunshots came from over the rise.

They ran, Luke in the lead with Brian behind her. The others brought up the rear, leaving Sheriff MacLean sucking air with his hands on his hips.

The air was thin and her breathing strained, but she moved fast, her body fueled by adrenaline more than oxygen.

Reaching to the other side of the scree slope, she scrambled up the rise and paused at the crest of the hill. There was a steep decline on the other side covered in jagged rock and more loose scree.

From her vantage she could see it all happening below. Rachette was at least a football field's length down the slope and scrambling over a rock outcropping. He stopped and aimed, and then his handgun flared, a ball of smoke drifting on the wind.

The sound of the shot reached her an instant later.

Following Rachette's aim with her eyes, she saw movement further below. A man running steadily downward, hopelessly out of range of Rachette's department-issue Glock. It would have been a difficult shot with a sniper rifle.

Brian came up next to her straining for breath. "Shit, there's no air here."

"Down there."

He took in the scene and brought his radio to his lips. "We need a chopper in the air now."

Luke whistled through her teeth and Rachette turned and put a hand up to shade his eyes. He pointed in the direction of Gene Fitzgerald and turned back around.

Fitzgerald had disappeared into a meadow filled with low trees bent by the wind.

"Come back up here!" She waved her hand.

Rachette ignored them and fired off two pointless shots. He was moving fast and fell. A second later he got up and continued at the same pace, his footsteps long and risky.

"Damn it." She scanned the landscape above Rachette and saw nothing out of the ordinary. No gaping dark mine entrances. But from the uphill vantage she doubted she would be able to.

Brian was on his radio talking to the helicopter pilot, pointing him in the right direction. Below a chopper's engine was whining and the rotor began spinning.

"I'm going down."

"Wait a minute," Brian lowered his radio. "One thing at a time. Let's capture our suspect, then we'll organize a rescue op."

Luke thought of Wolf lying in a pool of his own blood. Maybe standing in the dark without a flashlight, unable to see his hand in front of his face.

"Give me your flashlight," she said to Agent Wells.

The agent put a hand on it and glanced at Shecter, then back at Hannigan. "I'm the only one with a flashlight."

"No, don't give it to her." Brian put the radio back to his mouth. "Follow straight over our heads. Down toward the meadow at the bottom of this slope."

Below the rotors started chopping air. A few seconds later it powered up and left the ground, dropped its nose, and flew over the rise.

By the time it was passing over Rachette's head far below, Agent Luke was already skating down the scree slope, a flashlight in her hand.

Chapter 40

Every third step Rachette twisted his ankle, or slipped and lost his footing, sliding onto his ass and drawing more blood, but he felt none of it.

All he was thinking was he had six shots left in his Glock and an extra clip, so twenty-three shots left.

Charlotte Munford was possibly dead by now, and it was, under no uncertain terms, entirely his fault.

Panic constricted his chest and he upped his pace even more, slipping on a rock and landing on his ass again.

"Ah!"

The rock connected with his tailbone. He writhed in agony for a few seconds, clenching his eyes and baring his teeth, and then he got back up.

"You're dead!"

His voice echoed off the mountainside.

"Move, pussy," he said to himself.

He moved. This time keeping his feet underneath him.

If he would have been a man and married her, then her budding relationship with a serial murderer would have never happened. She probably would have never been in those karate classes at all, because she would have had a baby in her belly. Probably would have never even crossed paths with Gene Fitzgerald.

"I'm so sorry, baby," he said it again. "I'm sorry."

"—come in!"

Rachette ignored his radio. He understood the situation. The chopper was in a better position to find Gene Fitzgerald. But they would need somebody on the ground too. And he was going to be that guy. And there was going to be a lot of blood in the end of this scenario. He was certain of that.

"Wolf has been buried—we need your help getting back to him!"

Rachette stopped, wind-milling his arms to keep his balance as he looked up the mountain. He put the radio to his lips. "What?"

He failed to recognize the male voice. "I said, Wolf went into the mine and it collapsed! We have to get back to him from the opposite way! We need your help!"

For the first time he noticed he had tears streaming down his face. Wiping them with his sleeve, he looked down the slope, seeing no sign of Gene Fitzgerald anymore.

"I'm on my way."

He made his way back doing double time. His lungs burned, his legs cramped, and he was beginning to feel nagging pain in his left ankle.

When he reached the mine entrance, there were two FBI agents waiting there. One of them he recognized as the Assistant Special Agent in Charge, Todd. The man was wide-eyed with concern and holding out his hand.

"Please hand over your flashlight."

Rachette made no move to hand over his flashlight. "Where is he?"

"Somewhere in there. Special Agent Luke went in after him. Did you come out of this entrance?"

"Yes. Why did she go in there? What happened to Wolf?"

"The entrance you chased Gene Fitzgerald into collapsed right after Wolf went inside to go after you."

ASAC Todd held out his hand.

"And she's trying to get back to him? To the entrance?" Rachette thought back on the winding route they had taken to get to this spot. There had been forks after branches after splits. "There's no way she'll get back to him."

"Give me the light."

Rachette shook his head. "I'll catch up to her and lead her there."

"No you—"

"I just came out of there. I'm the only one that knows the route. It's my boss. I'm going. Besides, you look like you're going to pass out."

ASAC Todd hesitated.

Three agents summited the mountain above them and started scrambling down.

"They have flashlights. You can follow when they get here." He slipped inside.

The first thing he did was angle the light to illuminate the ground. It was dusty, showing clear footprints. There were three sets of them— his, Gene's, and now Luke's on top of them both going the opposite way.

It was an idea he'd had to come up with at the first intersection he'd come to earlier—to follow the tracks on the ground. Before that, his rage-filled mind made him too quickly to act and too slowly to think. Now he was numb, pure determination as he moved through the tight space.

"Agent Luke!"

He kept his light on Agent Luke's small shoe prints and slowed, listening for a response that never came. Then again, he doubted he could hear much over the panting in his head.

Again he moved, this time even faster. A few seconds later he slowed to a stop because the footprints disappeared.

"Shit," he breathed. The panic came back. He remembered following footprints most of the way. Never losing them.

Turning around, he saw the dot of light behind him. While traveling the opposite way, he would have been following the light at this point, unconcerned about the lack of footprints.

Turning back to the darkness, he pointed his beam and continued onward.

I'm coming Wolf. I'm coming.

He blanked out from his mind the possibility that Wolf was crushed under rock. That's not how Wolf was going to die. Rachette was going to be long in the ground before Wolf ever was.

He came to a junction of three tunnels and stopped. *Shit.*

It was still too rocky. He couldn't see where he and Gene had come out of earlier, much less where Luke had gone into.

Bending down, he put his flashlight beam close to the rock and saw a tiny scrape—a pebble etching the rock beneath it.

Left.

"Luke!"

He turned back around and saw the miniscule pinhole of light. Yes. He remembered coming out of one of these tunnels and seeing that pinhole for the first time. But he hadn't turned around and pointed his flashlight behind him to check which one it had been.

Damn it.

He bent down and saw a miniscule scuff mark on the ground of the center tunnel, too.

Shining his beam up the left hole, he willed himself to recognize something.

And then he did.

There was a small pile of rocks on the ground. His aching knee was a reminder that he'd fallen over them earlier. He was sure of it. He remembered getting up from the fall, forging ahead, and seeing the dot of light.

Instinctively, if he had been Agent Luke and had to guess, he would never have chosen the left tunnel. It looked to be going the wrong direction. The entrance was straight or to the right, she probably would have thought.

But she might have seen the scuff mark up the left tunnel.

"Agent Luke!"

The response came a second later.

"Help!"

He turned to the center tunnel.

It had definitely come from one of the two tunnels to his right. "Agent Luke!"

No answer.

"Agent—"

"Help!"

Center tunnel.

His sanity wavered like a rippling pond. Charlotte was already fighting for her life because of him. Perhaps dead already. The only man he would gladly die for was up the other tunnel, possibly already dead or dying. And why had Wolf gone into the tunnel? To follow him. And what about Patterson? How many people were going to die because of him today?

He turned around and saw the unobstructed pinpoint of light impossibly far in the distance. What was taking them so long?

"Help! I'm in here!" Luke's voice had a shrill desperation. The highest register it could go without blowing out her voice box.

"I'm coming!"

He ran as fast as he could without falling flat on his face. The flashlight beam quivered and shook ahead of him.

This was good. It was better to have two of them. But what if she was hurt? That was going to slow things down more.

Hang on Wolf.

He breathed heavily now, going balls to the wall. Crouching. Sprinting. His back ached. There was plenty of time for hot tubs later.

Move!

It came up like a head on collision—a gaping hole in the ground that seemed to be hiding in plain sight, just over a rise and looking like a shadow at first. Then it was no shadow.

He was already committed to a forward lean, his foot outstretching for the next step that was going to land smack dab in the middle of the hole.

"Watch out!" Luke's voice was right on him now.

His brain shut off and he twisted, landing on his chest and clawing at the ground with outstretched fingers. His palms slapped the dirt, just as the flashlight clattered and then disappeared, along with all the light in the world.

He was sliding, his legs over the hole up to his waist. His balls connected hard with a rock and his abdomen twisted with sickening pain. His fingertips burned and were going numb, but his death grip on the ground had halted his backward momentum for the time being.

"Help."

Her voice was weaker. Right next to him.

"I can't hang on," she said.

Jesus. She must have been clinging to the edge of this thing a foot away from him. He considered reaching over, but any more weight added to his and they were both going to go over the edge.

It was pitch black. Blacker than being in the middle of nowhere, space, Star Trek style, black. No, blacker than that. There would have been stars for the Enterprise at least.

And it was horrifying.

He gritted his teeth and clawed forward. Every muscle in his upper body was tensed, flexed to the max and vibrating. A few seconds later he was fully out of the hole, his knees and feet back up on flat ground.

Reaching back to find the edge, he brushed against Luke's fingers.

"Help, I don't have a foothold. There's nothing there. I'm hanging." She spouted the words quickly, like he had mere seconds to act or else she was letting go.

He lay on his stomach and reached over, clamping onto her slender wrist.

"Do you have me?" she asked.

"I have you."

The added weight was instant. She let go, giving up the burden of keeping herself alive to Rachette.

The sudden limpness of her arm was hard to grasp. What was once hard muscle, was now a wet, slippery noodle. She slipped until he caught a firmer purchase on the knobs of her forearm bone. Then she slipped some more.

There was blood on his hand, he realized.

Shit-shit-shit.

He reached over and clutched with his other hand, getting a grip solid enough to bend iron. Of course, now he was in no position to lift her up. She was light, but not that light.

"Hello!"

A voice came up through the tunnels.

"Help!" His voice was a screech, filled with the fear of failing another human being, of killing another person who dared put their lives in his hands.

There was a light beam that swept over him for just an instant. It was faint. Whoever it was must have been far.

"We're in the center tunnel! The center … shit."

His body started to slide forward. Something about both arms being extended over the edge of the precipice.

"Climb up."

Luke groped with her other hand, catching his forearm and then she let go.

"Ah," she said, "my hands are cramped. I can't hold on."

"I got you."

He slid forward some more.

"I have to …" The last time he'd been holding her with his right hand she had slipped in his blood. So this time he let go of his right hand and held on with his left, bringing his right to his side to get a handhold on something.

It was a disastrous move. He clutched at flat ground covered in gravel for a few seconds, then felt her slipping from his left hand just like she had been with his right, not only that, his body was sliding forward again.

He spread his legs wide, catching the outside of his feet on both sides of the tunnel.

Yes!

He reached down and grabbed her arm with his other hand.

"Shit," she said.

"Yeah … help!"

"I'm coming," the voice said. It was still far but there were thumping footsteps now.

One second his right foot was plastered to the wall, and then next it was swinging out wide. He must have had a mere millimeter of grip on a point of a rock, but right now he had nothing and his left foot was no longer gripping the edge of the tunnel, but pushing him away, toward the precipice.

He flexed his feet up and dug his toes into the rock.

That seemed to work, but if he dared breathe, move a single muscle to swallow, he felt the grip would give way to sliding again.

"Help!"

Footsteps were coming fast. One pair of them. A bouncing beam of light that was painting the other side of a hole ten feet away.

Luke reached up and grabbed again with her other hand, this time getting a hold on one of his forearms.

"No, don't."

It was too late. The movement had jarred him loose and he was sliding continuously now. His pecs were all the way over the edge. The gravel on rock was like greased ball bearings underneath his upper abs.

"Sorry," he said.

A twirling light went over the edge with him, and then it felt like he'd been pinned by a rock on his ankle, stopping his slide.

Rachette felt Luke's second hand slip and release at the sudden jarring, and felt her arm slip through his wet hands—past the wrist. Their fingers were hooked into one another.

"Wait, don't pull me yet," he said.

He got a firmer grip on her arm and yelled, "Pull!"

Chapter 41

Light streamed inside the hospital room windows onto the back of the sobbing woman sitting next to the bed.

The machine beeped. The vitals were unchanged. The squiggly lines were the same as they'd been for five days. The patient was still in a coma.

A woman slipped into the doorway next to him and squeezed his bicep.

Ignoring the pain shooting up his shoulder from the five stitches and the deep bone bruise, he looked down. Not that he had to. He'd smelled her first.

Wolf and Lauren locked eyes and said nothing to one another. Nothing needed to be said. She was here for Charlotte. She was here for him.

The surprise of seeing her green eyes faded as quickly as it came, replaced by a warmth that radiated from his chest to his extremities.

"It's nice outside today." Charlotte Munford's mother was speaking to her unconscious daughter on the other side of the room. "You can feel autumn in the air out there. I'm looking at some shimmering aspen leaves. A few of them are floating on the wind. You should see this."

Charlotte's mother looked down at her daughter and started sobbing again.

Heather Patterson was all the way inside the room, standing behind Munford's mom. She put a hesitant hand on the woman's shoulder.

"Excuse me." A tall man Wolf didn't recognize stepped up behind him and Lauren. They moved out of the way, and when the man smiled his appreciation Wolf realized it was Munford's brother. They had the same facial features.

"You work with Charlotte?" he asked.

"Yes." Wolf shook his hand. "I'm David Wolf."

"Ah, I've heard about you. I'm Ben. I'm Charlotte's brother."

"How's she doing today?"

Ben raised a cup of coffee to his lips and nodded. "She's a real tough bastard. She'll be fine." There was no hesitation in his voice.

Lauren sniffed and leaned into Wolf.

Ben turned to Patterson. "Hi, Heather," he said.

While Patterson and Ben small-talked, Wolf took the opportunity to look down at Lauren again. She was dressed in pink scrubs, her auburn hair tied back loosely, revealing the tattoo of musical notes behind her ear.

It had been six days since they'd seen one another, six days since they'd spoken, or broken up, or whatever they'd done that day at the fair.

It seemed like a year ago since he'd last felt her touch. Even in the present situation, with Charlotte Munford hanging in the space between life and death a few feet away, it was pure relief for Wolf. Like a muscle cramp that had finally eased.

Lauren met his gaze with arched eyebrows, leaning into his arm once again. With a glance at her watch, she said, "I have to go. I'll be back around, Ben. I have to go do my rounds."

Ben nodded. "Thank you, Lauren."

Wolf turned in the doorway and watched her leave.

She walked down the hall and glanced back at him, brushing a strand of hair behind her ear before disappearing through two push-doors.

He watched the doors bounce back and forth, finally resting motionless, the image of her leaving replaying in his mind.

When he swiveled back to the room Charlotte's mother was staring at him.

He straightened, feeling flush in the heat of her gaze.

"Have you guys found him?"

Ben turned and looked at him, too.

Wolf shook his head.

***

"Do you know where he is?" Patterson shook her head and pocketed her phone. "He won't answer."

Patterson and Wolf stood outside the automatic doors of the hospital sipping coffee. It was brisk for late August, and the scent of autumn rode on the wind.

Wolf shook his head, turning his face to the sun and closing his eyes.

"Where is he?" Patterson asked.

"Your guess is as good as mine."

When he opened his eyes she was staring at him. "Your guess is better."

"He's looking for the Jeep. When I talked to him two days ago he was up at the mines again. Looking for more clues we missed. I told him to come into the station, get a change of clothes. Get some food. Regroup with the rest of us … Rachette has his own investigation going on right now and I'm not going to stop it."

The coffee was burnt tasting. Grounds slipped through the lid onto Wolf's tongue and he spit them out.

Patterson shook her head. "I still can't believe the way he got out. Like a freaking secret agent escape hatch or something."

After running forward to avoid the catastrophic collapse inside the mine, Wolf had made his way through the tunnels easy enough by following Rachette and Gene's trail, and then heard Rachette and Luke struggling and had saved them by a hair from dropping into a hole that had opened up under Luke's weight, who had taken the wrong tunnel to find him.

During the rescue Wolf had lost his light, and so had Luke and Rachette, so their walk out had been slow going until Agent Todd and his agents came in to help them out.

In the end they'd lost valuable time, and to compound their loss, Gene Fitzgerald had apparently been prepared for such a situation all along.

Once they exited the mine, the helicopter pointed them all to another hole Gene had disappeared into. They went in with guns drawn but never found Gene. What they did find, however, was a plausible escape route that dropped their stomachs and had Wolf's churning ever since—an underground ore car track tunnel that went down at a steep angle, coming out over a half mile away on the other side of the mountain, in a completely different valley.

They followed the tunnel to the end, and when it finally came out in daylight, they had found tire marks. Tire marks that materialized in the mud from nowhere and went down the mountain back into the Chautauqua Valley, which meant the car had been parked there all along for a quick getaway.

Since then they'd identified the tires as BF Goodrich LT 235/75R15, which had a distinctive off-road tread that was old and worn. Furthermore, the axle and tire spacing narrowed their vehicle in question to a Jeep, either CJ7 or Renegade. A solid lead they were following up on with every means possible at the FBI and department's disposal.

"Escape plans, working in the morgue for God's sake. That freaking case he carried everywhere?"

She nodded back toward the hospital entrance. "Lorber's still a mess."

If Tom Rachette had taken the news of Charlotte Munford's coma the worst, then Dr. Lorber was in a close second place. It had been Dr. Lorber who had hired Gene Fitzgerald from the Fort Lewis College School of Forensic Science two years ago. With every waking breath the

ME was kicking himself for not seeing the signs earlier. For not putting it all together.

"And I gotta tell you," Patterson turned to him, her eyes like blue shimmering diamonds. "I'm kind of a mess, too."

Wolf put his arm around her.

"No," she shrugged him away. "I'm trying to say something."

A gust of wind passed by.

"Okay. What?"

"When we find this bastard, I'm … done."

Wolf's nerves tingled in his entire body.

"Shit. You're pissed."

"What?" He shook his head. "No. But … you're quitting?" He started to wonder if he'd heard her right.

"Yes, I'm quitting. I have to. My son doesn't even care when he sees me anymore. He just stares at me, like, with this cold expression. I mean, he's only thirteen months old, but I swear he either hates me, or just doesn't even know who I am. I am going to beat my mother-in-law with my own two fists if she reminds me of it again."

Both of her eyes were streaming now.

"And Charlotte. All I can think of is she was right underneath me when we were stuffed in that trunk. It was my weight that put her in that coma. What if it was my bodyweight that ends up—"

Wolf pulled her into his arms. She sobbed hard now, letting it all come out.

When she was done they broke from one another.

"You know none of this is your fault, right?"

She sniffed and nodded. "I still have to quit."

"I understand, Heather. Believe me. I understand."

She lifted her chin and nodded. "Thank you. I just have to."

"You don't have to explain."

"I think I'm going to get my PI's license. My father and aunt have a ton of connections with every law firm in the state, and they need investigatory services all the time. I know, it's like calling in a favor from daddy … but if it means I can see Tommy every day then I'd move back in with my parents if I had to."

He was glad she already had a plan in place that kept her in the investigation arena. She was good. One of the best, and to let that talent go to waste would have been painful to watch.

"Check that," Patterson said. "I wouldn't move in with my parents. They're annoying as crap." She cracked a smile and Wolf broke into a smile too.

Patterson shivered and craned her head. She searched the landscape, scanning the sage fields and the edge of the trees.

He knew what she was doing. She was looking for *him*. Wondering if he was watching them right now.

The sight of her concern sickened him and stirred the rage within.

"I just keep thinking about that case," she said.

The silver case.

Upon clearing out Gene Fitzgerald's car, they had found his silver ME's assistant case. The ever-present fixture to his hand. The case that he'd been carrying at Sally Claypool's body. At her situation room meeting. At Attakai's house. The case he'd carried around with him like it contained his daily necessities, but that he'd never actually opened.

The feds were still trying to account for the three other ears found inside.

Patterson looked at her cell phone. "What time's the meeting today? One o'clock?"

"One o'clock."

Regroup and recommit to the task of finding the man—that's all they had been doing for each of the last five days, and today would be no different.

Wolf pulled out his cell phone and gave it a cursory check as well.

He paused and raised it, getting a better look.

"What?" Patterson read his face.

Wolf dropped the phone back in his pocket. For a long moment he stared into the distance.

"What's happening?"

"Nothing." He blinked and shook his head. "I'm glad about your decision, Heather. Really."

She looked confused for a second then nodded. "Thank you, sir. You have no idea how much that means to me."

"Listen," he said, "I'm going to head back inside. I need to talk to Lorber about a few things. I'll see you back at the station. One o'clock."

"Wait, what was that?" She pointed at his pocket. "You just got a text message about something, didn't you?"

"We'll talk about it later at the meeting. You head back to the station."

Walking inside the automatic doors, he was unsurprised to hear Patterson's shoes squeaking behind him the whole way.

Without talking, they walked down the hallway at full speed, through the doors to the formalin smell of the morgue wing, and burst into Dr. Lorber's lab.

Lorber was bent over a deceased old man, cutting a Y-incision into his chest. He stopped and looked at them over his glasses. "What's up?"

Wolf hesitated.

"Yeah," Patterson said. "What's up? You're here to show Lorber your phone but not me?"

Wolf pulled out his phone and held it up for them to see.

Chapter 42

The scent of gunpowder still hung in the air, along with a gutted animal stench.

"Rachette!" The sound of Wolf's voice echoed through the trees and came back to him unanswered.

Rachette's SBCSD SUV was parked at the curve, along with an old Jeep CJ7 with a faded, dented, warped exterior. It was parked with its nose downward, and its door was hinged all the way open, the wind bumping it back and forth against the hood.

Patterson's SUV came crackling around the corner and squeaked to a stop. She and Lorber got out and joined him at the edge of the road.

Patterson drew her gun, then seemed to think better of it and put it back in her holster.

Lorber made a show of sniffing the air.

"Where is he?" Patterson asked. "Rachette!"

The curve on County Road 17 was dirt, ruts, and dense forest emanating with the sound of a burbling creek.

Rachette's first text message had been a statement: *I'm on County 17. West of the highway 8 miles. Parked on a curve.*

The second text message had been a picture.

The third had been another statement: *I have one bullet left.*

It was cool, the breeze picking up and bringing in some unthreatening clouds, and again the scent of blood and viscera.

"Jesus," Patterson stepped off the edge of the road and into the trees, clearly smelling the same thing. "Rachette!"

"Careful," Lorber said. "At your feet."

Patterson kicked a brass shell casing out of her path. "Whatever. Rachette!"

They fanned out and walked through the trees.

"Rachette!"

"Rachette!"

A short distance later they came into a clearing and saw the scene that had been digitally delivered to Wolf's phone.

Gene Fitzgerald was lying on his back in some grass and wildflowers. The flies had set in anywhere there was blood, which was to say the flies had set in everywhere on his body.

The ground sparkled with spent brass at Gene's feet. There was also an empty magazine.

"Rachette!" Patterson put her whole lungs into it.

"Here."

The close proximity of Rachette's voice startled them all. He was only ten yards away, leaning against a rock with crossed legs. He had a bloody hand pressed to the side of his abdomen. In his other hand, resting on his lap, was his Glock. His finger was threaded through the trigger guard.

I have one bullet left.

"I found him." Rachette smiled and started laughing, then clenched his eyes shut and raised his face to the sky. He was in agony as he convulsed in a hybrid of laughing and crying.

Lorber stepped up to Gene's corpse and stared down. "Damn. You sure did." Lorber kicked the foot. "Good riddance you sick fuck!"

A flock of birds took flight from the meadow.

Rachette relaxed and gazed at Gene. "I was on my way down into town and I saw a Jeep. He was driving the opposite way. Could have sworn I saw Gene in the windshield with those glasses of his. So I turned around.

"He must have seen me flip a U. Parked here and tried to ambush me. But I was ready. Had my gun out the window and pushed him into the trees with a few shots. Then we had it out. Apparently he wasn't trained in the art of shooting like a Sluice-Byron County deputy is." He bared his teeth and closed his eyes.

"You're hurt," Patterson said. "We have to get you to the hospital."

Rachette lifted his gun, aiming at himself. He stopped short of putting the barrel to his head and then dropped the gun back to his lap.

"No . . ." Patterson froze. "You're not gonna do that."

"I'm not?" Tears slid down his cheeks. "I should. I deserve it. I killed the only girl that ever loved me."

"You didn't kill her, Tom. She's in a coma. She'll pull through. Come on, give me the gun."

"What if she doesn't?" he asked. "I put her in that coma. What if she's a vegetable all her life because of me?"

She went down on one knee. "Gene Fitzgerald put her in a coma. If she doesn't wake up, then Gene Fitzgerald did that to her. Not you."

Rachette stared through his partner. "I went and visited her at the hospital. You should have seen the way her mom looked at me. She told me it was all my fault. Yelled it in my face. Spit on the ground at my feet. And she's right. I left her at the altar. She would have never been with this monster in the first place if I hadn't done that."

"Rachette …"

Rachette lifted the gun again, this time gritting his teeth.

"No, Tom!"

He pressed the gun against his temple. Clenched his eyes.

"You were scared," she said quickly. "That's okay. Please, Tom. Put the gun down. Lower it."

"I was a pussy."

"Please." She held out her hand. "Please."

He opened his eyes and lowered his arm. "I'm a pussy now. I should do it, but I can't. I should—"

"You were scared of becoming just like your father."

The forest was dead silent.

Wolf dared a long breath, but didn't dare blink. Every muscle in his body was clenched.

"I get it," she said, her voice soothing. "We all get it, Tom. We all understood the minute you didn't show up for that thing. Okay? *Charlotte* understood. So stop beating yourself up for that. And this guy? This guy had us all duped. This guy was a sicko who had us all duped."

She stretched her arm even more. "So why don't you give me the gun, okay?"

Rachette clenched his eyes and bared his teeth, and then he sobbed with bouncing shoulders.

Patterson edged forward, and Rachette left the Glock on his leg and put his hand over his eyes.

She pounced and plucked the gun from his lap, ejecting the single bullet still in the chamber, and then racked the slide a few times for good measure. Dropping the magazine, with a grunt she reeled back and threw it into the trees. It clattered off a log and skittered off a boulder.

Rachette's eyes were open now, watching his partner. "That's my piece."

Wolf pushed past Patterson and bent over Rachette. "Are you shot?"

Rachette said nothing.

He pulled Rachette's hand away and looked.

"What's it look like?" Lorber came up behind him and bent down. After a few seconds of ripping fabric and close study, the ME looked up. "It's through and through. Doesn't look too bad. Considering how he looks." Lorber thumbed back toward Gene.

"Got him good, huh?" Rachette asked.

Patterson was over near Gene's body. Wolf and Lorber joined her and Wolf got a good look for the first time. The wounds were in all the right places.

"This isn't going to be good." Lorber was looking at the ground. "He shot him God knows how many times, then reloaded and shot him sixteen times more." He looked back at Rachette, not bothering to lower his voice. "I'd say an IA investigation's going to call this a bad shoot."

"You think?" Patterson shook her head.

"If DA White has anything to say about it?" Lorber looked at Wolf. "Yeah."

"He shot Rachette. It's self-defense." Patterson shook her head. "Whatever. Let's not worry about that. Let's get him to the hospital."

"The first four or five shots, sure, self-defense. Then …" Lorber upturned his hands.

"Give me a gun," Rachette said.

"Shut up," Patterson said.

"You know … it would be a piece of cake," Lorber said. "We pick up the brass, then use hydrofluoric acid on him … or just dump him in one of those mine shafts. Hydrofluoric acid would be better. It'll dissolve everything else and we can remove the bullets. Then we take a few gallons of gas and douse this area, light it on fire to remove any forensic residue?" He shrugged his bony shoulders. "Of course after two rain storms it would all be gone anyway. Not that anyone would be looking up here for—"

"No." Patterson's mouth dropped open. "That's not what we're going to do."

Rachette stared at them with dead eyes.

Wolf said nothing.

"I don't know." Lorber held his hand out to Gene's corpse. "Your partner might go to jail for this. I mean, he cleared his gun on him. Then reloaded and cleared it again. Hey, I'm just saying. I'm all for it if you guys decide to get rid of the body."

Patterson looked pale, and not because of the smell coming off of Gene.

"What do you think?" Lorber turned to Wolf.

He studied Lorber's face and found no trace of irony in his voice. The man was dead serious.

"Deputy Attakai's sitting in jail because of this same thing," Patterson said. "Don't you see the irony in that?"

"Attakai's sitting in jail because there was another killer out there he didn't know about." Lorber studied the body, put a hand on his chin like a sculptor studying a lump of clay.

"Jesus." Patterson walked away.

"Justice is done," Lorber said. "Shoot him thirty times and put him in a hole for the rats to eat. And nobody else's life is ruined." He turned to Wolf, extending a long pointer finger. "Wait a minute. You didn't want to show Patterson your phone. You agree. You …" The tall ME let his sentence die, because Wolf was shaking his head.

"Why not?" The heat in Lorber's eyes threatened to melt his glasses. "This guy killed how many women? Ruined how many families? Munford's in a bed drooling on herself. We can't stop any of that from happening anymore. But Rachette's going to go to jail for this, and we have the ability to stop that right now. I think we need to do it."

Wolf walked past the tall ME. "Let's get Rachette up to the road."

"Hey!" Lorber clutched onto Wolf's shoulder.

Wolf froze and looked at Lorber.

The wild look in Lorber's eye dissipated like a cooling car cigarette lighter. Dropping his hand, he shut his eyes. "It's all my fault. I just want to fix it. I want to …" He widened his eyes and looked into the woods.

The sound of sirens floated on the wind.

Chapter 43

Sheriff's vehicles and FBI Tahoes choked the county road. Two news helicopters hovered overhead. The noise of radios and thumping rotors invaded the forest, and yet a family of deer stood a few hundred yards up the road cocking curious stares.

Wolf was sipping a cup of coffee at the side of the road, enjoying the light drizzle that drifted from the slate gray clouds above.

"Damn, that's a lot of lead he pumped into him." Special Agent Hannigan came out of the trees with Luke following close behind.

Luke had an FBI ball cap pulled low over her face. Underneath the bill her skin looked pallid. "I didn't know Rachette had it in him to do such a thing. Don't blame him," she said. "Just . . . haven't seen what thirty hollow points would do to a man before."

Hannigan slapped Luke on the shoulder, making her flinch. "It's over, though."

"Yeah." She gave him an annoyed glare. "Thanks."

The big man looked at both of them and left. "I'll leave you two."

With Hannigan gone she turned toward the dirt road and took off the ball cap, letting the drizzle hit her face. "Aw. Dang that was disgusting."

She sucked in a breath and pulled the ball cap back onto her head. "You hear about Mary Attakai?"

"No. What?"

ASAC Todd came out of the trees and paused at the sight of them talking, then nodded and walked on.

Luke sniffed and watched Todd walk away. "She came into the La Plata Sheriff's Office this morning and recanted her previous statements, then confessed to being the one who shot Fred Wilcox."

Wolf raised his eyebrows. "What did she say?"

"She said she saw Wilcox was following her and she led him out to the fracking well. Then she got out and blew him apart with a gun she'd been carrying ever since the attack. Then she called Hector and her brother. They came down and buried everything with an excavator rather than tell anyone. They didn't want her going to jail." She looked into the forest. "Attakai's been taking the heat this whole time for her. Remember Hector at the house?"

Wolf pulled the corners of his mouth down and nodded.

She leaned toward him. "Wait a minute. You knew about her doing it, didn't you? How did you know?"

He shrugged.

She punched him in the arm.

"Ah … that's the bad arm."

"I'm sorry," she leaned into him and put a hand on his bicep. "I'm sorry."

Her body was pressed up against his, and she backed up a split second after the awkward realization hit them both.

Wolf said, "I didn't know when we were talking with Mary. Though Hector's behavior makes sense now. He was watching her close, making sure she didn't slip up and say anything that would get her in trouble.

"I suspected she might have done it after Mansor and I talked with Attakai. Attakai went and started looking into Wilcox's life after he and Hector buried him, because he was wondering if his sister might have killed the wrong guy.

"Think about it, his sister shoots a guy to shreds and then calls him. He gets there and sees a bloody mess. He hears the story from his sister that it was the guy—it was him, she swears it. But he knows she was drugged up that night she escaped and her memory might have been fuzzy. He wonders if his sister's stable. But Attakai's protective, and so is Hector, so they bury Wilcox.

"They would have seen the blood in the Explorer, seen the collection of newspapers, and probably been pretty sure Wilcox was the killer, but Attakai starts second-guessing himself, so he goes and does some checking—searches Wilcox's house, goes to the funeral home. He convinces himself that it was Wilcox who was the killer. Then he leaves town, unable to face what they did, unable to face the families with dead daughters and sisters and him knowing the real truth and not telling the real truth, and so he comes up to Rocky Points."

Luke nodded.

Wolf said, "Then Sally Claypool was killed and put on display next to the river."

Luke nodded again. "And Sally had a missing ear. It was pretty much the same MO. He was probably freaking out. Probably thought his sister killed the wrong guy two years ago. That his fear was true, that they *did* bury an innocent guy out there."

"Which explains why he called his sister immediately after Sally Claypool was found," Wolf said. "Probably asked her how sure she was back then about Fred Wilcox. Because right then it looked like she was pretty wrong."

"But it was Gene." She shook her head. "He ... followed Attakai? That's why he was in Rocky Points?"

Wolf shrugged. "It looks like it. Let's go back to that day Mary Attakai killed Fred. Gene and Fred must have been in constant contact after Mary's escape that night. It was their one big screw up, and it was major. They probably met every night, talking about what they were going to do about Mary. What did she see? What did she tell the cops? Gene was careful. He covered his bases, never left a trace of himself on any of the victims. He would have told Fred to get rid of Mary. She was a liability.

"So Fred's mission would have been just that above all else. Then maybe Fred calls him one day, says, 'Hey, her brother left her alone. I'm on her tail. I'll call you back.' Or whatever, but, maybe Gene knew that Fred was going after her."

Luke nodded. "Then Fred gets whacked by Mary."

"Right. And then Gene's wondering what happened. His partner went silent. No status report, no nothing. But there's no official news of Fred's death. Nothing plastered all over the front pages or on the television, so he's wondering what happened? Did Fred leave? Did he run? Why? And, not only that, if Fred did run, now *he's* a liability to Gene."

"The broken window at Fred's place," Luke said. "So Gene's freaking out about Fred now, so he goes over and breaks into his place— checks it out. Maybe he removes the collection of toes, maybe he wipes the place down because he's left prints there."

Wolf nodded. "Then he sees Mary Attakai is still alive. He watches her and Deputy Attakai."

"But then Attakai heads north," she said. "And Gene goes north, too. Because he's wondering what Deputy Attakai is doing?"

Wolf shrugged. "Maybe Gene figures out Fred's cousin is up here, so he comes and interrogates him, pretending like he's a PI. That's why he asked his cousin if anyone came looking for Fred. Because he thought Attakai came north on his trail."

Luke squinted one eye. "But Attakai gets a job up here in Rocky Points and settles down. That probably confused the crap out of Gene."

"Probably," Wolf said, "I think it would start to look like the Attakais had done something to Fred at that point. But there would still have been the niggling doubt that Fred just up and left. The uncertainty of the situation would have hung over his head."

"So he gets a job up in Rocky Points? He's been sitting on your ME's team for two years."

Wolf nodded.

He tried to remember the first time he'd met the man and realized it was only this spring. Professionally, the only time they crossed paths previously was during high-stress situations. Crime scenes. One of them being at Lauren's house. The other, he would have been on his way to the hospital with a blown-off pinkie. It had been Charlotte Munford and

Patterson who had introduced him socially—a new addition to Patterson and Munford's martial arts dojo.

Scrunching her face, Luke said, "I guess the cell phone thing starts making more sense. He probably carried that thing around for the last two years, wondering if it would ring. He probably called Fred's phone every once in a while, just to see if it was on. And then we go off and call it one day."

Wolf nodded. "And then he probably found out about the truck down south somehow. Which confirmed for him that the Attakais killed Fred."

Luke's eyes widened.

"What?"

"Remember I said we called Fred Wilcox's phone twice and the second call we got an answer?"

"Yeah?"

"Agent Wells made the call. He was trying to draw out the call, you know, give us more time to triangulate it. He talked about the truck being pulled out of the ground. He talked about the Explorer and how we found the phone in the center console."

"That's what triggered Gene," Wolf said. "The phone call told him everything he'd been wondering for two years. Fred was dead. The Attakais did it. So he killed Jeremy Attakai's girlfriend. He planted the phone at his house."

"He planted it the day we searched his house, didn't he?"

Wolf nodded, remembering that Gene had been the first to enter Jeremy Attakai's bedroom that morning. "Looks like it. He wanted to expose what the Attakais did."

"And he got his wish, and then some."

They stood in silence and watched the helicopters thump overhead.

With an outstretched hand she turned to him. "I'm leaving."

He nodded and took it. "Drive safe."

"To Seattle."

He raised his eyebrows. "That was fast."

Now they held hands. Neither of them letting up on their firm grip.

She shrugged. "I told you, I was looking at other options."

"Did you hear Patterson was quitting?" he asked.

"No. She didn't tell me that. Are you serious?"

Wolf nodded.

"Shit."

"I'm glad for her. She needs to see her family more," Wolf said.

"Yeah." She pulled her hand away, their fingers sliding apart.

"Seattle." Wolf nodded. "I was stationed in Tacoma, you know."

She nodded. "Yes. I know."

"I'll hook you up with a crotchety old General if you want."

She smiled. Then she reached up and clamped her arms around his neck. Her body fit against his like he had put on a well-worn pair of leather gloves.

Her breath was hot in his ear. "I love you." Letting go, she landed back on her heels and locked eyes with him. "But not like she does."

"I love you, too."

She laughed but it wasn't a laugh. "But not like you love her."

He said nothing.

"So … you should figure it out with her."

He nodded. "Probably."

Chapter 44

Wolf's backpack dug into his shoulders and his legs were a dull, lifeless version of their earlier selves.

"You all right?" Lauren was well in front, looking lighter on her feet than he was. "You want to transfer some stuff out of your pack to mine?"

He shook his head. It was the damn cooler and its contents inside—an entire five-star dinner and bottle of chilled wine. Well, as five-star as one could get without an oven. It was his secret, and his burden to carry.

"Nah, I'm all right," he said. "You said three miles?"

"Yeah. Three miles."

Lauren would have normally smirked. Would have normally called him a wimp or worse. But these were different circumstances. This was a weekend backpacking trip together to talk things out. Right now their relationship was still on uncertain terms. The effortless quips would come later. If at all.

The last few days Wolf had been busy wrapping up the Van Gogh case and Lauren had been working her new day shift at the hospital and keeping it to Ella and herself at night. So they hadn't actually resolved anything. Still hadn't had "the talk", but they had come to a mutual decision that they would have "the talk".

Lauren had suggested the weekend backpacking trip, which had surprised Wolf. If she had any intention of breaking up, then he could think of no worse venue. To suggest such a trip was an unspoken statement of devotion, of a commitment that she wanted to work things out with him.

Three days earlier she had come into the station and asked him on the trip. As soon as the words left her mouth she had gone red-faced. Because to accept the invitation was for him to state the same level of commitment she was showing.

When Wolf had not immediately responded, she had said, "Never mind. Stupid idea. We could just … go get a cup of coffee when you have a free minute."

Wolf smiled at the memory of their hug that followed. "I'd love to," he had said.

And now, as sweat pooled at the small of his back, his skin chaffing like his shirt fabric was made of two-hundred-grit, he was thinking about a soft booth at the Sunnyside Café.

"Here it is," she said from the crest of the hill.

He climbed the final switchback and took in the sight of the hanging valley. Widely spaced pine trees jutted from a carpet of green grass and multi-colored wildflowers.

In the center was a turquoise lake surrounded by boulders and sloping scree walls that cascaded down from thirteen thousand foot peaks. Patches of snow spotted the gray slopes, veins of melt water filling the valley with the soundtrack of rushing water.

"Perfect," he said.

"Yeah." She looked relieved at his approval.

He had never been to this spot, which was a critical coincidence for him. There was no way he was going to do this in a valley filled with memories of him and Sarah rolling in a tent.

They walked into the trees near the water and set down their packs.

"Good spot?" she asked.

Turning a full circle, he nodded his approval.

While he stretched his back, Lauren watched with a half-smile on her lips. "Must be getting old, huh?"

He gave her a warning glare.

Her smile lit up the valley. "What do you have in there, anyway?"

With a shrug of his shoulders he said, "The usual, I guess. I just must be beat from last week."

She leaned her backpack against a log.

He watched her body move under her slim-fitting jeans and long sleeved shirt.

"Did you hear about Tom and Charlotte?" she asked.

Of course he had. The lore had swept through the valley. "Yeah, he told me."

"Oh," she smiled, "you got his version?"

Wolf smiled back. "Yeah. So?"

"What did he say happened?"

"He said he went in to see her after his surgery, and she woke up from the sound of his voice."

"Ha!"

"She didn't?"

"No. She woke up before that. Then went back to sleep, like regular sleep, and woke up when he came barging in, running into her bed with his wheelchair. I was there."

"Ah," Wolf said. "So the speech about undying love? The kneeling down in front of her with the ring and she cries and accepts his proposal and insists they get married then and now? Right there in the hospital?"

Lauren closed one eye. "If by speech, you mean tears pouring down his face, words spewing out of his mouth, begging for forgiveness on his knees, blood coming out of his stitches … then yes, that's what happened."

"And she just said yes? After all he did to her?" he asked.

She nodded. "She said yes. It was probably the most awkward I've ever been in my life, standing there in the midst of the whole scene."

"If it was so awkward, why didn't you leave?"

Lauren shrugged. "I was in there taking vitals when he came in."

"That explains nothing."

She smiled, her face turning red. "He just launched into it and kept going. And I had to see what happened next. It was like a, more than a car wreck, like a bus crash. A bus explosion. Had to watch. And besides, it was romantic."

They stared at one another for a second.

Romantic.

"What's going to happen to him, anyway?" She asked.

He scratched his chin. "We'll see."

"I heard from Margaret that DA White was pushing to press charges against him, but he's willing to look the other way if she and MacLean promise to endorse him for the election?"

Wolf shrugged. "I think that's the gist of it."

That was the black and white, but the underworld of politics always operated in shades of gray.

Margaret had told Wolf the story about her and White's lunch date. Margaret said that in between mouthfuls of food, the DA had danced around the topic of Tom Rachette's shooting of the serial killer that had tormented Colorado for years, using cryptic language to get a point across without actually coming out and saying what he meant, but she'd picked up the subtleties clear enough.

Currently, the DA was reluctant to take the position of being lenient on the deputy without the backing of influential people should he encounter some pushback. Lasting, permanent, backing of influential people.

She wrinkled her forehead. "You think they're going to do it?"

"I hope so."

She thought about it some more. "You think their endorsements would get White re-elected?"

He shrugged again.

After another few moments of contemplation, her forehead slackened and she turned to her gear.

"Let's set up the tents." He unstrapped his tent off his backpack.

"Tents?"

"Yeah, we want to get it over with," he said. "Then we can relax, and …"

She looked past him and rubbed her neck.

Shit. He'd gone three minutes without screwing it up and now he was crashing and burning.

Two tents!

That implied they were going to be sleeping in separate tents. Alone. *Damn it.* The talk about Rachette had thrown him off. No. It was the box that was throwing him off.

"Wait," he said.

She shook her head, looking at him like he was hopeless.

That wasn't anger. It wasn't disappointment. Her eyes were smiling.

She walked up to him and put a hand on his chest. "David."

"Yeah?"

"Do you know where Tom bought that ring all those months ago for Charlotte?"

Wolf slid his eyebrows down. "No."

She put her arms around his neck and pressed her body against him. Her eyes narrowed, focused on his lips. "Gonsch Jewelers. The guy in town on Main."

She leaned back abruptly and watched his face, delighting in what she saw.

"Know how I know that?" she asked.

"No."

"Melanie Gonsch, his daughter, works at the hospital, too. She's a blood tech. I told her about the whole thing. About Tom and Charlotte."

Wolf tried to look mildly interested.

"And then she told me she heard from her father there was another cop in there just recently. Of course she told me. She can't keep a secret to save her life."

He exhaled and looked at the lake behind her.

She reached up and kissed him, her lips pressing against his, her mouth opening and her tongue sliding into his mouth, seeking his. They kissed the most passionate kiss they'd ever kissed. It was like they'd invented something new.

She pulled away. "The answer's no."

Blinking, he stood frozen, a continuous noise coming out of his open mouth.

Again she leaned back, delighting in the sight of his brain shutting down and rebooting.

"What ... why?" he managed to finally ask.

She held onto him tighter. Pressed her body harder into his. The smile melted from her face. "David. I don't want to get married."

"O-kay."

"But," her eyes filled with tears, "the fact that you got that ring? The fact that you were willing to ask me . . . wait a minute, you were going to ask me, right?"

He smiled and nodded.

She burrowed her face into his chest. When she looked back up there were tears streaming down her cheeks but her eyes were calm. "The fact that you were willing to do that says so much. I just want what's good for Ella. But I also want what's good for you. And I don't want to push you into becoming the father of a six-year-old little girl, either. You don't have to do that. I just—"

Wolf put a finger under her chin and lifted it.

They stared at one another. Speaking without speaking. To use words would only complicate things.

"My house is so much better than yours," he said.

She blinked, pulled her eyebrows together. "What?"

"Will you . . . move in with me?"

Putting her head on his chest, she laughed. When she raised her eyes again, Wolf saw she was thinking it through, and to him it looked like she was rapidly convincing herself it was a good idea.

"Here." He pried himself from her arms and got on one knee. "Lauren Coulter. Will you spread your flowery girl crap all over my house?"

Her face dropped. With a mock scowl she put both hands on his shoulders and pushed.

When he landed on his back, she stepped over him and sat down slowly. Bending over, her auburn hair fell onto his face as she pressed her breasts onto him, and then her entire, negligible, weight. She reached one hand down and massaged him through his jeans and he immediately returned the favor through hers.

Her breath was hot in his ear.

"Yes," she said.

With an involuntary shudder he said, "Good."

THE END.

Thank you for reading. If you enjoyed Signature, I would appreciate it if you would help others enjoy this book, too. Here's how...

Review it. Please tell others why you liked this book by reviewing it on Amazon. It doesn't have to be much. Your thoughts go a long way with helping others know if they'll like the book, and a long way helping my efforts as a self-published author. If you do leave a review, please let me know with an email to jeff@jeffcarson.co so I can thank you personally. Otherwise, thank you very much for your support.

Lend it. Lending is enabled for this book, so please feel free to share this book with a friend. They just need a Kindle, or a free Kindle reading app for their other smart device.

Recommend it. Please help other readers find this book by recommending it to friends, readers' groups, and discussion boards.

You can sign up for Jeff Carson's new release newsletter and be the first to find out about new David Wolf novels and other works (which are always discounted for the first 48 hours). Just sign up at the following link:

http://www.jeffcarson.co/p/newsletter.html

As a thank you for signing up, you'll receive a complimentary copy of Gut Decision: A David Wolf Story about Wolf's harrowing first few weeks in the department as a rookie deputy.

David Wolf Series in Order

Sign up for the newsletter and keep up to date about new books (which are always discounted for the first 48 hours) and receive a complimentary copy of Gut Decision by clicking here --
jeffcarson.co/p/newsletter.html.

19703874R00204

Printed in Great Britain
by Amazon